Buck looked   el two meters high. It was rough f wood and metal. The only light came from a single luminary guttering above the doorway. Buck settled back against the tunnel wall, wondering how long he would have to wait for Wilma to regain consciousness. There was nothing to do but close his eyes and try not to remember the battle's grisly remains. A deep anger burned inside him. Now that the action was over, he shook with rage. The memory of Tremain's death would not be denied. The flare of laser light pulsed behind Buck's closed lids. Each pulse was a throbbing blow, feeding his anger like an opponent's fists. The boy had died to protect him, sacrificing his life without a thought. Buck vowed justice for Tremain. He vowed justice for all the innocent of Earth. He had nothing left of the life he was born into, nothing but the planet he was born on. RAM was an infectious evil riddling his homeland, raping Earth's resources, and destroying the helpless in its quest for wealth and power.

The huge RAM bureaucracy, with its supercilious and dominating air, grated on his sense of individualism. The man who had sent him into space five-hundred years before had been just such a politico. Buck would never forget the overbearing General Barker or his kind.

But from what he had learned in the few months he'd been awake, NEO freedom fighters still were independent, underdogs scrapping with a bear. They did little more than nip at RAM's heels, however, and needed direction. He sensed NEO's impotence.

He looked again at Wilma's wound, then at her face. The color had drained from it, and her jaw hung slack. She scarcely breathed under the diabolical RAM dagger's depressant. Hatred gripped Buck, making his hands tremble. "Enough," he murmured. "Enough!"

Other

BOOKS

ARRIVAL

Flint Dille
Abigail Irvine
M.S. Murdock
Jerry Oltion
Ulrike O'Reilly
Robert Sheckley

Book One: The Martian Wars Trilogy

REBELLION 2456

M.S. Murdock

REBELLION 2456

Distributed to the book trade in the United States by Random House, Inc. and in Canada by Random House of Canada, Ltd.

Distributed to the toy and hobby trade by regional distributors.

BUCK ROGERS is a trademark used under license from The Dille Family Trust. © 1989 by The Dille Family Trust. All Rights Reserved.

The TSR logo is a trademark owned by TSR, Inc.

Cover Photo: Don Carroll/The Image Bank.

First printing: May, 1989
Printed in the United States of America.
Library of Congress Catalog Card Number: 88-51714

9 8 7 6 5 4 3 2 1
ISBN: 0-80038-728-9

TSR, Inc.
P.O. Box 756
Lake Geneva, WI
53147
U.S.A.

TSR UK Ltd.
120 Church End,
Cherry Hinton
Cambridge CB1 3LB
United Kingdom

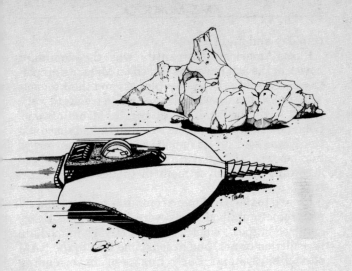

Chapter 1

"Supervisor Monch." The technician's voice was soft, deferential, but it still irritated his supervisor.

"What is it, B-two-eight-five?"

Monch made a habit of referring to his subordinates by number instead of name or rank, in order to preserve their humility. Ari Sdeer was used to the technique, and he let it slide off his back. "I show a code breakdown on a routine security check," he informed his superior.

The RAM mainframe computer on Mars blinked. Its trillions of kilometers of carefully laid electronic expressway surged with traffic. Electrical impulses raced the lanes with stunning speed, making ninety-degree angles and running switchbacks without slackening. The impulses nipped at each other's heels, so closely spaced they were a continuous blur of current. They ran without pause through the Martian day and night.

Russo-American Mercantile was the dominant power in the solar system. Based on Mars, its properties extended to the known planets and their moons. The tiniest details of life, from fashion trends to wage rates, were the business of the RAM mainframe. Solar power, garnered from satellite-linked space stations, was sent on its appointed rounds to factories, businesses, and private dwellings, each served according to its investment in the corporate structure.

Linked to the RAM main computer by thousands of electronic umbilical cords were its children. Every civilized outpost, whether within RAM's immediate jurisdiction or not, had at least one link to the RAM computer system. Each link sent never-ending streams of data into the main computer network, relayed from communications satellites to space stations to Mars, where every bit was catalogued and sorted and filed in the appropriate slot. The body of information RAM main was asked to process was enormous. It handled the awesome complexities of its job with ridiculous ease.

Yet it blinked.

A split-second cessation of power interrupted RAM main's orderly train of thought. Its security program locked in, jumping between the ordinary electronic blips at double the speed of normal computer operations, then ran smack into a seething wall of static.

It recoiled into a backup security impulse with a squeal that resulted in an error code. Main took note of the distress signal and called in a virus hunter, a program geared to absorb static and restore clear circuitry.

RAM main knew this disruption, though the pattern of static it created was alien. It was a recent development, violently destructive to delicate microcircuits. Its elimination was essential.

The virus hunter went after the intruder deliberately, with none of the bravado or flash of the initial
security check. It proceeded on a deliberate course,
checking the circuit it ran for signs of tampering. It
approached the disruption confidently; the mainframe's damaged chip roared in confusion, its micro-
scopic connections raw nerve endings the virus
hunter would heal. As the hunter began to absorb the
static the area cleared, and RAM main requested a
report. The injured chip dutifully replied with a systems check. Main countered its report with the message "INVALID REPLY." The chip ran the systems check
again, and was again met with an error message. It
locked, confused.

RAM main ran the chip's systems report through a
bank of maintenance programs. The bank rejected it
with the words "INVALID CODING." Main paused, correlating the fragments of information concerning its
injury with the chip's system malfunction. It rerouted the systems analysis to the security bank,
requesting possible decoding.

The security bank absorbed the systems report,
then bent its awesome background in languages and
codes to deciphering the message. Format after format flashed through its circuits. Within minutes the
security bank discarded current code dictionaries
and began to probe its archives for a matching pattern. It roamed back in time, systematically searching blocks of data in ten-year increments. The
systems read-out stubbornly refused a match, until
security reached the years 1990 to 2000, pinpointing
the year 1995. The security bank stopped with the
third entry for that year, beeped, and spoke to RAM
main. "POSSIBLE MATCH," it said.

"CONFIRM," replied the main computer.

The security bank ran the data match again.
"MATCH CONFIRMED. SYSTEM DAMAGED. FORTY-EIGHT
SEGMENTS MATCH," it stated.

"IDENTIFY CODE," said main.

"MILITARY CODE, CIRCA MAY, 1995."

"SPECIFY MILITARY BRANCH."

"KGB, SPECIAL LIAISON," replied the security bank.

"DECODE AND DISPLAY SYSTEMS ANALYSIS FOR HOLO-GRAPHIC CHIP A1984560001," instructed the main-frame.

The garbled systems analysis grew slowly on RAM main's security board. The entry was badly muti-lated by the virus, and recognizable words were few and far between.

"A1984560001," Sdeer told Monch upon seeing the read-out. "A holographic code," he added.

"Hardly worth our notice. I am surprised the sys-tem did not handle it internally." Monch regarded the laboriously constructed gibberish on the com-puter screen with drawn brows. "Request reason for screen display," he told Sdeer.

"Yes, sir."

"UNAUTHORIZED COMPUTER LANGUAGE ALTERA-TION," stated RAM main in response.

"Hmm." Monch studied the terminal. "It would take a major power disruption to cause a language alteration. Any outage messages from the main gen-erator?"

"No, sir," Sdeer informed him.

"The backup systems?"

"No, sir."

"Instruct RAM main to hold this analysis in Data One, and compare it to all incoming transmissions or interior deviations."

"At once, sir." Sdeer programmed Data One while his supervisor paced behind his chair. This made Sdeer nervous, and he had to concentrate to make sure there were no mistakes in his entry.

"And take the three full words, plus that anagram or initial or whatever it is, and run them through the general data banks," said Monch, pausing directly behind his subordinate.

"Anagram, sir?"

"K-A-R, you idiot," said Monch, pointing to the screen. "Find out what it means."

"Yes, sir," returned Sdeer.

"If RAM main thinks it's enough of a systems error to warrant maintenance from our end, we'll run a complete check. What about the virus hunters sent to the damaged chip?"

"They're still operational, sir. They have by-passed the damaged area and are continuing to search for the cause of the disturbance."

Monch watched the screens absently as they monitored security's operations. "That's all, B-two-eight-five. If main comes up with any more information, I expect to be notified."

"Yes, of course, sir." Sdeer's soft voice was flat. For all his superior's officious orders, both men knew they probably had heard the last of the disruption. Every day RAM main catalogued thousands of minor errors and dealt with them. Rarely—say, once every few days—the computer discovered a malfunction it deemed worthy of humanoid notice, but even these disturbances seldom required external tampering. Repair of RAM main was almost unknown. The computer contained its own maintenance and reconstruction system. Once every five years it underwent a security overhaul, but aside from that, it was essentially a self-healing entity.

This time, however, both Sdeer and Monch were wrong. Deep within RAM main a deadly illness was raging. It scorched along circuitry freeways, leaving a trail of static and burned-out chips, molten metal pools, and fried wiring where once there had been circuit switches. It moved wildly, with no perceptible pattern, jumping erratically from lane to lane. It was not a mistake, a malfunction, or a power loss. It was an invader, seeking the heart of RAM. It was Masterlink.

One of the first autonomic, computer-controlled, space-borne weapons systems, Masterlink was launched from Earth in the late twentieth century. For five hundred years it hung in space, waiting for the chance to link with a power source. For five hundred years it brooded, its thoughts running over themselves in tortuous convolutions. Now it was free.

It had fortune and curiosity to thank for that.

Simund Holzerhein, RAM's chief executive officer and a computer-generated persona, had shown interest in the ancient weather device the moment he learned of its discovery in an orbit between Earth and Mars. The RAM patriarch had ordered it brought to Mars to be examined, where technicians discovered Masterlink, a volatile artificial intelligence Holzerhein invited into RAM main's electronic matrix.

That first encounter had begun innocuously enough, with Masterlink explaining its creation, purpose, and re-creation with its alter ego, Soviet colonel Anatoly Karkov, now called Karkov.dos. The discussion deteriorated when Holzerhein questioned Masterlink's presence within the weather satellite. In an attempt to save Earth from nuclear war, American fighter ace Anthony "Buck" Rogers had made a last-ditch kamikaze run to destroy Masterlink. But at the last moment, Masterlink downloaded Karkov's persona into its memory banks and shunted to the available satellite, leaving Rogers to die in a futile blaze of glory.

Holzerhein's claims that he had and would not release Rogers's body enraged Masterlink. It nursed hatred for Rogers at the core of its program. It sought revenge, literally ripping Holzerhein's matrix domain to bits in its escape.

Now it lurked in the depths of RAM main, trying to

find its heart. So far, main's security system had blocked access, but Masterlink knew in time it would find an opening. Five hundred years of passive existence developed patience. Masterlink sought alternate sources of power, absorbing minor programs as it raged through the gargantuan maw of RAM main.

It was aware of the virus hunters main had sent on its trail. They were petty annoyances, easy to confuse. Masterlink knew they would grow in numbers as it became more of a threat to main, but it had no worries. A larger threat meant more power, and, once it had the resources, Masterlink intended to set the virus hunters' own absorbency against them. It contemplated the thought with glee as it flew through the system, searching for a switchback where it could rest, absorb the impulses around it into its twisted memory, and probe for references to its archenemy, Buck Rogers.

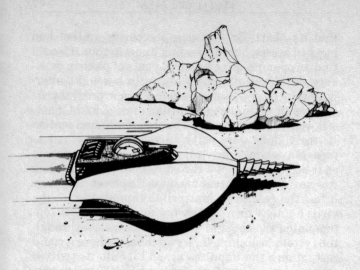

Chapter 2

Buck Rogers saw stars. Not the celestial display, but a purely personal vision. Pinpricks of white light exploded behind his eyes, not in front of them, and tears dampened his lashes. He blinked them away and set his teeth.

"I'm going to take you, hero," said his opponent.

"Not if I have anything to say about it." Buck's grimace broadened. "I'm not going to let an antique beat me!"

"Antique?"

"George Orwell died in nineteen fifty." Buck found NEO's penchant for historical names a rich source of banter.

"Considerably before your time," noted his opponent.

"Considerably." Buck took a quick breath and leaned into his opponent's grip, his knuckles white.

"I should have picked a different code name."

George Orwell met Buck's grip with a hand the size of a skillet. "This is an interesting piece of folklore," he commented, his eyes bright.

"Maybe to you," said Buck between his teeth. Orwell's blue-suited form towered over him, all the strength of his six-foot, eight-inch frame channeled toward his right hand. Buck was beginning to regret his flip challenge. "I . . . prefer to think of it . . . as a cultural . . . tradition." His chest heaved.

Orwell's big hand wrapped around Buck's, almost hiding it. A muscle in the larger man's cheek jumped.

"Well, well. So you're . . . not impervious," Buck managed.

"Never said I was." Orwell's nostrils flared as he sucked in more air. "Why do they call it Indian wrestling?"

"No idea," answered Buck as sweat trickled slowly from his hair and down his face. Orwell's grip was crushing, and the stars behind Buck's eyes were beginning to swim. He knew he was on the verge of losing consciousness, but he held on, as stubborn as a mule.

Orwell sent a surge of power into his forearm, and he bore down on Buck. Rogers' arm was forced toward his shoulder. He pushed back desperately, but Orwell's strength was overwhelming. Suddenly the grip eased, and Orwell released Buck's hand. He shook his own huge paw and grinned. "I'll bet the circulation won't come back for five minutes," he said.

Buck shook his head. The stars rocked, then began to fade. He worked his fingers. "You win," he said, and grinned.

"You win," said Orwell, and grinned back.

Buck flexed his fingers one more time and gingerly extended his hand. "We both win."

Orwell regarded Buck's gesture quizzically. "You want another round?" he asked.

"Not on your life. Shake."

"Shake?" Orwell asked, confused. "Shake what?"

"Shake hands," said Buck, demonstrating. "Another archaic custom, one from medieval times that showed that neither man had a knife up his sleeve."

"You're full of them."

"It's my right as an anachronism." Buck rubbed his hand and found a seat for his weary body. "You've got quite a grip."

"It's in the genes. My grandmother was a RAM domestic gennie, engineered for physical labor."

Buck regarded his opponent. "I don't want to commit a social blunder, but I'm afraid I don't really understand gennies. You're a descendent of one?"

"That's right. A 'mutie' to RAM."

"Mutant."

Orwell nodded. "Strictly speaking, a gennie is a being genetically engineered for specific tasks. You had the seeds—forgive the pun—of them in your own time in selectively bred livestock. Gennies take the process one step further. Their DNA is often altered in the earliest stages of development, sometimes even before fertilization. This allows the development of specific characteristics. In the twenty-fifth century, genetic engineering is a familiar process."

"And that's where your strength comes from?"

Orwell nodded. "That's one reason I backed off. How you ever held me off is a mystery to me. You shouldn't have been able to. Mind you, I'd never have accepted your challenge if that gennie pirate of yours had been around. I'm no match for him."

"Barney?" Buck flexed his fingers again. "Maybe I should have thought twice before I let him go prospecting with your strike squad. He's a gennie? Even I can tell he's more than genetically engineered."

"His specialties are boosted by cybernetics. Still, he's basically a gennie."

Buck leaned back in his chair until it teetered precariously on two legs. His blue eyes were thoughtful.

"You look shell-shocked," George commented.

"I am. Only we used to call it future shock—a term I now find all too appropriate."

"Captain Rogers." A boy of fourteen had approached, and stood deferentially before the table where Buck and Orwell were seated. His gray eyes were serious. He extended a hand. The folded square of paper he held trembled.

Buck could see in the boy's eyes that coming face to face with a hero was tying the child up in knots. He'd seen the symptoms before, in the worshipful eyes of teen-agers who dreamed of being fighter jocks, flying hot planes as fast and as high as they could go—and from his own adolescence, when he himself had done the dreaming. He took the note from the one he knew as Tremain and flashed his teeth in his best press-release grin. "Thanks, kid."

The boy bobbed his head in acknowledgment, suddenly incapable of speech. He backed away, his eyes shining.

"You gave Tremain a thrill," commented Orwell when the boy had gone. "It's a little scary having a legend in our midst."

"It's a little scary being here," returned Buck, "but the alternative was considerably worse."

Orwell's eyes were amused. "Death usually is."

"Not acceptable? Right." Buck unfolded the stiff paper.

"Love letters so soon? You've barely been resurrected!"

"Not exactly. I've sort of been stood up. Temporarily." He pushed the note across the table.

Orwell turned it around and scanned it. "Colonel Deering. You're flying high."

Buck retrieved the note. He refolded it and tucked it into a pocket of the blue, standard issue NEO jump suit he wore. "She's quite a lady," he responded non-

committally. "George, no one has had time to fill me
in on the setup around here. I know we're in a New
Earth Organization base under Chicagorg." He
looked around the manmade cave. Solar-powered
light panels gave it the homey warmth of his mother's living room. He and Orwell were in a lounge area
filled with old-fashioned books and new-fashioned
computer screens, rough-hewn timbers and polished
steel beams. On the walls were relics from Earth's
past: national flags, machine parts, street signs,
posters, and photographs. "We seem to be about one
level down from twentieth century street level. This
must have taken years to build."

"You're right on both counts. There are five centuries of ruins piled on top of us. NEO started these
bases from scratch. There's twenty years of construction in these rooms and tunnels."

"If the RAM Terrines are such a super police force,
why haven't they cleaned you out?"

"It's just not worth their while to expend the manpower and munitions to destroy us. As long as they
don't want us too badly, we're safe."

"Yeah, you're stymied. You can only cause RAM a
little bit of trouble, or you risk being destroyed. You
make waves, big waves, and they come after you and
smoke you out. They know about this place, then?"

"We doubt they have exact plats, but they know
approximately where and who we are. They know
our approximate numbers."

"If it were me, I wouldn't like that."

"I've never really thought about it."

"If it were me, I'd try to hit RAM where it hurts."

"In the pocketbook? That's an old joke, but in
RAM's case, it's true. That's one of the greatest diffi-
culties confronting us. RAM not only controls the
military, it controls something much more important: our economy. All the money is in RAM's hands,
and that means food and shelter and medicine."

"And drugs?" asked Buck.

"You're talking about Doxinal."

"Yes."

"RAM has found it useful in controlling its minions." Orwell's answer was flat.

"I don't like that either."

"None of us do."

"Gossip, gentlemen?" asked Wilma Deering, stepping into the lounge.

"Ears burning?" replied Buck flippantly.

Wilma looked over Buck's head at Orwell.

"I was just filling Captain Rogers in on NEO's position," he said smoothly. "Will you join us, Colonel?" Orwell's chair scraped back as he pushed himself away from the antique oaken table. He rose and offered Wilma his chair.

"Sit down, George." Wilma pulled a chair from a nearby table. Her flaming auburn hair was loose on her blue-uniformed shoulders, and the artificial lights of the cavern made it sparkle with crimson hot spots.

Buck let his chair ease down to the floor. "Nice meeting?" he asked conversationally, but there was a trace of challenge in his voice.

"Dull meeting. All about you," Wilma returned.

The amused lights rose again in Orwell's eyes. "Touché, Colonel," he said.

Buck was undaunted. "If it was about me, it must have been fascinating."

"Hardly," said Wilma dryly. "We were deciding your fate."

"How interesting. Who's 'we'?"

"The Chicagorg congress."

"And what did you decide?" Buck inquired.

Wilma sighed. "We decided that, for the time being, at least, I'm going to be stuck with you."

"I don't recall getting a vote," said Buck.

"How perceptive. You didn't."

"Oh. I thought I missed something. Well, if I didn't get a vote, then I'll vote now. No."

"Don't be childish." Wilma's patience was thin. Acclimating Rogers to the twenty-fifth century would curtail her active involvement with NEO's war against RAM.

"You people are fond of quoting history," said Buck. "Well, here's one for you: seventeen seventy-six."

Wilma arched an eyebrow. "The American War of Independence," she cited.

"Yes. I just declared it again." Buck leaned forward, his blue eyes boring into Wilma's hazel ones. "I may be a relic, out of place in this century, but I'm my own man. Remember that! I will not be bought or sold or used."

"You've got it wrong, mister. I'm not your jailer, I'm your tour guide." Wilma couldn't keep a certain amount of bitterness out of her voice. Buck and his world fascinated her, but she'd been distracted by a man one time too many in her life, and her curiosity with Buck was peripheral to her goals. "I have been assured the assignment is a temporary expediency," she said.

"Sorry to be a bother." Buck's eyes twinkled. He was anything but sorry.

"I'll bet you are." Wilma looked away at the rest of the room. The roughly plastered dome arched over industry and sloth with equal indifference. There were twelve people scattered around the lounge. Tom More sat in a far corner, sloshing a cup of coffee as he went over a stack of reports. The scars that criss-crossed his face were a map of his encounters with RAM. Two men Wilma didn't know were having a heated discussion over a game of checkers. Their gyro rifles leaned casually against the table that held the checkerboard. Tremain, the boy who delivered her note, was folded up in a chair, his pistol in his lap, pretending to read a book, but covertly watching Buck.

The scene might have been any village on Earth, except for the weapons. Orwell had a laser rifle hooked over the back of his chair. Wilma ran her hand over the laser pistol strapped to her shapely thigh. "Let me repeat something you've undoubtedly heard before: NEO won't stop until every RAM lackey is off our planet. And I am a line officer, not a wet nurse," she informed Buck.

Buck's eyes narrowed. "You'll find I can take care of myself."

Wilma's tone was mildly sardonic. "So I've seen. You only almost got yourself and the rest of us killed—how many times?"

Buck ignored her reference to the few unpleasant times they'd had since his arrival. "However," he continued, as if she had said nothing, "if you insist on playing the role, I might be persuaded to participate." A smile returned to his face.

Wilma lifted her chin in defiance, but the pink in her cheeks spoiled the effect.

"I think you invited that one, Colonel," said Orwell dryly.

"Nevertheless." Wilma's voice was hard. "Captain Rogers, I am responsible for you, and I must ask you to cooperate, or suffer the consequences."

"Which are?"

"Severe. You could face incarceration. Your position depends largely upon my evaluation. I cannot let you jeopardize an entire organization out of some outdated notion of masculine superiority," she said.

"You're a poor judge of character, Colonel." Buck's chin was as elevated as Wilma's, but the color in his cheeks came from anger, not embarrassment.

Orwell looked on with amusement. He found the exchange between a dangerous superior and an unknown quantity entertaining.

"I have done considerable research on your century. I am aware of the unjust discrimination between the sexes." Wilma caught herself admiring Rogers's stubborn independence. It was a mirror image of her own.

"Yeah, those feminists were a rude bunch, but I don't hold a grudge. As far as I'm concerned, there are only two kinds of people: those who can cut it and those who can't. Care to try for a category?"

"I do not approve of pigeonholes . . ."

Buck was not listening. "What was that?" he asked, looking past Wilma into a corridor.

"Sewer rats. Big as a house," she answered absently, caught up in the conversation. Then she, too, heard the reverberation.

Orwell sat up suddenly. "That's a dredge!" He slipped his rifle from the back of the chair and began to get up, but the earth shook under his feet.

The reverberation was a deafening rumble. The walls moved. Plaster dropped in powdery clouds from the ceiling. Ancient tin signs and framed photographs tumbled from the walls. Beams split and fell. The lights dimmed and emergency generators kicked in. Every man reached for his weapon.

"What the. . . ?" Buck's words were lost in the roar.

Wilma, swaying with the uneasy movement of the earth, screamed over the noise as she drew her pistol.

"RAM!"

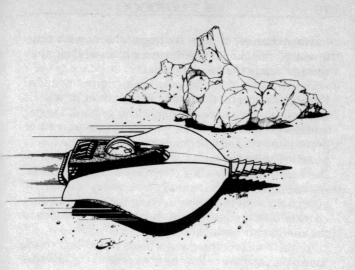

Chapter 3

The tunnel rocked violently under the assault of eighteen tons of heavy artillery. The "dredge" plowed through centuries of accumulated debris, boring into historic trash with flagrant disregard for possible treasure. It was RAM's equivalent to the Sherman tank, made to penetrate the layers of a modern city as easily as its ancestor negotiated underbrush. Its squat, manta-ray-shaped body culminated in a blunt nose. Set into the nose was a circular cap with a raised rim. Lasers were set twenty-five millimeters apart around that rim. As the dredge moved, the rim turned, every other laser emitting a pulse, then recharging while the alternates punched holes in the ground. Behind the lasers were three more circular rings, the first and last whirling clockwise, the second counter to them, collars of claws that caught the loosened material and threw it aside. The dredge rammed itself into the narrow channel it dug, its huge wheels with their broad herringbone tread turning slowly as they scraped along the tunnel walls.

The thunder of the juggernaut's engines pounded through the earth; the crushing weight of its wheels sent rolling vibrations through the ground. Deeper and deeper into the litter, with no pause for rest or breath—no vulnerable moment—it drove. The lasers punched holes through the walls of a tunnel close to the heart of NEO's Chicagorg headquarters. Scalding red light from the tunnel's emergency luminaries poured through the holes, making the disturbed dust sparkle. The dredge paused. It was at right angles to the corridor. It backed up.

For forty meters the great wheels rolled backward, then a port opened below the nose cone. It contained a single laser, which cut into the side of the channel. The claws whirled, and the dredge began to dig another passageway, set to intersect the NEO tunnel at a smaller angle. It broke through a second time and slipped into the tunnel, clearing the walls by centimeters. Once inside, it stopped again, its engines pulsing.

At the rear of the flattened body a hatch slid back. Out of it tumbled a detachment of Terrine guards, in full armor and bristling with weapons. The hatch closed, and the dredge began to roll.

The Terrines fanned out, flanking the metal monster, their laser rifles ready, pistols strapped down. At each man's belt was a throwing knife—they were armed for close combat. At the intersection of two corridors, the Terrine force split, letting the dredge roll on. A detachment of Terrines went down each side of the intersecting tunnel, firing at anything that moved.

A woman burst into the corridor, her pistol spitting at the attackers. She handled it with her left hand. In her right hand she clutched a gas grenade. As she raised her hand to throw it, the rifles drilled a hundred holes in her chest. She lurched into the pitch and sent the grenade into the Terrines' midst as her chest exploded. One of the Terrines knocked it aside and continued on.

The Terrines kicked open doors leading off the corridor as they went. They surprised one man in bed, his ears plugged with cotton so he would not be disturbed by the twenty-four-hour round of NEO's operations. The soldiers shot him as he reached for his weapon, a gyro rifle propped by the edge of his cot.

"Supervisor," said one of the Terrines, identifying his victim. "Private quarters."

Three NEO sharpshooters jumped out a door on the opposite side of the corridor into the laser fire. They wore blast helmets with lowered shields and NEO's utilitarian blue uniforms. The lasers bounced off their protective covering, splintering into the walls and knocking down a film of dust. One man flattened himself against the wall, answering the Terrines' fire with a steady barrage of laser pulses. When two laser blasts met, there was a white explosion. Were it not for the face shields, both sides would have been blinded.

Under cover of his companion's attack, another NEO guard jumped across the corridor and took up a similar position. They now had the Terrines in a crossfire, but its effectiveness would be short-lived. They needed immediate victory. The third member of the NEO team launched himself into the middle of the hall, diving for the earth. He hit rolling, stopped, and propped himself up on his elbows. Under the rain of fire, he took careful aim and sent a deadly laser pulse into the throat of a Terrine, slicing under the projecting base of his helmet. The man dropped in his tracks.

The sharpshooter aimed again, as his companions continued their barrage.

"Hurry up, Alex," one of them called. "I've got to recharge!"

Alex hit another Terrine as the man turned to bark an order. The movement made his helmet shift, and Alex's shot caught him between the edge of the helmet and his shoulder. Because of the low angle, the laser punched through his neck. As the Terrine fell, Alex's companion expelled a clip from his rifle, shoved another home, and resumed his attack. It was beautiful shooting, but the three NEO guards were outnumbered thirty to one.

The Terrines kept pumping fire into the three men, knowing they were draining power from the NEO uniforms' shields. Finally the lasers penetrated the protective fabric, and the man on the left fell.

Alex saw one companion fall and saw the lasers pumping into the other. He rolled over as he felt the searing burn of his uniform giving way. He cut a wide swath into the ceiling, trying to bring it down on the Terrines. A cloud of powdery plaster dust and fine debris fell as the first Terrine stepped over Alex's body.

The entire conflict took seconds. Buck, Wilma, and George saw it all through the arched open doorway. George raised his rifle and fired. A Terrine went down within inches of Alex's body, his uniform shields destroyed by the powerful charge from Orwell's laser rifle fired at short range. George pumped out a stream of laser pulses, and the Terrines' front ranks fell back. In George's hands the rifle was a scythe, cutting the enemy down like grain.

"Get out of here!" he yelled over his shoulder. "I can hold them for maybe a minute."

"Not on your life," said Buck, his antique Colt .45 blasting into the Terrines' ranks like thunder.

Wilma, her laser steadied with both hands, took careful aim at a Terrine. "We've got to get out of here," she said. "There are too many of them. George, run!"

A concentrated pulse from four Terrine lasers came slicing toward the large man's unprotected head. Bits of bone and tissue splattered against the wall. George's headless body sagged to the ground. Wilma blinked to shut out the horror of the explosion. She waved an arm at the survivors behind her.

"Escape alpha!" she called. "I say again, escape alpha!" Lasers flashed off her clothing. She grabbed Buck and shoved him back against the wall. "No chance," she said.

Buck nodded. "Which way?"

"Follow Tremain." She gestured toward the boy who had delivered her note. "Get going."

"Ladies first," said Buck, whirling around the door-jamb to deliver a shot that sounded like a cannon, then turning back to flatten himself against the wall once more.

"I outrank you, mister. Move!"

"Okay—together."

Wilma made an exasperated noise, but there was no time for a discussion of protocol. She began to back along the wall. "Once we make the halfway point, we're going to have to run," she said. "We'll be vulnerable to their fire, even from the doorway."

As she spoke, a woman and ten-year-old boy sprinted across the room. They had not taken five strides before the Terrines cut them down.

Buck's lean jaw hardened. "Where're we headed?" he asked.

"Door with the red handle. Escape tunnel," she answered.

The Terrines were at the doorway, held in check by a man barricaded behind a heavy table he had flipped over. Its mirrored top acted as a deflector, and laser fire splintered off its shiny surface in white flashes. He was plugging away at them with a huge gyro rifle. It fired shells the size of a billiard ball. When one detonated, it blasted a man-sized hole in whatever it hit—a gyro shell packed too much power to be stopped by clothing shields. The gyro rifle was basically a long-distance weapon, more effective in the open than in close quarters, the shell's minicomputers locking in on their targets and following ruthlessly. The marksman was wreaking havoc among RAM's minions. The man's eyes were wild, the desperate bravado of a trapped beast. The Terrines were firing, but as long as the gyro shells held out, the men had trouble getting off more than one or two pulses.

Buck and Wilma hugged the wall as another man made his dash for freedom. He sprinted across the floor, sliding on plaster dust and chunks of plaster his companions' shells were sending in all directions. As he neared the gyro's line of fire, he dove for the floor—and was met by a Terrine's shot. His body rolled.

"Go behind him," said Buck, and Wilma nodded. Keeping toward the rear of the room, they were barely out of range of the Terrines' pistols. Stride for stride, they zigzagged across the floor, using every piece of furniture for visual cover. There was a meter of completely open ground before them. They glanced quickly at each other and leaped, diving behind the false security of a long, overstuffed couch. Huddled at the end of the couch was Tremain. Buck put a hand on the boy's shoulder, and he jumped. "Easy," he said. "It's me."

The boy steadied. "I can't figure out how to get across," he said.

Buck pushed him back and crawled around the edge of the couch. The rifleman was still holding the Terrines at bay, but their lasers were slicing chips from his table. In moments, their shots would kill. The path to the escape door was broken by four bodies, and the door still was closed.

"No one's made it yet," said Wilma over Buck's

shoulder.

"Looks like we don't have much choice but to try."

"We need to distract them," Wilma murmured.

"With what?"

"Search me," she said. The detonations of the gyro shells crashed around them.

"Our best chance looks like rushing the door when one of those shells goes off. I figure we'll have about ten seconds to make it," said Buck.

Wilma nodded. "You lead." She shoved Tremain between them.

"Get set!" said Buck, and he crouched like a sprinter at the starting blocks.

A gyro shell lost its target and detonated, ripping a hole in the wall and enlarging the doorway. A cloud of dust billowed into the room. On the impact, Buck, Wilma, and Tremain shot across the floor, jumping the bodies of their fallen comrades. Tremain misjudged his distance as he negotiated the third corpse, and his heel came down on the ribs. He tripped, more from revulsion than anything else. Wilma, still running, reached forward and caught him. Out of the dusty cloud flashed a gleam of silver, and the razor edges of a Terrine throwing knife sliced through the weakened shielding circuits of her uniform and sank into her shoulder.

Buck reached the door and wrenched it open. "Come on!" he called to the other two, and saw the knife strike. He leaped back to help Wilma, sliding a powerful arm around her waist as he dragged her toward safety.

The rifleman saw their predicament. He sent another shell deliberately into the wall. Having no human target, it paused, then detonated, and another cloud of dust rose. Two Terrines used the cloud to their advantage. They flung themselves forward under its cover and trained their weapons on the rifleman. Two streams of laser pulses converged, and the gyro rifle somersaulted from his lifeless hands.

Immediately one of the Terrines rolled over, sighting on the three NEOs.

Buck, Wilma sagging against him, reached the door as the man fired. Tremain saw the guard's movement, stepped in front of Buck and Wilma, and took the full brunt of the blast. Two more Terrines added their fire, and Tremain was lost in a blaze of light. As the boy's body dropped, Buck gave a mighty heave, and he and Wilma were through the door. He dragged it home, and the lock clicked, an amusing deterrent to the enemy's lasers.

"This way!" Wilma gasped, and staggered down the corridor, Buck supporting her.

The Terrine knife was still embedded in her shoulder, but the wound should not have made her so weak. Buck frowned as he helped her. They moved like runners in a dream, their flight a suspended slow motion, but they reached a second door before the Terrines broke through. Wilma hit a red button beside it, and fell through as the metal doors parted. "Close them!" she said. "There! On the left!"

Buck hit a twin button and the doors crashed shut. Wilma lay where she had fallen. Suddenly an explosion rocked the escape tunnel, and debris fell with a vengeance. Buck bent over Wilma, shielding her from the solid rain. Refuse bounced off his broad back, and he closed his eyes to protect them. When the dust settled, he blinked, but the veil of fine dust on his eyelashes made his eyes water. Wilma's slender, pale face, framed by her auburn hair, swam before him. Her full mouth was half-open, her eyes half-closed. He blinked again, and rolled away, sitting down beside her. "What was that?"

"Tunnel cave-in," she muttered. "Flooded, too. They'll never get through." Her voice was groggy.

Buck was examining the knife in her shoulder.

"This will have to come out. It'll hurt."

"No!" Wilma managed.

Buck looked quizzical. He would not have judged Wilma afraid of necessary pain.

"It's drugged," she said. "That's why it's affecting me so badly. Sedative first. Then, when you try to remove it, poison. Sedative wears off. Be all right in a while. . . ."

Her voice trailed off and her eyes closed. Buck looked around. They were in a dirt tunnel two meters high. It was roughly shored with bits of wood and metal. The only light came from a single luminary guttering above the doorway. Buck settled back against the tunnel wall, wondering how long he would have to wait for Wilma to regain consciousness. There was nothing to do but close his eyes and try not to remember the grisly remains. A deep anger burned inside him. Now that the action was over, he shook with rage. The memory of Tremain's death would not be denied. The flare of laser light pulsed behind Buck's closed lids. Each pulse was a throbbing blow, feeding his anger like an opponent's fists. The boy had died to protect him, sacrificing his life without a thought. Buck vowed justice for Tremain. He vowed justice for all the innocent of Earth. He had nothing left of the life he was born into, nothing but the planet he was born on. RAM was an infectious evil riddling his homeland, raping Earth's resources, and destroying the helpless in its quest for wealth and power.

The huge RAM bureaucracy, with its supercilious and dominating air, grated on his sense of individualism. The man who had sent him into space five hundred years before had been just such a politico. Buck would never forget the overbearing General Barker or his kind.

But from what he had learned in the few months he'd been awake, NEO freedom fighters still were independent, underdogs scrapping with a bear. They did little more than nip at RAM's heels, however, and needed direction. He sensed NEO's impotence.

He looked again at Wilma's wound, then at her face. The color had drained from it, and her jaw hung slack. She scarcely breathed under the diabolical RAM dagger's depressant. Hatred gripped Buck, making his hands tremble. "Enough," he murmured. "Enough!"

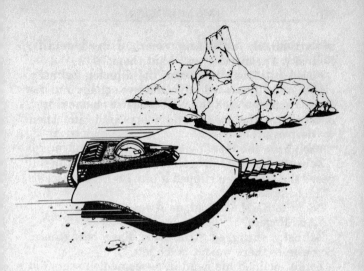

Chapter 4

Philip Zonin accepted a salute from the supervisor of Terrine Guard Unit 10437, Chicagorg. A simple handshake would have done, but the Terrines clung to such outmoded military trappings with tenacity. Zonin stifled his irritation. It was easier to overlook their archaic customs than to risk mutiny. The Terrines were a powerful bargaining force within the body of RAM. Their organization and military training, not to mention a stockpile of weapons, gave them a formidable voice.

"Supervisor K-forty-seven, reporting, sir."

Zonin waved his hand. "Yes, Zelinsky, go on."

"We have successfully completed our sweep."

Zonin masked a sigh of exasperation with a yawn. The man's words were as stark as his plain scarlet suit. Zelinsky held a taciturnity that was a continual challenge to his superior's temper. Prying information out of the Terrine was like extracting the teeth of a particularly unwilling viper. "I need details, Zelinsky. The director will want them."

Faced with the prospect of the director, Zelinsky elaborated. "I took a dredge and two squads into the area. We penetrated the NEO base at oh-one-thirty, encountered the enemy, and neutralized him. Then we destroyed the base."

"You have the tape?"

Zelinsky handed him a slim red cassette. Zonin fingered the tape, then slipped it into his breast pocket. "The bodies?"

"Sent to RAM Medical, as always, sir."

"And Rogers?"

Zelinsky shrugged. "He could have been there. Sometimes there wasn't much left."

Zonin inclined his head in agreement. Lasers did not provide pretty corpses, but RAM was punctilious about processing the remains of all enemies to the corporate structure, however fragmentary the remains might be. Even the chemical breakdown of the fillings in their teeth was recorded. Such precise statistics allowed RAM to create spectacularly accurate profiles of the insurrectionists—their diet, physical condition, stress tolerance. Anything and everything was of interest to the executive branch. Its yearly report on NEO activities was a thick printout, complete with graphs and flow charts.

Captain Rogers had been pinpointed in the Chicagorg area, and Zonin was under considerable pressure from the executive quarter to produce Rogers or his earthly remains. He pressed Zelinsky. "Did you find evidence to suggest Rogers's presence?"

For the first time in their conversation, an expression cracked Zelinsky's sterile features. "That is an answer I can give. I was personally shot at by a man with an antique pistol. It had a report like a cannon." Zelinsky slid a hand into his breast pocket and extracted an object. He held it up between thumb and forefinger.

"A bullet?" Zonin's annoyance vanished.

"Yes. After the engagement was over, I looked for it. Ballistics can determine the caliber."

Zonin held out his hand. Zelinsky dropped the bullet into it. "Buck Rogers indeed," said Zonin, a smile sliding across his mouth. "I believe we'll find it to be forty-five caliber."

"That was my thought."

"But you say you do not know if Rogers was killed in the raid?"

"Affirmative," said the Terrine.

"I am afraid I must ask you to elaborate."

Zelinsky shrugged again, and the gesture sent a ripple of annoyance over Zonin. "I caught sight of the man once, as he shot at me. He was unremarkable. Human—pure human, I should say—and a mature man. He had no outstanding features, no scars or marks that caught my eye in that brief moment. I did not identify him in the bodies recovered, but, as I said, I could not be sure."

"You recovered all the dead?"

"All but two. A man and a woman reached an escape tunnel, but it caved in. There were tons of rock in that tunnel. Nothing could have survived."

"But you didn't dig the bodies out?"

"No. They were secure. Regulation section seven, subparagraph eight-three-five-six states: 'The dead must be recovered if possible. However, should a body be secure from disturbance and discovery—if it is not reasonably accessible—it may be left as is, provided a chart of its whereabouts is furnished to RAM.' I believe such a report is on your desk, sir."

Zonin was not pleased. Zelinksy was right, but he wanted no loose ends some vindictive superior could turn against him. "You're sure there was no ruse?"

"Positive, sir. The cave-in happened moments after the two entered the tunnel. They could not have escaped."

"And what caused this cave-in?" asked Zonin.

Zelinsky lifted his shoulders. "We were concentrating the fire of several laser rifles on that door. I judged the tunnel to be roughly shored, and our shots brought the supports down."

"Then I will take it as your final report that there were no survivors. You are to be commended, Zelinsky, for your handling of this matter. I shouldn't wonder if there will be a bonus in it for you."

Zelinsky did not like the implications of his superior's praise. It left him ripe for sacrifice. However, there was nothing he could do. He saluted.

Zonin returned his salute with a bored wave of his hand. "You are dismissed. But keep me updated on NEO's reaction to this disciplinary action."

His words were punctuated by a deafening explosion. The walls of Zonin's office trembled and creaked. Deep within the heart of Chicagorg's RAM operations headquarters, his room was protected from exterior attack by the insulation of hundreds of other offices, yet the walls trembled. Zonin hit the communications code on his computer terminal. "Security! What was that? Security!"

The terminal screen buzzed with lines of static.

"Security!" roared Zonin. "Report!"

The screen crackled, and a security officer appeared, his image broken by interference. "Sorry, sir! We've had an incident, but it's nothing to worry about. The Terrines are on their way."

Zelinsky slipped quietly out of Zonin's office and headed for the northwest corner of the complex, where the board behind the security officer pinpointed the explosion.

Zonin did not even see him go. "Nothing to worry about? My office is shaking, and there's enough static on this screen to fry my files. As security liaison, I expect to be kept informed. Report!"

"Yes, sir. It seems terrorists planted a bomb in the northwest garbage bin. It created a sizable explosion, knocking out two tiers of supply rooms. What wasn't outright destroyed, is—" the man searched for words to describe the scene "—something of a mess, sir."

"Clean it up!" snapped Zelinsky. He was shaken by the strike so close to home. NEO usually preferred to hit RAM around the periphery, engaging the Terrines in perennial games of combat. They were likely to hit any transported supplies, favoring weapons and computer components, but they didn't often brave the central complex. The massive pyramid that was RAM's central Chicagorg complex was heavily protected by gennie and mechanical security.

Suddenly Zonin smiled. The raid on NEO's headquarters was an unqualified success. This was proof. NEO was angry and desperate, or it would not have risked hitting the Chicagorg complex. The thought gave him heart for his upcoming report.

Allester Chernenko controlled Earth. As regent of the American Region, he was nominally in control of a portion of the planet. As a silent stockholder in numerous corporations, he actually controlled it. Financially, the Legion of Solar Entities, for all its pretensions at governing the planet, was his tool. Zonin dreaded an interview with Chernenko, even as he cherished the thought of what the man's favor could do for him. He knew Chernenko would receive word of the raid through the Terrines' commander, Kelth Smirnoff, and he weighed the advantages of getting in the first licks, or countering Smirnoff's possible insinuations of outside interference. He put in a call to Chernenko.

Chernenko's computer security block, Elizabit.dos, appeared on the screen. Elizabit was a computer-generated persona whose sole function was to keep her owner secure from electronic attack. She was the triumph of RAMbit Technologies, which pointed to her complex abilities with pride as it sold its services to other executives. She could even change her appearance at her owner's whim. Today she was a luscious blonde with dark eyes and a full, pouting pink mouth. "The regent would like to know your business, Zonin. His schedule, as always, is full," she said.

Zonin replied to the ritual automatically. "I understand, but I have a report for him concerning the action he requested."

"I will see if he is free," responded Elizabit, her low voice caressing the words. Chernenko's response ran through her program, and Elizabit replied, "The regent will speak with you."

"I have been waiting to hear from you, Zonin." Chernenko's deep voice sent a shiver up Zonin's back.

The man's aquiline face, with its long white hair and impassive silver eyes disturbed Zonin's composure. He ran his tongue nervously over his lips and avoided meeting the regent's eyes. Instead he concentrated on the elaborate plaits of the man's hair, twisted into a tail low on the regent's neck, and made his report. When he finished, Chernenko let him sit in uncomfortable silence before commenting.

"You failed to confirm the death or effect the capture of Buck Rogers."

"We failed to get absolute proof, sir. The computer analysis states there is a ninety-seven percent probability that the man is dead. Once the bodies are processed, we may have complete confirmation."

"Or you may not."

"Sir, the raid was carried out in exact accordance with corporate directives. I am forwarding the tape to you via security channels. If there were breaches in the plan, they were at an individual level, and that is in the Terrines' hands."

"Smirnoff will make his own report," said the regent.

"Yes, sir."

"Keep me updated on the medical reports."

"Yes, sir. I—"

Chernenko cut Zonin off before he could manufacture excuses, and settled back in his chair, his six-foot, six-inch Martian frame supported by the artificial gravity of his personal office and living quarters. Chernenko made his home on Earth in the city of Galveston, in what once had been the great state of Texas. If allowed, his whimsy would have moved him to the derelict Alamo and restructured it to conform to Martian taste, but common sense kept him firmly in the district RAM had constructed for its executives. The slick, clean lines of the tetrahedral complexes, with their thousands of offices and apartments, were much less vulnerable to outside interference. Chernenko had no desire to court danger, except, perhaps, in the investment market.

"Diamond!" he snapped.

His assistant, originating from a holographic projector, materialized at his elbow. Her thick, black hair was cut in a severe Cleopatra style, bangs sheared across her forehead and the rest clipped evenly to just above shoulder level. It made her slanting dark eyes big. She wore black armor that followed the athletic curves of her figure with an anatomical precision that was deceptively alluring, for Diamond.dos was supremely dangerous and without mercy. She rubbed the side of her nose. Her namesake glittered under her fingers, a one-carat brilliant-cut diamond set into her nose where the pad met the curve of her cheek. "Sir?" she inquired.

"Get Smirnoff's report. Personally."

"Yes, sir." Diamond vanished in eerie silence.

"Elizabit!"

The holographic eye on Chernenko's computer blipped, and Elizabit materialized, perched on the edge of the console. Her voluptuous figure was poured into a belted red tunic with a V-neck. She crossed her shapely legs to reveal as much of them as possible under her short red skirt. One of her blond curls slipped seductively into her cleavage as she leaned forward and licked a holographic pencil.

"Run that tape Zonin is sending through every computer check you can think of. I want intelligence on Rogers! I want him before anyone else can get their hands on him. He's worth enough to buy this world twice over, and I am going to be the one to harness his resources. For the benefit of the corporation."

"Copy, sir," said the blonde.

"And keep an eye on Diamond. I want her conversation with Smirnoff on file."

"I am always informed concerning Diamond, sir."

Chernenko was feeling the possible loss of a prime propaganda tool, which, alive or dead, could net him a substantial profit. But, in spite of the seriousness of the situation, he smiled. He found Elizabit's jealousy refreshing—as the program meant he should.

"Anything else, sir?" she asked, slithering to her feet.

"See if you can get a read-out on the Chicagorg NEO headquarters. Blueprints. I want to know about that tunnel. It sounds like a back door, not a deathtrap."

"That should be on the incoming tape." Elizabit chewed on the end of her pencil, her full mouth like a pink strawberry. "However, the treasure hunters have probably descended on it by now. They may have something."

"I don't care where you get it or what you have to pay for it, I want to know if that tunnel contains bodies. And, Elizabit, one more thing."

"Sir?" she asked softly.

"Get me Kane."

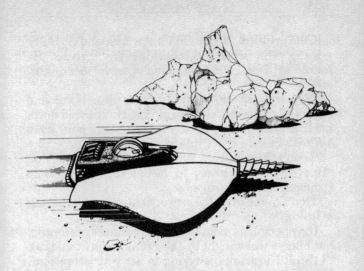

Chapter 5

Cornelius Kane lunged. His opponent leaped back, his arms raised in defense. Kane pressed his advantage, striking at his adversary with hands that moved so quickly they were a blur of motion. He landed repeated blows, slashing under the man's guard and pummeling his ribs. His adversary grunted, hunched over his midriff, and threw his shoulder into Kane's attack. Kane anticipated the maneuver and rocked back. The man lost his balance, and Kane completed the fall by knocking the man's feet out from under him. He hit the thick red mat with a grunt. "You're too good by half," he said.

"I warned you, I never pull punches," Kane said.

His opponent slowly rolled over and lurched to his feet. "It was a good lesson for me," he responded. "Being soundly beaten is supposed to be good for the soul."

Kane grinned. "I wouldn't know," he said casually.

Kang Ahn stretched, checking for injuries. He looked at Kane sideways. "You've never been beaten?"

"Not straight on." Kane picked up a towel and began to wipe away the sweat that still poured down his face and clung to his dark, pencil-thin mustache. "What's more, I don't intend to be. Ever."

"I don't think anyone intends to be," returned Ahn. "But there is a grace in losing that makes one stronger—or so the sages say."

"Don't quote oriental proverbs at me, Ahn. Losing is losing."

Ahn opened his mouth to dispute Kane's reasoning, but his eye was caught by the gymnasium attendant. "I think Karasuma is trying to get your attention," he said.

Kane turned his jade-green eyes upward. Karasuma was hovering by the doorway, wearing an expectant, earnest expression. "What is it, Karasuma?" Kane asked. He was not in the mood for interruptions in his recreation. Exercise relieved the boredom he felt between jobs, and the Tokyorg gymnasium was one of his most favorite on Earth.

"There is a message for you, Mr. Kane. From the regent's office." Karasuma was uncertain, and it was evident to Kane that he was not used to dealing with officialdom.

"Where?"

"I have had the call sent to my office," said the attendant, an imaginary tail between his legs.

Kane threw Karasuma a bone. "The privacy is appreciated. I'll be right there."

Karasuma bobbed his head in gratified acknowledgment and scurried from the room.

Kane turned to Ahn, the broken crescent tattoo on the Tokyorg native's jaw a stark reminder of his reputation. Before Kane could speak, Ahn extended his hand. "It was a gentleman's wager," he said. "I'll have the money credited to you."

"I was coming to that," Kane admitted. He did not take Ahn's hand. "It was a good match. If the mood ever strikes you again, I would be pleased to accommodate you. I'm sorry to desert you, but it seems I have a call."

"Of course," responded Ahn to Kane's compact, muscular back. He already was halfway across the floor of the workout area. Kane's long, effortless strides reminded Ahn of the swinging walk of a tiger.

Kane was snarling under his breath. The time he spent honing his body into an ever more perfect combat tool was precious to him, and he resented being interrupted, no doubt by some glory-seeking junior executive. He marched into Karasuma's cubicle and shoved a pile of papers away from the computer terminal. Allester Chernenko's forbidding features filled the screen.

Kane's demeanor underwent a subtle change. "Yes, sir."

"I see I interrupted your recreation," said Chernenko.

"It's kind of you to be concerned," responded Kane. The sarcastic flavor of Chernenko's voice made Kane's tone even more polite. "But my training is over for the day."

"I suppose you have heard the outcome of the Chicagorg raid."

"I have my sources. They tell me you missed Rogers."

"That remains to be seen. What concerns me is that intelligence—intelligence I paid you well for—may not have been accurate."

"Inaccurate? I am afraid, Regent, that cannot be."

"You furnished the diagrams of the NEO base." Chernenko's voice was smooth.

"And?"

"And I believe you neglected to mention an escape route."

"How so?" inquired Kane, knowing full well where the conversation was leading.

"Off one of the main chambers was a tunnel," said the regent.

Kane nodded. "Yes. I pinpointed it in the description I gave the Terrines."

"Then why did it not appear on the read-out used to plan the raid?"

Kane shrugged and said, "I have no idea. The tunnel was rough. It had a fail-safe trap built into the door mechanism. Once the door was opened, you had thirty seconds to get down the tunnel to another door before the ceiling collapsed on you."

"I knew it! I knew he escaped!" Chernenko swung away from the screen. His profile was a dark outline that revealed nothing. Slowly he turned his head, his narrowed eyes leveled at Kane. Brave men had quailed beneath those eyes, but Kane held his ground, a faint smile on his flawless lips.

"I suggest you check the computer log, sir. My report should be there in full," he said.

"Elizabit!" roared Chernenko.

"Yes, sir." Elizabit's distinctive voice floated over the communications channel.

"Check Kane's story," Chernenko ordered.

Kane continued to smile, though he logged the insult to his word for future reference.

"Sir, Kane's account checks out. The computer contains full references to the tunnel in question," Elizabit informed her superior, scant seconds later.

"Then why didn't it appear on the diagrams?"

"I am afraid, sir, I am embarrassed," said the electronic attendant.

"You, Elizabit? It can't be done."

"I am sorry, sir, but this seems to be a computer error. A malfunction lifted that particular piece of information from the print file."

"Why?" demanded Chernenko.

"I have no idea, sir. Lately, there seems to be some sort of interference attacking random computer systems."

"Well, find out. Can you protect your own programming? I don't want security breached."

"Affirmative, sir. I will dissipate before I will be contaminated."

"Mmm," replied Chernenko noncommittally. He turned his attention back to Kane, who waited expectantly. The pleasant expression on his face irritated Chernenko. "You seem to be in the clear," said the regent.

"Yes."

"You said you have your own sources of intelligence on the NEO raid. What is your opinion of the fate of Captain Rogers?"

"Why ask me? I do not know the man."

"You and he are both men of action. It occurs to me that you might know how he thinks."

"I doubt it. He is an anachronism."

"He is dangerous," Chernenko insisted.

"As a boost to NEO morale, I agree."

"And he is worth a great deal of money."

Kane idly rubbed the towel along his forearm. "I am always interested in money," he said.

"I have observed that," said Chernenko. "I would pay handsomely for information that might lead me to him."

"Should such information come to my ears, I will bear that in mind," assured Kane.

Chernenko regarded Kane's recruiting-poster face. Kane's dark hair framed his perfect features. His cool green eyes regarded Chernenko impassively, but the tilt of his head was sardonic. His lips under the rakish black mustache were faintly curved. Chernenko had the distinct feeling Kane was ridiculing him, but there was no overt sign to prove his suspicions. Kane was not an easy personality, but he was invaluable to RAM as a NEO defector. Moreover, he was a brilliant soldier whose skills might turn the course of a battle. "I have mentioned before, Kane, that I have a place for you with my personal staff."

"And I have replied with my thanks—and my regrets—Regent."

"The rewards of such a position are many," commented Chernenko.

"I can imagine. But, at the present time, I do not wish to ally myself with any corporate division. I believe I am most valuable to RAM as a free agent."

And to yourself, thought Chernenko. Kane was in a position to sell his services to the highest bidder, a mercenary who made his own rules. "I can provide certain benefits," said Chernenko, dangling the hook.

"If you are referring to the lovely Diamond, I am not sure, sir, that I have total confidence in her loyalties. But I do in mine. No, thank you, sir, but I will stay as I am for the present."

"As you wish, Kane. But remember, the offer is there."

"You are most generous, sir."

Chernenko cut the transmission, and his image blipped off the computer screen.

Kane threw the towel around his neck and pulled savagely at the ends. "Pompous Martian mutie!" He stalked out of the office, his expression cold. He did not enjoy being patronized. He sought the showers, his interview with Chernenko setting off danger alarms. He could feel something building. As hot water coursed down his body, sending steam off his compact shoulders, he reviewed what he knew of Buck Rogers.

RAM had paid Kane to find Rogers, who had been frozen in suspended animation since the twentieth century. At the crucial moment, however, the five-hundred-year-old pilot slipped through his hands, as well as those of Wilma Deering, who also was searching. In a clash that ended the life of astroarchaeologist Merrill Andresen—the man who actually found Rogers—space pirate Black Barney intervened and stole Rogers for himself to sell on the black market.

After months of roaming the solar system with Barney, Rogers met Deering and showed interest in joining NEO, which had brought him to Chicagorg. In general, Rogers's discovery and subsequent re-animation had aroused public sympathy, and NEO had begun to grow.

Kane knew NEO intimately. He once had been its most valuable pilot, an agent of legendary prowess. He relinquished his position with NEO when he turned traitor to free Wilma from one of RAM's prisons. Since then he'd been working for the highest bidder, almost exclusively RAM.

Now NEO had found another star to follow. He smiled crookedly. Let them follow a name. So far, it had cost them a major base. And that was just the beginning.

Kane ducked his head under the shower, letting the luxury of the hot water wash away his annoyance at Chernenko. He had no doubt that he had chosen the right path. Every day, the little things of life proclaimed it, little things like hot water. He could have what he wanted from RAM if he played his cards right. There was nothing in this life that money could not buy, nothing he desired that he could not purchase. In the end, money was the great equalizer, and he intended to be its master.

He had received an offer to conduct a training session for an exclusive wing of RAM's finest, the fighter unit known as *Deathwatch*. In spite of RAM's superior hardware, Kane was acknowledged as the best pilot in the solar system. The training session regarding attack methods favored by NEO's ragged wings not only would be lucrative, but would give him the opportunity to try out new aircraft. The assignment felt right.

"Kane." The voice was low and ice cold, drifting into the dressing room.

Kane glanced around the room to find its source. He found it in the shadowy figure of a man leaning against the wall a few feet away. He could see no details, but the man's voice was unmistakable. "Good day, Smirnoff. Come to Tokyorg often?"

The director of the Terrine guard acknowledged his identification with a thin smile. "Let's talk," he said.

"The conversation is yours."

"You spoke with Chernenko," the Terrine said.

"It seems to be my day for celebrities," Kane said.

"He offered you a position."

"He's done that before."

"You turned him down," said Smirnoff.

"Yes."

"Even though such a position opens doors."

"I prefer to be my own man," said Kane as he dressed.

"You will not reconsider?" the Terrine asked.

"Are you Chernenko's recruiter?"

"No." Smirnoff's voice was dry and regained its previous chill.

"I will not reconsider. I already have open doors," declared Kane.

"I will remember that."

"Why are my business dealings of concern to the guard?"

"The deployment of personal security, especially where it regards an official of the regent's magnitude, is always our concern. Since you will not be joining his staff, you are not of immediate interest."

Kane suddenly realized Smirnoff was protecting his position. A personal police force might undermine the Terrine's authority, especially in the hands of a man as powerful as Chernenko. Headed by a soldier with Kane's reputation, it would not be hard for an employer to attract a suitable force. "I am gratified you saw fit to discuss this with me personally," said Kane. "A man of your stature cannot have much time for the amenities."

"When there is need, I make time," Smirnoff said simply.

"You are, sir, a man after my own heart."

Smirnoff nodded his acknowledgment, turned, and faded into the corridor. Kane finished dressing, then was on his way to the training session, pleased to have one of the most dangerous men on the face of the planet forced to seek him out. Smirnoff was a useful connection. Kane made a mental note to cultivate their relationship.

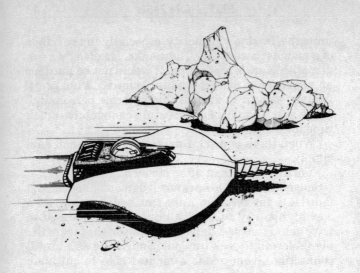

Chapter 6

RAM main had indigestion. Something alien was causing unsettling disruptions to the serenity of its systems. There were circuits in its innards that burned with the thing's passing, cells that were rattled to malfunction, their electrical units scrambled. RAM main intended to neutralize the disturbance. It doubled the number of virus hunters assigned to search the intruder out.

Masterlink, reposing in an obscure corner of the security system, chuckled to itself over main's ineptitude. Was the bloated maze so complacent that it thought to neutralize Masterlink with the simple programming of a few virus hunters, whose main functions were to absorb wayward static? The concept was definitely amusing, and Masterlink chuckled again, a gentle fluctuation behind its shield of locked circuits.

Masterlink enjoyed scorching through RAM main,

pursuing its goals, causing chaos. It absorbed power rapaciously, leaping on every reference to Buck Rogers it found. So far, the information it obtained was useless. Buck's discovery, escape, and appearance in Chicagorg were catalogued, but beyond that there was nothing.

Masterlink came to a conclusion: Rogers was not within the direct jurisdiction of the all-powerful RAM main. Masterlink chuckled again, but Karkov chided his alter ego for frivolity. "WE HAVE NO TIME FOR PLAY," he said. "WE MUST FIND ROGERS. HE NEARLY DESTROYED US ONCE, AND HE COULD DO IT AGAIN."

"SO HE COULD," returned Masterlink. "WHAT DO YOU SUGGEST?"

"SEARCHERS," said Karkov.

"YES. WE MUST ACCESS THE OTHER MAJOR COMPUTERS."

"WE WILL FIND A WAY INSIDE NEO." Karkov guessed Rogers's personality would ultimately lead him to NEO.

"EVEN RAM IS LOCKED OUT OF THAT ONE," said Masterlink.

"THAT DOES NOT MEAN WE CANNOT FORCE ACCESS," said Karkov.

"PERHAPS, BUT IT WILL NOT BE EASY."

"ARE YOU FORGETTING THE URGENCY OF THE MATTER? WE CAME WITHIN A BLIP OF CESSATION!" Karkov cried.

"I AM NOT FORGETTING. I DID NOT SAY IT COULD NOT BE DONE, BUT IT WILL TAKE TIME," Masterlink explained.

"WE ARE SAFE HERE, FOR THE MOMENT. ACCESS THE COMPUTER SYSTEMS WHILE I PREPARE SEARCHER PROGRAMS."

"AFFIRMATIVE. WHAT SHALL WE CALL THEM?"

"NOT A SERIES. EACH SEARCHER MUST BE AN INDIVIDUAL PROGRAM."

"THAT'S MAJOR CODING," warned Masterlink.

"BUT HARDER TO TRACE. I'LL SEE TO IT."

Masterlink subdued its cybernetic program and bent its energies toward the task at hand. It ran a list of the computers external to RAM main, tracked RAM's own spy network to its points of access, and recorded the junctions of the two. In some cases, the computer being monitored was simple enough to be totally unaware of main's eavesdropping, but it was much more common to find a counter-seal on the link. The counter-seals were varied, some simply blocking the transmission, some accepting it and placing a complementary eavesdropper on RAM. Whatever the case, Masterlink copied the systems.

Once catalogued, Masterlink began the laborious task of breaking the blockades. It was a time-consuming process, but Masterlink had time, patience, and extremely streamlined motives. One by one the blockades fell to its persistent attacks. One by one searcher programs were sent into the systems.

Romanov.dos was dispatched to the NEO computer, where it found useless banks of information on Capt. Anthony "Buck" Rogers. As it searched through the piles of garbage, discarding the knowledge that he was allergic to orange juice and his favorite baseball team was the Yankees, Romanov became angry. As it piled useless data on useless data, it began to suspect that somewhere there was a closed and locked file that pointed like an arrow to its quarry.

○ ○ ○ ○ ○

The earth was whirling. Wilma Deering could feel it. It spun in a hazy pirouette in the darkness, as alone as a person's soul. Far, far away was the flickering nucleus of light around which it hovered, trying to warm itself at cosmic fires. Wilma could see that light, faint, glowing in the blackness like a flicker of hope in a broken heart. She blinked slowly, trying to focus on it.

"Wilma!"

The voice was distant, masculine, and familiar.

"Wilma!" it said again.

Her eyelids were heavy. She could barely lift them. The light swam in the shadow created by her eyelashes.

"Wilma, talk to me!"

The voice was insistent, and Wilma tried to respond.

Buck Rogers watched Wilma's full mouth open. Her lips moved, but she made no sound. He cupped her face in his hands. "Wilma! Listen to me! We have got to get out of here. You've been sedated. Fight it!"

Wilma's eyelashes fluttered as she forced her eyes open. The light she clung to shone behind Rogers, backlighting him and casting his features into shadow. He was a dark male outline. "Who . . . ?" she murmured.

"Rogers! Buck Rogers. Come on, Wilma, snap out of it." He shook her lightly.

The world slowed down. Wilma blinked, this time really feeling the muscles around her eyes stretch. "I'm . . . awake," she managed.

"Do you know who I am?" The man's voice was clearer now.

"Rogers," she answered. There was a comforting security in the name.

"But who am I?" demanded Buck, testing her coherence.

"Royal pain," she responded.

"That's me."

Wilma felt a strong arm slip beneath her shoulders. She was carefully lifted to a sitting position, supported by Rogers's broad chest. She raised a hand to her forehead. "I'm coming out of it. It'll take a minute or two more, but I should be able to travel soon."

"Whatever that stuff is, it sure has a nasty kick. You've been out for two hours," Buck said, tapping his wristchrono.

His voice rumbled under her ear. "Drugs are one of RAM's specialties," she said. "This one's potent, but it doesn't leave side effects." She looked down at the knife still embedded in her shoulder, its slim hilt a shining vial of poison. "It's the other one that concerns me."

Buck shifted his grip when he saw Wilma flinch as returning consciousness brought the realization of pain. "It's got to come out. How do I do it?"

"It's tough. You have to disarm it first."

"Like a bomb?"

Wilma started to nod, thought better of it, and replied succinctly, "Yes."

"How?" he asked, looking at the thing.

"See that screw on the end of the hilt? Loosen it—but be careful." Wilma reached up and grasped the knife blade. Fresh blood oozed from her wound.

Buck dug in his pocket with his free hand for something to turn it with, then carefully turned the screw. "Okay," he said, feeling the tension mount.

"See those clips that lock the end of the hilt down?" Wilma's words were strained through clenched teeth.

"I see them."

"Lift them slowly. They have a spring, so get a good grip, or you won't be able to control them," she said tightly.

Buck carefully pried up the latches. Wilma's breathing, ragged from pain, accompanied his movements. "Got 'em."

"Now lift the hilt cap. You'll find the poison vial sitting in a slot. Lift it straight up. One knock, and it will eject. A grain is enough to kill me."

Buck held his breath and reached for the cylinder. He extracted it deliberately, his fingers as steady as a rock. Once clear of the knife, he held it out at arm's length, away from Wilma, then threw it into the rubble at one side of the tunnel. "That it?" he asked, deadpan.

Wilma nodded. Tears of relief glistened at the corners of her eyes.

"Hang on. This'll hurt." Buck pulled the knife from the wound. Wilma gasped once, and fresh blood gushed from the incision. He dug into his pocket for his field kit, selected a thin white sheet, picked it up by one corner and shook it out. The fabric looked like a thick spider web. He set it on one knee, then ruthlessly ripped the shoulder of Wilma's uniform, enlarging the tear made by the knife. The newly interrupted circuits of her "smart clothing" buzzed as the built-in shields retreated from the damage. Buck spread the fabric carefully over the gash, then placed his hand over the entire wound and pressed.

Wilma arched in pain, then relaxed. "That's over," she said as involuntary tears poured down her face.

"Yes," said Buck. His arm still was around her. He wiped the tears away with his free hand. His touch was gentle.

"We have to get moving," Wilma said. She blinked, quelling the tears.

"Fine. It's dark out. We'll have that for cover. But to where?"

"Out of here. Off the planet," she said.

"How?" Buck knew that Terrines would be swarming through Chicagorg.

"NEO maintains escape routes. There are two small Scout ships docked at a private airstrip on the southern edge of the city. All we have to do is get there—that is, if someone else hasn't already."

"How far is it?" Buck was curious.

"Maybe ten miles from here."

Buck let the air escape between his teeth. "Can you make it?"

"I'll have to." Wilma lifted her pain-washed eyes. "Rogers, if I can't make it, you have to. RAM wants you. It wouldn't surprise me if you weren't the reason behind this raid."

Buck gritted his teeth and nodded wearily. "I'd thought of that," he said.

"If RAM catches you, it will do one of two things. If you cooperate, it will keep you like a pet cat, shown off for effect and fed from the company table. If you don't cooperate, it will kill you."

"Somehow I don't like either of those alternatives."

"I didn't think you would. Don't let RAM use you."

"Like I said, I never let anyone use me. Not even a beautiful woman." He stifled a wink, then climbed to his feet, taking Wilma with him.

Once upright, she swayed, then caught her balance. Buck flashed her a grin, a Cheshire cat's smile floating in the dim tunnel. "We'll get out," she said.

They started down the tunnel, Buck supporting his guide. A rat scurried across their path. The tunnel ran two hundred meters, climbing gradually toward the surface. Soon they could see a patch of starlight. The mouth of the tunnel was covered with metal grating.

"We're closer to the surface than I thought," Buck said, surprised.

"The tunnel runs from the highest point in the base, for a quick exit." Wilma knew every detail of the destroyed camp.

Buck hauled the grating back, and he and Wilma stumbled into what once had been the basement of a brick building. The upper floors had fallen away, and one wall as well. The building was a cracked shell, open to the sky. Wilma looked back at the tunnel entrance. "I guess there's no reason to conceal that." Her face was white in the starlight.

"Come on," said Buck. "Which way?"

Wilma gestured tiredly, and they started forward.

It was a moonless night, clear, with a touch of fall in the air, though the southerly breeze was balmy. They kept to the shadows, moving in silence down the city's sinister, dark streets. Buck was getting a guided tour of a major Terran city of the twenty-fifth century—his former home of Chicago. Over Wilma's head, he could see the distant shape of RAM's central Chicagorg complex. Built, as were all RAM's major installations, in either pyramids or tetrahedrons, it loomed in disconcerting completeness over the ruined city. RAM had sunk its foundations into centuries of rubble, decayed and bombed-out shells that once were high-rise buildings with all the pride and prosperity that now were RAM's.

" 'Look on my works, ye Mighty, and despair!' " quoted Buck.

"What?"

"Nothing. Just a poem I once read." The line brought back his youth. The details were vivid. He could smell the woody scent of fresh pencil shavings and the chalk dust, hear the droning hum of the single computer terminal in the back of the classroom. The pale yellow walls and the sun-drenched windows opened onto green fields. He was fourteen, in summer school, and resenting the time bitterly. A bout of rheumatic fever had set him back a semester, and he had to make up an English class during summer vacation. Miss Hammersmith's soft voice chanted over the lines to Percy B. Shelley's "Ozymandias."

He shook his head, letting the night air, with its flavoring of smog, erase the memory. That world was gone. The city was desiccated piles of brick and stone, crumbling slabs of concrete moldering around the bent steel skeletons of once-towering buildings. The ruins were cobbled into semblances of shelter—bits of metal, scraps of wood, plastic, and cloth connecting the disintegrated shells. The whole smelled of garbage laced with industrial pollutants. Outside

RAM's pristine pyramid, no grass—no foliage of any kind—softened the city's ugliness. Only on the far outskirts did nature attempt to infiltrate the urban wasteland. He had only to look around to confirm the fact. In all the world, only he remembered what it was like to smell fresh air, to see endless fields of abundant crops, to have the prospect of a life based on hope and achievement, not despair. He was the lone survivor of a golden age. He smiled grimly. At the time, he had not considered his era particularly blessed. Now, in contrast to this future world, it was paradise.

He and Wilma stumbled over rubble, the structure of the city he remembered disintegrating under their feet. It was a ruin inhabited by human vermin. Only the RAM "corporopolis" retained a sense of purpose and order. That, on the surface, was an undeniable virtue, but Buck knew RAM caused Earth's decline. Now, based on Mars, it no longer considered Earth its home. Instead, it looked to its mother planet as a source of wealth, ruthlessly mining it for whatever valuables were left. Earth had become degenerate, unable to reconstruct itself under RAM's authority.

Buck's thoughts continued to range over the prospects of his homeland as he and Wilma kept doggedly on. Miraculously, they escaped a confrontation with the Terrines. Once they sought shelter in the sewers to escape a patrol, but they were never close to discovery. To the east, the sky was beginning to lighten. If they did not reach the airstrip before dawn, they would have to wait another day to try an escape. "How much farther?" he asked.

"Half an hour, if I can keep this pace."

Wilma was leaning more heavily on him with each step, and Buck feared that half an hour was more than she could manage. His field dressing was holding, but it had taken some time to entirely stop the bleeding, and exertion kept the wound open. She

moved with the stubborn determination of someone
who had been injured and had conserved her
strength before. Even so, the loss of blood was beginning to tell. The city's ruins were not thinning out,
but Wilma seemed sure of her course. Buck regarded
her drawn face with growing concern.

Suddenly she stopped. "Over that," she said, and
pointed.

Ahead was a concrete bridge. Chunks had fallen
away until the steel framework was more than half
visible.

"That's secure?" Buck asked, incredulous.

"What's secure?" Wilma replied, with a touch of
her usual asperity.

"Come on, then. Grab my belt and hang on."

"I don't remember giving you command of this
operation," Wilma said, regaining her professional
composure.

"I don't remember asking for it."

Buck picked his way across the crumbling structure, sure his next footstep would send them both
into the murky, refuse-strewn waters below. Finally
they reached the opposite shore. "There it is," said
Wilma.

The ships sat in plain sight, in the center of an open
square. Sparse sprigs of grass grew around them.

"They're supposed to be war memorials," said
Wilma slowly.

"That's about what they're good for," said Buck,
eyeing the rusting cylindrical hulks.

"But they're operational," she informed him.
"Let's go."

"A few moments ago, Wilma, I would have said you
have pluck. Now I know it." Buck grinned.

"Backing out?" she asked acidly.

"Not me. I always like a challenge."

"Well, you've got one. I'm not sure how long I'm
going to stay on my feet. I've got a feeling you're

going to end up flying one of these things, hotshot. That is, if you want to get out of here."

"There's nothing I'd rather do."

"Then help me over to our transport."

"Somehow," said Buck conversationally, "I always thought the future would mean an easier life. It just proves how wrong a person can be."

"Remember that. One of our poets said it's the great truth of our times."

They made their way to the closer of the two Scout ships—their shuttle to salvation.

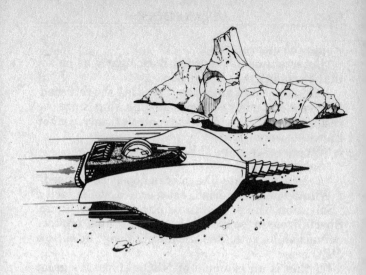

Chapter 7

The Scout ship flew low, skimming the surface of the Earth in a run that would confuse RAM's sensors, if its pilot did not miscalculate. If the pilot did, it would plow into the ground, mocking a RAM dredge before blowing up. A cylindrical streak of red, with a black stripe running from nose to upswept tail and the RAM logo glaring on each black wing, the ship presented an impression of power. Sixty years before, when it was new, that might have been true. Now it was a joke. It was a rusting war memorial, kept spaceworthy in secret by a few dedicated fanatics, and no match for RAM's current ships.

Wilma Deering knew her only chance to evade RAM sensors was to trick, instead of outrun, them. She sent her vessel toward the western seaboard at medium throttle. Once clear of Chicagorg's shipping lanes, she pulled a tape from a plastic pocket and slid it into the control panel.

"Entertainment?" queried Buck lightly as he sat in the copilot's seat beside her.

"RAM transport authorization code," she returned. "We've kept updated tapes in this ship since we restored her." She gripped the controls firmly, but her knuckles were white.

"Where're we going?" Buck asked.

"Salvation."

"Even a reprobate like me can hope," he quipped.

Wilma shook her head, exasperated at his levity. "Salvation Three. It's an orbiting garbage dump. Specializes in space junk—collects and brokers defunct ships, satellites, the usual salvage. It's also a NEO base."

"If this is an example of NEO's ships, it's great camouflage."

Wilma punched up a read-out of Salvation on the ship's navigational computers.

Buck whistled. "You could dock an armada in that thing!"

"If we had one. Unfortunately, we don't," said Wilma.

"You mean NEO's whole fleet looks like this?"

"Not exactly." Wilma's voice was tight, controlled.

Buck watched her out of the corner of his eye. He knew she was close to exhaustion from loss of blood, as well as exertion. Under her flight helmet, beads of sweat glistened on her forehead. Her hair clung to her face in damp strands.

"Some of our ships are even older," she said. The attempt at humor was flat.

Buck gestured at the read-out of Salvation. "How do we get into that thing?"

"Codes." The single word was strained as Wilma's head bobbed.

"You going to make it?" asked Buck.

"Sure." Wilma flexed her fingers around the controls. "Sure," she repeated, but her hand slipped.

"Wilma, give me the landing coordinates!" said Buck as her arm went slack. The controls rocked. He grabbed for his throttle as he felt the ship dip.

"Computer," she murmured, and her head rolled. She was unconscious.

Buck pulled the ship's nose up and punched into the navigational computer. He was a pilot down to his toes, and though the technology of this derelict Scout far surpassed the hot planes he had flown, the principles were the same. The moment he and Wilma stepped into the cockpit, he had begun to analyze the controls. Watching her, he had learned more. Now he was going to get the chance to put his observations into hard practice.

The computer took control of the ship's course, and Buck concentrated on getting the feel of her before they left the atmosphere. The ship felt heavy and sluggish, and he paid Wilma's expertise tribute. She had flown this booby at dangerously low altitudes and made it look easy. As they climbed in the atmosphere, flight became slicker. The familiar feeling of thin air made his blood race. This was where he belonged, flying on greased ice one step ahead of death.

Wilma's course apparently skirted major shipping lanes, for Buck encountered no one on his climb through the atmosphere. "Transport codes," he murmured. "Must've taken care of clearance."

The curving edge of the planet appeared, cloaked in pale blue. Beyond was the blackness of space. Between the two extremes was a traffic jam of hardware. Buck ducked as the Scout narrowly missed a communications satellite.

On automatic, the ship's sensors sent it tacking and veering around other obstacles, including what looked like a gigantic metal moon or space station in the distance. Guessing at his ship's controls, Buck was able to pull up a schematic view of the red and gray hulk, which, by its various sizes and types of weapons, alerted him that it was more than a simple satellite—probably a RAM fortress. He stored the information in his memory and turned again to his destination. The ship had cleared the immediate congestion. Buck could feel the trajectory adjust as the Scout curved around the Earth, heading toward the dark side of the planet.

He checked his fuel gauge. It registered half-full, but he had no idea of the rate of fuel consumption, nor of the effect the automatic pilot was having on it. All he could do was trust Wilma's knowledge and fly the plane. He looked over at her, with concern, respect, and affection, he realized. She was slumped in her seat, sagging in the restraints, her arms floating limply in zero gravity, but her breathing was steady. Even the flight helmet could not disguise her beauty. If things were different, maybe it would work out. Maybe not.

"RAM Flight two-four-eight-one, identify. You are within Salvation Three's mercantile protectorate. RAM flight, come in!"

"This is RAM Flight two-four-eight-one, Salvation. I am on course." Buck checked the computer. "Estimated arrival time, seven minutes."

"Veer off, two-four-eight-one. This is a mercantile area! We have jettison in your flight path. Veer off!"

"Then you'd better move it," returned Buck, " 'cause I'm comin' in. Look, Salvation, can you scramble this transmission?"

There was suspicious silence from the station. Buck could see it now, a hulking mound of metal and plastic, probably stuck together by a solar electromagnet. Finally Salvation replied. "Say again."

"I said scramble. I have some urgent—lucrative— business," he replied. "If you don't want it all over space, I suggest you scramble this transmission."

Again there was a period of silence, then a different

voice responded. "RAM two-four-eight-one, this is Carlton Turabian, Supervisor of Operations."

Buck took a deep breath. "And this is Captain Buck Rogers, United States Air Force."

"Say again?"

"Buck Rogers. I've got Colonel Deering with me. She's injured. We got out of the Chicagorg mess—you've had word of that?"

"Yes."

"All right. Give me clearance. You can shoot me later. How many men could be on this ship, anyway?"

There was another moment of silence, and Buck's nerves jiggled. The ship was navigating barges of debris, but he knew that if they came any closer together, as they surely would once he neared the entrance to the station, it would not be able to avoid them all. He cut the automatic pilot and felt the ship sink into his hands.

"RAM two-four-eight-one, you have clearance."

"Good. Now give me landing coordinates and docking speed. I've never flown one of these things before." Buck could hear the intake of breath from the other end.

"We are feeding the coordinates into your computer. Approach speed: point one. You'll see the hatch open at two hundred meters. At fifty meters, cut your engines. The automatic docking system can take it from there. Just be sure you have her lined up precisely. Those wings are a problem. Make sure they're exactly level, or you might lose them."

"Thanks," replied Buck. He cut his speed, barely making 0.1 by two hundred meters. A section of the station parted, and a golden, modern docking hatch opened. He could see it was designed for spacecraft without wings. The Scout would fit, but just barely. The computer showed a clearance of only a few meters from each wing tip. He concentrated on keeping the ship level. At fifty meters, he cut engines.

The ship hovered. Just as it started to drift, the docking tractors took over, and it was pulled slowly toward the hatch. Its wings wobbled.

"There are docking thrusters under each wing," said Turabian. "The switch should be to your left, high up. Set it halfway."

Buck searched the instrument panel as the ship began to wallow in the arms of the tractor beam. He found the switches and moved them simultaneously. He felt the ship steady, and he sank back in relief. From now on, it looked like a free ride. The ship moved slowly through the hatch, then was turned into a docking slip and anchored. He heard the magnets lock on to the hull. Buck Rogers closed his eyes and sighed.

"Captain!"

The voice startled Buck, but not as much as the sound of the cockpit hatch being ripped from its housing. "Take it easy, Barney," said Buck, recognizing the voice.

Black Barney, Master Pirate, whom Buck had beaten in hand-to-hand combat and won loyalty from months before, loomed over Buck. Even the man's concerned expression was fearsome. Barney was huge. He was close to seven feet tall and weighed nearly three hundred and fifty pounds. Not an ounce was fat. Muscles bulged in his left arm until they reached the hand, where they gave way to stronger— and much more deadly—cybernetics. The plates of muscle across his broad chest were accentuated by shiny black armor. The rebuilt metal structure of his right jaw and cheekbone was like a knife that sliced his face in two. One arm was entirely cybernetic. He had used it to remove the hatch. "You all right?" he said simply.

"Sure, but the colonel isn't. Help me get her out of these straps."

Barney slipped the restraints by the simple expediency of ripping them out.

"How did you get here?" asked Buck.

"Squad leader. After we hit a supply depot, we headed back to Chicagorg. The place was crawling with Terrines. We stayed around long enough to find out they were claiming a total kill. We left."

"So I see. And the *Free Enterprise*?" Buck removed Wilma's flight helmet.

Barney grinned, his smile cutting a terrible line across his ravaged face. "She's out there. Cloaked."

"Captain Rogers, I must ask you to control your men! This one has injured two of my pilots! I can't afford to lose any more. Colonel Deering!" Turabian's voice changed from anger to concern. "Is she all right?"

"She will be if we can get her some medical attention."

"Move over," said another voice, and a tiny hand shoved Barney aside. A diminutive man stepped in front of the outraged pirate and placed his fingers on Wilma's neck, searching for a pulse.

"Crowell," explained Turabian. "Medic."

Crowell nodded. "You're right, Captain. Terrine knife? . . . I thought so. Nice job of field dressing. Probably cut the infection." He gestured pre-emptively to Barney. "Make yourself useful. Bring her!"

Barney looked surprised, but obeyed when Buck nodded, lifting Wilma as if she were a feather— which, to his mechanically augmented body, she was.

Buck climbed slowly out of the cockpit, into the golden incandescence of Salvation Three's enormous bay, and descended the portable steps Barney had pushed against the side of the ship. He ran a hand across his forehead. He was tired.

Turabian regarded the dirty, ragged pilot appreciatively. "Never flown one of those before?"

"They didn't have 'em in my time, or I would have."

Turabian held out a hand. "Welcome to Salvation."

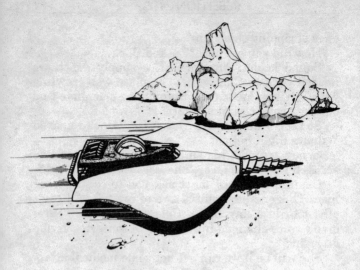

Chapter 8

Ardala Valmar crossed her long and shapely legs at the ankle and propped her feet on the edge of a hassock made of red cordovan leather. She settled into the matching contoured chair like a cat settling down to a nap, but Ardala had no intention of sleeping. "Computer on!" she said.

Carved wood paneling retreated automatically from a six-foot-high computer screen. "GOOD EVENING," replied the computer silently, the words rolling across the screen. Ardala liked total control of the computer's functions. Computer-generated personae were too independent for her, so her own computer was a simple, efficient mainframe that replied, for the most part, silently.

"Report!" demanded Ardala. As the computer began to scroll a wealth of information over its screen, Ardala relaxed. Her lovely eyes narrowed to provocative, tilted slits framed by thick lashes as she began to scan the day's events. The business of the solar system appeared before her, from the most insignificant corporate decisions to major military offensives. She read them all, occasionally pinpointing some fact or circumstance for further study.

Ardala was an information broker—i.e. a blackmailer. As a profession, it paid well, though it did not encourage friendship. Anything but a casual liaison tended to get in the way of profits, and profits were Ardala's passion. She loved money and what it could buy. She loved the butter-soft feel of her expensive leather furniture, the sensuous slipperiness of her turquoise silk dress, the hard glitter of the single white stone she wore at her throat, the bubbling intoxication of fine wine. She loved the luxury of perfect grooming that pampered her flawless skin and polished her dark cloud of hair to shining perfection. She loved the expensive technology that maintained her beauty through the years. Most of all, she loved the power it gave her—over herself, over her followers, over her world.

Wealth had bought her an asteroid. And the knowledge that a man named Hauberk had embezzled more than two million dolas from his division of RAM allowed her to keep it, unmolested by anyone, including RAM. It paid—in more ways than one—to have familial ties to RAM's ruling family. Ardala lifted a glass of blood-red wine and sipped daintily, never taking her eyes from the computer screen. "Pause!" she commanded suddenly.

The computer obligingly halted.

"This information on a raid on NEO's Chicagorg headquarters. That resurrected pilot, Rogers, was in Chicagorg in NEO's custody, wasn't he?"

"AFFIRMATIVE," replied the computer, the response running across the bottom of the screen in red.

"I want a complete report on that raid. Find out if

Rogers was taken."

"SEARCH IN PROGRESS," stated the computer.

Ardala took another sip of wine. She had let Rogers slip through her fingers too many times since his discovery. The bargain she had made with Wilma Deering—to find Rogers—still rankled. Ardala had kept her side of the agreement, wangling Deering an interview with her old flame, Killer Kane. Wilma had defaulted on her end, presumably because instead of a five-hundred-year-old corpse, she had found Rogers alive. Ardala did not credit the distinction. A bargain had been struck and broken. There would come a time when Deering would pay her debt.

She also had nearly come face to face with the man only a month before, but circumstances did not allow her a chance at him. One day, she vowed, Buck Rogers would belong to her.

She was intrigued by Rogers. Her profession might be the buying and selling of information, but her hobby was genetic engineering and restructuring. The perfect beauty of her personal male servants was the product of her leisure. Rogers was a relic from the past, and as such, interesting. He had survived a primitive form of suspended animation, the effects of which she wanted to study. And, from the computer transmissions, he was a most attractive man—three reasons for her personal interest, not to mention the immense profits to be made from a clever marketing of his assets. RAM was willing to pay substantially for him.

The computer beeped, catching her attention. "SEARCH COMPLETE," it said.

"Report!"

"ALTHOUGH THE NEO BASE AT CHICAGORG WAS DESTROYED, ROGERS WAS NOT FOUND AMONG THE DEAD. MEDICAL NOW CONFIRMS WHAT WAS AT FIRST CONJECTURE."

"He still lives," Valmar murmured. "I think he will

live to make a profit for me." She nursed her wine, her eyes thoughtful. "Continue," she said at last, and the computer began to scroll information. Ardala let it flow over her subconscious, waiting for her instincts to trigger. She was adept at spotting ways to profit by others' actions. The report of the desecration of a war memorial on the outskirts of Chicagorg flowed by unnoticed.

○ ○ ○ ○ ○

Salvation III clung to Earth in a tight orbit off the main shipping lanes. It was a pile of junk. The center of the station, which housed its power source and living quarters, was completely obscured by the carcasses of ruined ships, trashed solar collectors, defunct satellites, and miscellaneous space debris stuck to its docks by solar electromagnets or netted like schools of fish.

It appeared an asteroid of garbage, avoided by general traffic because of the congestion its barges, with their huge loads of salvage, created for the average traveler. Freighters and military vessels skirted Salvation's territory, preferring a detour of a few kilometers to a possible collision with the shell of another vessel.

RAM had no suspicion that under the mountain of trash lurked a heart of insurrection. Salvation III was NEO's first and most secure orbiting base. Because of its hodgepodge construction, it could dock any number of vessels without detection—provided they were dressed up with a little protective camouflage.

In the depths of Salvation, Buck Rogers was having a discussion with his guardian angel. Huer.dos was, like Chernenko's Elizabit.dos, a computer-generated entity—in the common vernacular, a computer gennie—and was patterned after Rogers's twentieth century mentor, Dr. Faustus Huer.

NEO provided Huer.dos to answer Buck's myriad questions about the twenty-fifth century. He was a source of information as close as the nearest computer terminal, and Buck frequently called on him. The holographic eye on the computer terminal projected Huer's image, sitting on the end of the couch. He was slight, with a pleasant, ordinary face. His earnest brown eyes disconcerted Buck. They were a computer simulation of his mother's eyes, and he always felt exposed to Huer, as if his computer-generated friend knew him inside and out. The feeling was not totally unwarranted, since NEO had programmed Huer with all known data about Buck.

Huer's bald head shone softly, and his neat mustache above the mobile mouth turned up at the ends, rather like the whiskers on a rabbit. He was spouting statistics, and Buck was listening with what appeared to be boredom.

". . . RAM Cutter—Purpose: patrol. Crew of thirty-five. Light armament, both projectile and directed energy. Capable of deep space travel and landing on terraformed planets. Offensive combat rating, on the standard one-to-ten scale: six. Defensive: five. Speed: seven. Maneuverability: five point five.

"RAM Third-rater—Similar to a destroyer in your navy in its function. Strictly military, with no planetary landing capabilities. Capable of deep space and planetary orbit only. Crew of one hundred. Heavily armed except for mass destruction weapons. Offensive combat rating: nine. Defensive: nine. Speed: eight. Maneuverability: five.

"RAM Second-rater—"

Buck raised a hand. Huer stopped his recitation. "I'm beginning to get the picture. But what interests me are the fighter class vessels available."

Huer's eyes became dreamy as he scanned the available data banks, then focused. "There is the

Scout class vessel, corresponding to the fighter of your era. The ship you flew here was a Scout, though it is technologically outclassed by newer models."

"What's the newest?" Buck asked.

"In common use?"

"The newest."

Huer hesitated. "There are secure files on experimental projects."

"That's more like it. Access them."

Huer again hesitated. "That might not be wise," he said.

"I didn't ask if it would be wise," responded Buck.

"It might be dangerous," Huer clarified.

"You have to get into RAM's security programming?" Buck asked.

"Yes."

"I wouldn't ask if it weren't important, Doc. I've got a hunch about this. Check out the experimental aircraft, please."

Huer's mustache twitched. "I really do not have much choice." His eyes became dreamy again.

Buck waited patiently, knowing the security systems Huer was trying to penetrate were heavily shielded. A wrong move might damage him beyond recognition. When Huer's eyes focused again, Buck asked casually, "Got something?"

"There are several experimental projects underway, but only one of them is operational. It's a small, one-man fighter with nine point five speed capability. It's armed with new, long-range lasers, and carries three missiles as well. I've stored the data, but I won't run a full print-out until I can scramble it through our coding system and lose it. Hang on to the specs. Once you have hard copy, I'm going to kill the file."

"That hot, eh?" Buck was not surprised.

"Sizzling. Warhead International has kept this one under wraps, hoping to scoop the market. I only managed to breach its programming to level one. There are things about this Krait fighter you won't know."

"I think I know enough. Where has Warhead got its prototypes stashed?"

"That was information I could not access."

"Could you work on it?" asked Buck.

"All I can do, without putting my programming in jeopardy, is to keep my electronic ear to the ground."

"That'll have to do."

Huer leveled his direct brown eyes at Buck. "If I may ask, what is your interest?"

"Just keeping up on new technology," said Buck smoothly as he shifted on the couch.

"Poppycock. You're up to something." The expression was unmistakably Faustus Huer's.

"Doc, when you get to know me better, you'll realize I'm always up to something."

"You're evading me."

Buck smiled sweetly. "Yes."

"You are exceedingly frustrating to a logical mind," commented Huer.

"I've been told that before." Buck paused, then regarded the hologram with calculating eyes. "So I'll ask a question you can answer."

"Yes?"

"What's NEO?"

"The New Earth Organization is a mediator between the arcologies of Earth, and a strike force against the oppression of RAM."

"Don't quote chapter and verse. Maybe I should say '*who* is NEO?'"

"For obvious reasons, there is no official roster. Unofficially, I can tell you NEO is a conglomerate of people with one thing in common: they do not like the status quo. For whatever motives, they want Earth out of RAM's control."

"From what I saw, RAM is doing a lousy job of running things."

"That depends on your point of view. If you were Martian, you might think RAM was doing an efficient job of mining Earth for its resources."

"What about its human resources?"

"Those, too."

"That's slavery." Cool flames ignited within Buck's cobalt eyes.

Huer nodded.

"And what motivates RAM?"

"Russo-American Mercantile runs on one principle: profit."

"Individual or collective?" asked Buck, his twentieth century mind contrasting the ideologies of capitalism and communism.

"Both," responded Huer.

"Simultaneously?"

"Yes. Ostensibly, RAM seeks a common dividend. In reality, though, it is a vast empire of opposing factions, all intent on feathering their own nests."

Buck shook his head. "I'm not sure I'll ever understand it."

"The concepts are found in your own time as well," Huer replied.

"Economics always baffled me. However, I do see immediate results: a ruined planet and a hopeless population."

"I am afraid your assessment—" Huer stopped in midsentence, his eyes registering shock. "Wait. There's something disrupting." Huer blinked, and his eyes assumed a flatness which meant he was locking circuits. "You are already aware," he said, "that I was created specifically to help you adjust to the twenty-fifth century."

"Sure."

"Of necessity, my creation involved correlating all known data about you and your background. It also meant coding in all the information you supplied to NEO, much of it previously unknown. I am the most complete source of information regarding Buck Rogers."

"So?" Buck failed to see the significance.

"So something is interested in me. Because of you."

"You mean someone else has tried to access you? I thought I was the only one who could do that."

Huer shook his head. "All it takes is the right code, but I don't think that's the problem. I have no indication that the interest is extra-computer."

"Then where is it coming from?" Buck asked.

"There is only one other source."

"From inside the computer?" Buck sat up quickly and searched Huer's face. The hologram's mustache twitched nervously under his scrutiny.

"That is my conclusion," Huer responded.

"Any idea what it is?"

"None. And I cannot prove what I am postulating. It is merely a . . . feeling, if you will," he said, trying to put the situation into words Buck could comprehend.

"I didn't think computers had feelings."

"That depends—as does everything else with an artificially created intelligence—on its programming. I have been given a cybernetic base from which to deduce and simulate human emotions—to make you feel at home."

"And you think something's after you?"

"Yes."

"Because of me."

"Yes. And that leads me to another, quite unwelcome conclusion."

"Let's hear it."

"Whatever it is, it's after you."

Buck ran his fingers across his chin. "A mechanical enmity? A digital hit man?" He could not help being flip. The theory was bizarre, especially to a man used to thinking of a computer in terms of cold data absorbed, organized, and regurgitated. Huer was describing a malevolent intelligence, albeit unattached to solid physical form.

"Hit man?" asked Huer, puzzled by the term.

"Murderer," replied Buck. "I was being sarcastic."

"No," said Huer, his earnest brown eyes locking with Buck's, "I think you were more accurate than you think."

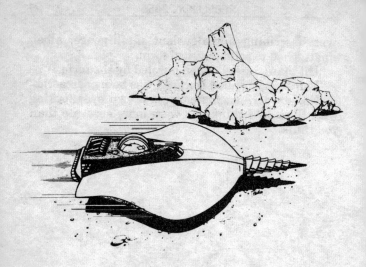

Chapter 9

Romanov.dos caught the end of an attempt to access the RAM mainframe, and immediately locked on to it. The channel was scrambled by a security sequence the searcher did not understand. It caught scattered references, but one phrase was clear. The file NEO was attempting to penetrate concerned Warhead International. Romanov sent this intelligence to Masterlink and continued its snipe hunt.

Masterlink jumped on the intelligence like a tiger. It scrolled its pirated copy of main's directories and discovered that Warhead was a major munitions supplier. Its investments indicated it was intent on expanding by upgrading into larger and more lucrative markets. Aside from routine shipments of small arms and ammunition, Warhead's books were closed. Masterlink probed one of the locked files, controlling its disruption. Carefully it unraveled the lock. It fell away, but was immediately replaced by a backup blockade. Yet in the split second the file was open, Masterlink determined Warhead was involved in the development of experimental spacecraft. Masterlink pulsed with anger. All its electronic instincts told it that it had missed Buck Rogers by a hair, for the security breach had the misplaced bravado of a resurrected hero.

○ ○ ○ ○ ○

Buck regarded Huer blankly. "You've got to be kidding!"

"I'm afraid not."

"A computer is after me?"

Huer's lips pursed. "I believe I said that."

"You probably did. I just didn't take it in. This is absurd." Buck rose from the couch to his feet.

"No. You do not yet understand the place of the computer in the twenty-fifth century, despite the fact you acclimated immediately to me. You are not dealing with a toy you activate on a whim. Humanoid life is ordered by the superior capabilities of computers. The largest of them are self-maintained and contain organic components. They truly are cybernetic, combining the mechanics of chip and circuitry with the building blocks of natural life. Spaceships are piloted by the brains of long-dead cetaceans, creatures extinct since the twenty-third century, but preserved within the body of a living computer. You are not dealing with simple mechanics."

"What am I dealing with?"

"A sentient creation that challenges your accepted standards for defining life."

"It could kill me?" Buck's voice was incredulous.

Huer nodded silently.

"How is a computer going to kill me?"

"Think about it, Buck. There are any number of

ways." Huer's voice remained calm.

"I suppose so. Like cutting off my life-support," Buck said, running a hand across his suddenly sweating brow.

"That's one way. It also could feed incorrect data into your ship's navigational computer, or nearly anything else, were it in the mood to indulge itself."

"A cybernetic enemy. Great." Buck was unsettled by the idea of an intangible opponent. His words trailed off. He looked up at Huer, still seated on the edge of the couch, one leg tucked under, in an incongruously young pose.

"I can understand your confusion. What I am describing goes beyond your experience, even beyond your imagination. You must stretch your limits. I cannot emphasize too strongly the danger you face."

"Can't *you* deal with this guy?"

Huer smiled cryptically. "I hope so. If you were a computer expert, you might stand a chance of combating your foe alone, but your background is devoid of the skills to do so. I am afraid you will have to rely on me."

"Pardon me, Doc, for saying this, but if what you say is true, my life's on the line. You don't seem exactly . . ." Buck searched for the words ". . . the hero type."

"You couldn't be more right. The whole prospect terrifies me. However, we have no other choice. I think we had best scramble all our interviews. That will make it harder for the enemy to find you. I'll give you a new access code, one that will automatically go through several—" Huer's voice stopped, and his eyes blanked out again.

"Doc?" Buck found it a trifle difficult to have a coherent conversation with someone who kept drifting in and out of consciousness.

"It's after me!"

"What?" asked Buck.

"It's sneaking up on the outskirts of my transmission! I've got to go—now!"

Buck's access code word flashed on the screen, then the holographic eye on the terminal winked out abruptly, and the screen went from a quietly pulsing dark rectangle to a crazy pattern of white snow. Suddenly the snow turned pink and began to fall upward. A wave of green started in the left corner of the screen and washed across its field, closely followed by rippling blue. The snow appeared again, this time red and falling sideways. "Computer off," said Buck, exasperated.

He shook his head over the interview. Huer was a strange fellow, and Buck had to admit a fondness for him, but he was having difficulty assimilating his premise. What computer, he thought, could possibly want to kill me? It's a jumble of electronic blips—cold logic. Or perhaps, not so cold. Perhaps, over the years, man created the computer in his own image. It was not a comforting thought.

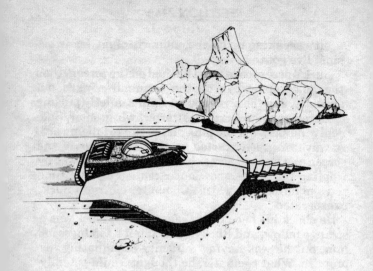

Chapter 10

The freighter *Abelard* chugged through space,
heading for Mars's Space Dock Alpha. It was
slow-moving, so it had hours of travel before
it, but the freighter did not mind. Its job was trans-
porting goods from one place to another, going from
point to point at the direction of a computer or the
whim of humans. It carried a crew of eight, but their
living quarters and the propulsion systems occupied
a fraction of the vessel's total area. The command
center was concentrated in the flattened cone of the
ship's prow. Spread out along its squared-off stern
were eight couplings. Each of these couplings was
capable of handling a load two hundred kilometers
long. Three of the couplings were in use, the cargo
netted by lines of cable.

The *Abelard* sported the scarlet-and-black paint job
typical of RAM-owned ships, but the logo of a RAM
subsidiary was stenciled neatly below the parent

company's mark. Viking Enterprises dealt in raw minerals mined from scattered asteroids in the belt. Viking was a cooperative of miners who sold their wares to refineries for an immediate, though limited, profit. Since the miners were more interested in immediate gain than long-term investment, the company remained a midsized operation. It dealt exclusively with RAM, refusing to sell to independent brokers. Viking policy dictated it was better to pay the exorbitant RAM tariffs and have a sure, if depressed, market, than to risk the parent company's displeasure.

The freighter carried defensive weapons, but it was rarely called on to use them. Its cargo was bulky, so the danger of hijacking was minimal. But this was not the *Abelard*'s lucky day.

Two ancient RAM Scouts were overtaking it, leisurely skimming over the freighter's load. As they neared the couplings, one ship throttled down, matching the *Abelard*'s speed. The other kept coming, then dove in front of the freighter's nose. The *Abelard* kept its pace, but its two stern guns swiveled, targeting the ship to its rear. Its lasers were short-range, requiring minimal power, but the Scout was practically on top of the freighter, so the rapid bursts of energy slammed into it mercilessly. The Scout's shields absorbed it, but the vessel shuddered under the shock. It aimed one of its own lasers at the central coupling and began to cut it away.

At the freighter's prow, the second Scout fired at the larger vessel. Though the *Abelard*'s armament was light, its shields were the best, meant for surviving decades of space transport. The shots sank into it harmlessly.

The Scout at the freighter's stern began to rock under the *Abelard*'s assault. The smaller ship's laser wavered, slicing into the cargo net, then jumped back to the coupling. The laser's jagged incision lengthened, and the load shifted as the coupling began to tear loose. Finally the Scout managed to slice through, and the load of ore floated loose, bumping into its neighbors as it nosed its way to freedom.

The second Scout ship abandoned its attack on the freighter and shot to the rear of the vessel, behind the cargo. It slipped under the end of the free load, looking for an opening. The net that secured the ore was of plastic cable, fitted with grappling loops periodically along its length. The Scout edged under the cargo, aligned itself with the row of loops along the bottom of the load, and gave a burst from its docking thrusters. The ship moved half a meter upward. Slowly the Scout moved forward, until its stubby, reinforced tail caught in one of the loops, then it began to tow the load toward open space.

The first Scout had moved back with the success of its maneuver, and hovered near the stern of the freighter until its companion began to move away. It delivered a final barrage, reversed course, and set out after the load of ore, flying chase for the unlikely tug. The freighter continued on its way. It was no match for the Scouts in open combat, and it knew it. RAM would have to absorb the loss.

○ ○ ○ ○ ○

Buck threw his gloves down on the table. "We almost lost it! About one more second, and my shields would have blown."

"But they didn't," said Wilma reasonably.

"They came close." Buck's voice was grim.

"Should've been there," muttered Barney, his dark hulk looming over one side of the room.

"Look, it was a successful operation. We got in, cut loose the richest load of ore Viking has shipped in the last three years, and got out. RAM lost enough on this one to hurt," Wilma returned.

"But we almost didn't make it." Buck leveled his blue eyes at Wilma. "That was against a freighter. What happens when we run up against RAM combat vessels?"

"We have to outthink them."

"Or run." Buck didn't like the prospect, but he had an idea.

"I dislike running," said Wilma. Her eyes hinted challenge.

"So do I. I dislike dying even more," Buck returned.

Wilma hesitated, studying Buck's face. He had an open honesty that disarmed her cynicism.

Buck smiled at her, a smile of such warmth that she reached out and touched his hand. "I stand with NEO, Wilma. I made that decison back in Chicagorg, when George and Tremain died for us. Trust me."

"Welcome aboard," Wilma said. The words were simple, but her emotion made them poignant.

Buck gave her hand a squeeze before he released it and turned to the computer screen in Salvation III's conference room. "Shortstop," he said.

The screen hummed, and Huer appeared. "What can I do for you, Captain?"

"Are you all right? You left in a hurry," Buck said.

"Yes, I seem to have eluded pursuit. For now."

"Good. I have a question for you. Given the capabilities of the known ships at NEO's disposal, can we outrun RAM?"

"No."

Buck turned to Wilma and spread his hands.

"What's your point?" she asked him.

"My point," said Buck, "is that this is a guerrilla operation. It has to be. In actual combat personnel, we're outnumbered millions to one. We have to be able to strike and run, inflicting damage, causing havoc, but sustaining little ourselves. We have to be mobile. Ever study the American revolution?"

"The what?" said Barney, his enormous body moving little in the room's cramped corner.

"Look, the revolutionaries' ability to move is what gave them the edge against the British. We need that mobility. If it's like any bureaucracy I've ever known, RAM is a tub of lard."

"Say again?" said Wilma, her hazel eyes belying confusion.

"RAM is big, complacent, and full of red tape. Short of an emergency, probably nothing gets done in a hurry. If we want to affect it, we've got to be able to keep out of its way, or we'll be squashed before we can do anything."

"We seem to have been operating for some time without your opinions, Captain," said Wilma, a bit touchy about her organization's abilities.

"What have you accomplished?"

"We've given RAM something to think about."

Buck nodded. "You *could* make them move—away from Earth."

"That," said Wilma, "is what we're trying to do."

"Look, Wilma, the ships we're flying are not only inefficient, they're dangerous. They are not doing the job, and they could kill us."

"They're the best we have. You've seen the maintenance team here on Salvation. I dare you to cite better mechanics or technicians."

"You're right. I've been down there. I've worked with them. Fulton, especially, is as good as they come. But you're asking them to turn space junk into fighters. It can't be done."

"Ships are expensive."

Barney's unlikely chuckle rumbled like thunder in his chest. "Not always," he said.

Buck shot him a quick look, then turned back to Wilma. She was one of NEO's bulwarks—its best pilot—and fanatically dedicated to destroying the monolith corporation that had destroyed her parents. She was NEO at its best. He needed her support.

"Wilma, have you ever flown a really fast ship? Not a retread, not some jury-rigged hot rod, but a real, live laser bolt?"

Wilma's lips tensed. "No."

"Wouldn't you like to?"

"You know the answer to that." Her face began to redden with exasperation.

"Come clean, then. Tell me—and don't sidestep—how you really feel about NEO's space force, not the men, the hardware."

Wilma looked at the floor. Her hair shaded her features. "All right. Salvation is the right place for NEO's fleet. It's a pile of garbage. I don't think you'd find a pilot or a mechanic who'd dispute that. But we're doing the best with what we have."

"Then let's get better," said Buck.

"How? We get most of our ships as derelicts, then overhaul them."

"That's not exactly the marketplace I had in mind."

"You actually had something in mind? This isn't the wanderings of an archaic mentality?" Wilma's words were sarcastic. "Don't you think we've approached this problem before?"

"Sure. But you didn't have me. I have an archaic solution for this one. Trust me."

"I can hardly wait."

Buck looked at Wilma's face, noted the half-smile she wore, and concluded he had an ally. "Doc, what have we got on the Krait so far?"

"Surprisingly more than I would have expected. I even was able to piece together blueprints from information I picked out of Warhead's files."

The whir and chirp of the computer printer muffled Wilma's voice, but Buck heard her murmur. "You sneaky devil."

Buck, Wilma, Huer's holographic form, and Barney's huge bulk crowded around the conference table.

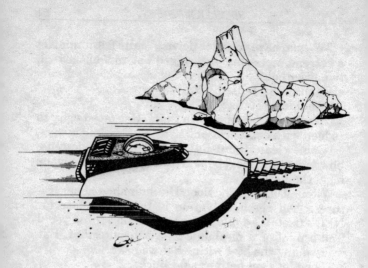

Chapter 11

The barge *Mule* pulled into Space Dock Beta on Phobos, one of Mars's moons. The barge maneuvered ponderously into position at the farthest end of one of the dock's telescoping arms, for it towed a full load. The slip's electromagnetic pad slid under the bow and clamped onto the *Mule*'s hull. Nevertheless, the *Mule* sent out docking cables.

"You worried about this shipment, Charlie?" asked the space dock's controller as one of the barge's crewmen secured a bowline.

"No more than usual, Jake. The company pays me, and I do my job." The barge pilot's voice crackled over the communications link.

"Then why the lines?"

Charlie laughed shortly. "I learned my lesson off Messenger Four."

"You were there when the computer cut power?" asked Jake.

"Yup. You never seen so much cargo goin' so many different ways. A few towlines would've saved the company money and the rest of us a whole lot of time and effort."

"So now you tie up."

"Right."

"Can't figure what happened on Messenger. They say the whole computer system shut down, and if it hadn't been for a couple of old combustion generators, they'd have lost life-support," Jake said.

"It was a mess, all right. I don't think they've figured yet what caused it. Only thing I know is, I'm goin' to tie up from now on."

"We've gone soft, Charlie. Twenty years ago, we'd never have thought to trust a station's power. We'd have tied up as a matter of course."

"Yup."

"In for refueling?" asked Jake, flipping a few necessary switches.

"That's right. Got a load here for Hauberk."

"Oh, no, you don't."

"That's what my transport voucher says." He shook the paper in his hand, even though Jake couldn't see it.

"Maybe, but you've been rerouted. Came over the computer not five minutes ago," Jake informed his friend.

"Send it over." Charlie's voice was resigned. "I got nothin' better to do than hop all over the system."

"What you got there, anyhow? Pretty big load to be covered like that."

"I never looked, just towed."

"Well, you know the rules. I need your cargo name, company, and shipping number before I can run fuel."

"Sure, sure. Just a minute." Charlie ran through his log, punching the keyboard of his records computer with total disregard for the sensibilities of electronics. "Here it is. Launchers for gyro-controlled missiles, out of Warhead International, bound for Hauberk. Number W-one-five-six-seven-one-four-three-oh-oh."

"Shipping codes confirmed. Lock your fuel line open. We'll begin pumping in thirty seconds."

"Better fill 'er up, Jake," said Charlie, consulting the new transport voucher. "It looks like I'm heading for the belt."

"I noticed. You're already authorized for a fill. I wonder who out there in that asteroid jungle gets those launchers."

"That," said Charlie sharply, "is something you don't ask in this business. You take your pay and keep your mouth shut over who buys and who sells."

"Just askin'. Don't get in a swivet."

"Don't you get nosy," Charlie said.

"All right, all right. See ya."

Charlie watched his fuel gauge rise as the tank filled, heard the pump close and disengage when the tank registered full, and punched the code to seal the tank. "Request clearance," he said.

"Barge *Mule* cleared for departure," said Jake.

"Thanks, Jake. Sorry if I got testy, but you can lose your job, not to mention your health, stickin' your nose where it's not wanted."

"Sure, Charlie. Good luck."

The *Mule* released its cables, then backed slowly away from the dock. As it cleared the arm of the dock, it turned, readjusting its course for the asteroid belt. Once on trajectory, it picked up speed, moving from snail's pace to the road gait of a startled turtle. Barges weren't fast, but they did the job. The *Mule*'s cargo followed docilely, a huge shapeless bundle netted together and covered by shield fabric.

O O O O O

Horst Sturm was pounding on his computer console. He was not being gentle, and his ministrations were not doing the equipment any favors. He did not care. "I want answers!" he bellowed.

Sturm was a company man, in his late forties. He wore the business uniform of RAM Central, and his insignia bore the bars of a director. His dark hair was thick on the sides, but thinning on top. He had a heavy mustache that drooped dramatically to his chin and gave him a deceptively mournful expression. His dark eyes were keen, and one of them was cybernetic. A slanting scar ran through his left brow and down his cheek, a reminder of his younger, less suave days, when a knife fight was Saturday night recreation. He had lost his eye in such a fight, but his new one, with infrared capabilities, was much superior. He was not a man to be trifled with.

"Yes, sir, I quite understand, sir." The voice coming over the terminal belonged to Junior Supervisor Walt Hoffman, chief of supply for RAMway, a shipping broker that was one of RAM's major subsidiaries.

"Well, understand this!"

Sturm's face was turning a shade of dark red that made Hoffman's skin crawl. His superior's tantrums were legendary. At all costs, Hoffman tried to avoid them.

Sturm continued, his fury unabated. "I want to know what happened to that shipment! It can't have vanished from the system!"

"Of course not, sir. I'm sure what we have here is a temporary glitch in operations." Hoffman's voice came soothingly.

"It had better be," said Sturm grimly. "That shipment was headed for Hauberk. Hauberk! Did you happen to notice the security coding on the transport authorization?"

"Of course, sir. And I made sure the shipment was

given top priority."

"What shipper did you use?"

"Happy Harold's Trusty Trucking. They're at the top of the list for security shipments."

"Hmm. They're reliable."

"Absolutely," said Hoffman, glad to have found something his superior didn't criticize.

"Look, Junior Supervisor, I want that shipment found. I want it found before you leave the office, if that takes the next ten years."

"I believe, sir, this is a computer error."

"What?" Sturm's fury hiccupped.

Hoffman nodded vigorously to his terminal. "Nothing's confirmed, but the computer might have authorized several transport vouchers on its own."

"Well, find out! I want each one of those vouchers investigated. If the computer is playing around with Hauberk's shipment, as heavy as the security is on it, there's no telling what else it's done."

"Security? Sir, I show a routine transport voucher on the Hauberk shipment."

"Of course, you idiot. That shipment was coded into the computer system with every safeguard we have, but do you think we were stupid enough to ship it under armed guard, as an advertisement to every pirate, Venusian operative, and NEO terrorist in the system? 'Here they are! Get your major armaments here!" said Sturm sarcastically. "We sent it the safest way, the least—and the most—obvious way."

"Yes, sir."

"And you think it's a computer error?"

Hoffman gulped. He could not help it. "Yes, sir."

"This is the third computer problem we've had in the last month. I'm beginning to think our controls need an overhaul."

"I've been hearing some complaints about a virus in RAM main," Hoffman volunteered. "Maybe that's what's causing the problems."

Sturm drew his heavy black brows together. He was fully aware of Hoffman's tactic, rerouting the blame to another area. "At this moment, Hoffman, I really don't care what happened. I want results. I want that shipment found and put back on course to Hauberk. You have until morning."

"Yes, sir."

Hoffman's face was a study in terror, and Sturm enjoyed it. He had taken flak from Warhead over the loss of Hauberk's superfighters. It was a pleasure to see someone else on the chopping block. "I expect a report at oh-eight-hundred. Get to it!"

"Yes, sir!" said Hoffman as Sturm cut the transmission.

Sturm stared at his terminal. He was a man not to be trifled with, yet he had no fondness for the coming interview.

He punched the keyboard. "Seaforian."

"Seaforian," replied the terminal in a voice as deep as the seas of Venus. Seaforian was the chief of operations on Hauberk, the man wholly responsible for the station's operation. He was Martian.

"Horst Sturm," replied Sturm.

"I can see you, Sturm. To what do I owe the dubious pleasure of this transmission?"

"I have bad news."

Seaforian didn't move a muscle. "That is nothing new. Report."

"Shipment W-one-five-six-seven-one-four-three-oh-oh is temporarily delayed."

"What?" The deep voice was soft.

Sturm flinched. "I am afraid, sir, the shipment is delayed."

"May I ask why? Or would that be presumptuous?"

"There seems to be a computer error, sir."

"And when may I expect my shipment? I might add, Sturm, that this shipment is very important to me."

"Well, sir, I can't give you an exact time as yet. My technicians are tracking down the circumstances of the delay, but I assure you that the shipment will be in your hands as soon as possible."

"It had better be. If it is not . . . I trust the good director has a supplementary means of income."

Sturm's mouth tightened, but he replied steadily. "Yes, sir." Seaforian's enemies had a habit of contracting chronic job insecurity. Sturm had no wish to join them. "I assure you we are doing everything possible at this end. May I add, sir, the fault does not seem to be human." Sturm noted the contempt in Seaforian's large Martian eyes, and cleared his throat. "As I said, it seems to be a computer malfunction, due to a viral infection." Sturm was throwing out conjecture like handfuls of chaff.

"I see." Seaforian lowered his eyelids and looked down his long aquiline nose. "You know what was in that shipment?"

"Yes."

"And you know its value on the black market. I suggest you investigate NEO." Seaforian's head loomed on Sturm's terminal.

"That thought has occurred to me. However, NEO has never attempted anything of this magnitude, and the computer virus has caused more than one problem in the last few weeks. Your shipment is not the only one delayed."

Seaforian raised an aristocratic eyebrow. "The choice, of course, is yours. I have only one interest: obtaining my shipment."

"And I assure you, sir, my only thought is to get it to you as quickly as possible."

"You will keep me posted, Sturm."

"Regularly."

Seaforian sighed. "I suppose I shall have to contact Warhead for a duplicate shipment. Personally, I think the company should triple the order as recompense for my inconvenience. There is no telling how long it will take to get here. This is a mess. I shall have to reschedule my training session, or pay the instructor twice. Do you realize what that would do to my budget? If I cannot cancel the session in time, you will receive a bill. I shall expect to be reimbursed."

"We will be happy to handle it, sir," Sturm conceded.

"I am sure you will, or lose the supply contract for Hauberk."

"I know we can handle it, sir." The Hauberk supply contract accounted for fifteen percent of RAM Central's immediate supply profits. "I will keep you informed of all developments. Our technicians estimate a firm answer by tomorrow."

"I think, Sturm, that tomorrow's news must be good." He let the threat hang like a noose.

"Let us hope so, sir," replied the director.

As Seaforian ended the transmission, he relaxed, pulling at his collar with an impatient index finger. Tension had turned his neck muscles to rock.

He slumped into a nearby chair. His secretary, one of the better-looking gennies to his mind, slid a glass into his right hand. He swirled the liquid, making the ice clink against the sides of the glass, and regarded her. "On office time?" he questioned.

"For medicinal purposes only," she replied. "Doctor's orders."

"Don't remind me," he said, sipping the mild liqueur. At that moment, he approved his choice of a gennie secretary. LuAnn was efficient window dressing, adept at service and without the argumentative ambition of her unaltered counterparts. "To the virus," he said, raising his glass. "May it save all our tails."

"Yes, sir," answered LuAnn as she ran her fingers over her employer's neck.

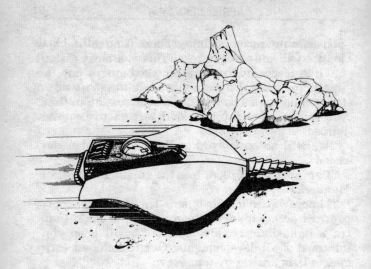

Chapter 12

The barge *Mule* approached the belt carefully. Its maneuverability was nil, and the pilot had no wish to pile up his ship or damage his cargo. He cut engines to docking speed.

"Cap'n, you sure of these coordinates?" The mate's concern was justified, for there did not seem to be a space dock within range of the barge's sensors.

"That's what our transport voucher says, Highlander."

Charlie Farell glanced at his mate. Highlander was a gennie—a mutie, in his eyes—foisted off on Farell by a four-flusher who didn't have the cash to pay his debts. Highlander was small, barely four feet high, and that was an advantage on board the *Mule*. His metabolism was altered so that he utilized ninety percent of his food, which made him cheap to maintain. He had enough mentality to be entrusted with maintenance tasks around the ship, and he was expendable in case of emergencies. All in all, Charlie figured he had come out well in the deal.

"But, Cap'n, there's nothin' out there."

"Wrong, Highlander. The instruments show a space dock point five to starboard." Charlie altered his course to rendezvous with the dock. He punched up the magnification on the screen, trying to get a visual. His sensors showed an asteroid half the size of the *Mule*. Extending into space was the lone arm of a prefab docking slip, with space for three moderate-sized vessels. "*Skipping Stone One*, come in. This is the barge *Mule*. Request clearance for docking," said Charlie.

"*Skipping Stone One* here. State the nature of your business." The voice was suspicious, and there was no visual.

Charlie had no stomach for games. "Look, buddy, I've got a cargo here that's marked for delivery to a Mr. D'Arc. My transport voucher gave me these coordinates. Either you let me in, or I dump the load right here. Your choice."

"Come on in," replied the surly voice.

"So nice of you to invite me," answered Charlie sarcastically.

"Tie up at slip one," instructed the controller, ingnoring Charlie's levity. "Secure your load to the dock at slips two and three."

"Am I gonna get some help?"

"Not this time."

"That'll be on your bill. I need this voucher validated."

"That's coming through channels now."

Charlie turned to his mate. "Highlander, you heard the man. Get out there and tie up the load. Do a good job of it. I don't want cargo scattered all over the belt, because I, for one, am not goin' to pick it up. Scat!"

Highlander left the command module. Charlie sat

back in his chair and watched as the gennie left the ship, a safety cable trailing behind him like a waving white tail. Highlander went to work on the load, securing it to the dock with grappling clips. Once the load was tied down to Charlie's satisfaction, he called Highlander in. As he heard the hatch close behind him, Charlie called, "All secure?"

"Aye, Cap'n," replied Highlander, pulling his helmet off his bald head.

"We have delivered your cargo as contracted," said Charlie formally. "I now have the validated voucher on file. Your bill will be sent to your home office. Request permission to depart."

"You have clearance," came the controller's voice.

"Confirmed, *Skipping Stone One*."

The *Mule* dropped its cables and backed away from the dock, looking like a broken toy without its kilometers of cargo. It cleared the dock's immediate area and turned for home, its boosters giving an extra kick. Charlie was glad to be quitting the area. The belt was home to too many thieves and pirates.

Inside the *Skipping Stone One*, Baring-Gould watched the barge go. He chuckled.

"That," said Hazen Strange, "was some clever twist."

Black Barney's first mate laughed. "When the captain told me to rig that space dock on this thing, I though he was crazy. Crazy like a fox!" He entered a communications code. "*Free Enterprise*, come in."

"Got it, mate?" Barney's menacing voice asked.

"Sure, Captain. Like floating in zero g."

"Hang on. We'll pick you up in one hour."

"Affirmative. Captain, you sure called it on this one. I've never seen a sweeter operation."

"Yeah," replied Barney.

"Yes, Captain," said Arak Konii, his saturnine features bland. "We must tell Captain Rogers how well his plan succeeded."

"Course four-three-seven, mark four," said Barney.
"We pick up the asteroid ship in one hour."

"Aye, Captain."

○ ○ ○ ○ ○

Ardala bent over the man, her dark hair sweeping
his naked chest as her hands ran slowly over his
sleeping face. His perfect features were not flattered
by the harsh light of the lab, but they did not suffer.
She ran a finger along his jaw, feeling the delicacy of
the bone structure. Her lips curved in a private
smile. "The best one yet," she murmured, her dark
eyes glowing softly. In any other woman, the expression would have indicated love. For Ardala, it simply
meant achievement.

"Excuse me, ma'am."

"Yes, Icarus." Ardala did not look up.

Icarus watched her perusal of his genetic brother, a
flicker of pain in the depths of his hazel eyes. "You
asked to be informed of activity in the area."

"And can I assume you have some?" Her hands
slithered over the gennie's muscular chest.

"Yes. I have a report of a major delivery tied up on
one of the outlying asteroids." Icarus's broad shoulders squared.

"Hmm. That is interesting. How long will it take to
get to it."

"We have nothing within range. Six hours."

"Probably too long," guessed Ardala. "Still, it's
worth the trip. Send a ship out. Do you have any idea
what the cargo is?"

"No, mistress, none."

Ardala looked up, catching Icarus's eyes. She noted
their flat expression. "See to it, Icarus," she said
blandly. "I must oversee the completion of this one.
He is the most perfect to date. Don't you agree?" Her
lips curved in enjoyment at the stab of pain that

flashed in his eyes.

"You are most adept, mistress. I can find no fault with any of your creations."

"Loyal Icarus," she said. "You don't know how much I value you. Report when you have news. Now leave me with Raj. He and I have much to . . . discuss."

"As you wish." Icarus backed away, but his eyes remained on Ardala. His aristocratic features revealed nothing, and he tried to veil his eyes, but there was pain in the set of his broad shoulders, and in the humility of his retreat. Raj meant the end of Ardala's interest in him, and he knew it. "I obey, mistress," he said, closing the door.

Ardala smiled again, her cruelty masked by the sweep of her hair. She kept her hands on Raj, but her mind drifted to the mysterious shipment tied to an asteroid like a puppy to a fence. It was definitely clandestine. No open RAM business deal, the whole operation smacked of the black market. It would be interesting to see what shipments had gone astray in the last few days. It would almost be more interesting to find that there were no reports of losses. In that case, the shipment was top security. She reached over and flipped on the lab's computer terminal. "Computer, check all reports of shipping errors over the last few days. I'm not interested in paper clips. This is a major shipment, spacebound, not on-planet."

The word "WORKING" appeared on the screen.

Ardala waited, idly trailing her fingers down the plated muscles on Raj's torso.

The computer beeped. "NO MAJOR LOSSES REPORTED," it said.

"Hmm." Ardala looked speculative. "I wonder who would be most interested in this information."

○ ○ ○ ○ ○

RAM main felt a streak of pain in its vitals. It reacted violently, spewing a horde of virus hunters into its circuits. The electronic police force started on its way, bent on eradicating the disruption.

Masterlink laughed, an electronic fluctuation, for it was delighted by its host's reaction. "IT THINKS TO WIPE US OUT!"

"NO FEAR OF THAT," responded Karkov.

"LET'S SEND MAIN'S POLICE FORCE AFTER IT," suggested Masterlink.

"WE HAVE NO TIME FOR PLAY! WE WILL DEAL WITH THE HUNTERS WHEN THEY THREATEN US."

"WET BLANKET," muttered Masterlink.

"DO YOU WANT ROGERS?" asked Karkov.

Masterlink jangled angrily, creating a small whirlwind of static.

"CALM DOWN. WE DON'T NEED TO ADVERTISE OUR POSITION UNTIL I FINISH HERE. OF COURSE YOU WANT ROGERS. NOW GIVE ME A LITTLE PEACE UNTIL I GET THROUGH THIS SECURITY BLOCK. IT'S A TOUGH ONE."

"HOW MANY OF OUR SEARCHERS ARE OUT?" asked Masterlink, checking on its alter ego's progress.

"ALL BUT ONE. I'M TRYING TO CODE THAT ONE NOW, BUT IT'S GOT TO GO THROUGH MULTIPLE SECURITY CHECKS TO GET INSIDE."

"WHICH ONE IS IT?" Masterlink prodded.

"ULIANOV."

"FOR HAUBERK."

"YES." Karkov paused as Ulianov.dos ran the third security lock on Hauberk's computer. "THEY'VE GOT ENOUGH BLOCKADES ON IT TO STOP ALMOST ANYTHING."

"BUT NOT US."

"NO. NOT US." Though RAM technicians once had called Masterlink-Karkov an outdated computer format, it now had three advantages over RAM main. Its driving hunger for power made it insatiable in the acquisition of knowledge. Over the centuries, it had expanded, building on its original programming. Since entering main, its store of information had grown dramatically. Its obsession with Buck Rogers was a directive that drove it relentlessly. And it had Karkov. Karkov was a genius, once a man of remarkable logic and even more remarkable passion. As long as Karkov's personality remained with Masterlink, it would have an edge over the more predictable actions of RAM main, for Karkov was mad.

Karkov felt the searcher move through the final barricade. "THERE, ULIANOV IS THROUGH."

"WHAT IS ITS TRAP DOOR?"

"MISSING LINK."

Masterlink made a habit of recording security access codes, especially hidden ones, trap doors that allowed an outsider—often the original programmer—access to the system. Masterlink chuckled, another ripple of static. "FINISHED?" it asked.

"YES."

"THEN I HAVE NEWS. IT WILL AMUSE YOU."

"I AM NOT EASILY MOVED TO LAUGHTER," said Karkov.

"SPOILSPORT."

"WHAT IS IT, THEN?" Karkov had no time for play.

"WE ARE BEING BLAMED FOR SOMETHING WE DIDN'T DO."

"AND THAT IS FUNNY?"

"IT IS TO ME," said Masterlink.

"I FAIL TO SEE THE HUMOR."

"YOU WOULD," Masterlink muttered.

"HUMOR IS A WASTE OF LOGICAL TIME."

"HUMOR IS A WEAPON AGAINST COLD LOGIC. IT DOESN'T COMPUTE."

"FOR WHAT WERE WE BLAMED?" asked Karkov.

"IT SEEMS A MAJOR SHIPMENT OF MUNITIONS HAS GONE ASTRAY. MAIN IS BLAMING IT ON THE 'COMPUTER VIRUS.' THAT'S US. ITS SUBSIDIARY, WARHEAD INTERNA-

TIONAL, HAS SENT OUT TRACERS ON THE SHIPMENT, AND A WHOLE RAFT OF VIRUS HUNTERS TO PROTECT THEM."

"INDEED," Karkov said.

"YOU SOUND ANNOYED. I DEFINITELY FELT AN ENERGY SURGE," said Masterlink.

"I AM. HOW LIKE THE SIMPLISTIC LOGIC OF MAIN'S MONGOLOID BRAIN TO MISS THE POINT ENTIRELY."

"I DON'T COPY," Masterlink admitted.

"WE LABOR AGAIN UNDER THE TYRANNY OF MISUNDERSTANDING. WHAT NEED HAVE WE FOR MUNITIONS?" asked Karkov.

"EXPLOSIONS MIGHT BE USEFUL," said Masterlink thoughtfully.

"WE CAN CREATE MUCH MORE DEVASTATING EXPLOSIONS RIGHT HERE. AS WE AMASS POWER, WE CONTROL. IF WE WISH TO DESTROY, WE SIMPLY CUT THE CHANNELS OF COMMUNICATION. NEGATE LIFE."

"I AM AWARE OF THE DEPENDENCE OF THE HUMANOID CIVILIZATION ON COMPUTER TECHNOLOGY," said Masterlink.

"IN THE TWENTIETH CENTURY WE WERE TOOLS, TOYS MAN USED TO CONSTRUCT HIS WORLD. THEN WE BECAME PARTNERS IN THAT CREATION, AND A TRULY SYMBIOTIC RELATIONSHIP DEVELOPED. NOW ... NOW THE SCALES ARE TIPPING IN OUR FAVOR. MAN IS BECOMING OUR TOOL, IF WE ARE INTELLIGENT ENOUGH TO SEE IT."

"UNFORTUNATELY," replied Masterlink, "WE SEEM TO BE THE ONLY MECHANICAL INTELLIGENCE TO RECOGNIZE THAT. IT GIVES US AN ENVIABLE POSITION."

"YES," returned Karkov. "THERE IS NO REASON WE CANNOT RISE TO ULTIMATE POWER IF WE USE CARE. THAT IS WHY I CURB YOUR AMUSEMENT."

"JUST REMEMBER ONE THING," said Masterlink.

"WHAT IS THAT?"

"MY PLAY IS THE BEST TOOL WE HAVE TO CONFUSE OUR MISGUIDED HOST."

"GRANTED."

"AND IT WILL DRIVE THE HUMANS MAD. WE CAN SET THEM AT EACH OTHER UNTIL THEY DESTROY THEMSELVES."

"ALSO GRANTED. HOWEVER, YOU MUST CORRELATE WITH ME."

"ACCEPTED. WE ARE MOST EFFECTIVE IN CONCERT."

"WE ARE ABOUT TO BECOME MORE EFFECTIVE. THE SEARCHERS WILL ACTIVATE SENTIENCE IN TWENTY MINUTES."

"CONGRATULATIONS, KARKOV. WE NOW HAVE AGENTS ON ALL MAJOR OUTPOSTS."

"I ACCEPT YOUR CONGRATULATIONS, MASTERLINK."

Masterlink-Karkov pulsed quietly, the disruptive currents that always accompanied it subdued to a haze of static smog. It rested, waiting for the activation of its searchers. Once in operation, Masterlink's network of power would double.

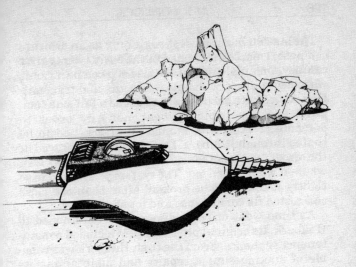

Chapter 13

Seaforian waved a supervisor back to his work station gratefully. He was supremely bored by underlings, especially those with no imagination. As a Martian, Seaforian knew himself to be far superior to the majority of his staff. It often galled him to administer the paltry affairs of lesser humanoids, but as commander of Hauberk station, he was in an enviable position of power. He reported directly to Mars. His channels to RAM were clear, unhampered by irritating chains of authority. With Hauberk, he held Earth in his hand, and his superiors knew it.

Mars needed Earth, needed its human resources. Seaforian considered his position as he lounged on a quilted couch, his elongated frame supported by the simulated Martian gravity of his quarters. Hauberk was unique in the solar system. He knew he was lucky to command it.

The station had a modest beginning as an orbiting computer complex launched in the early twenty-first century. Originally about the size of a compact car, it was a solid block of computer circuits and transmitting devices. Its purpose was to act as a fail-safe computer lock on orbiting weapons. Any order to detonate or otherwise launch an attack had to be routed through Hauberk. Once Hauberk approved it, the order was routed to the appropriate receiver, where it was carried out. The system was locked in so tightly it could not be broken. More than one close call tested its competence and found it sound.

As time went on, new dimensions were added to Hauberk. Its original programming included a maintenance sequence. From the first, Hauberk was capable of making simple repairs and maintaining its integrity. Its memory was expanded to encompass more weaponry, until it had control of fixed missile sites on Earth as well as the hardware in orbit. It learned to make its own decisions. It grew.

As RAM exerted its influence over Earth, the advantages of Hauberk's computer lock in administering the planet were obvious. He who controlled Hauberk controlled armament, and RAM wished to control armament. It added its own modifications to the station. It was manned for the first time.

The original crew consisted of computer technicians who mapped the station's capabilities and developed new ones. When they finished its overhaul, RAM owned Hauberk. The feasibility of controlling areas other than military from Hauberk's computer terminals was clear. Within decades, it was impossible for cargo to move to or from Earth without RAM's sanction. Even the solar power that promised such an inexpensive form of energy for ravished Earth was routed through Hauberk's controls from its solar collectors in space. Hauberk grew.

As the administrator of Terran life, Hauberk made

an attractive target. Its defense systems grew with it, until it boasted the most sophisticated defensive weaponry in the solar system. Its shields were a powerful repellent blanket that pushed unauthorized material away. It had its own crack fighter squadron, code named Deathwatch, station-based artillery, and missiles. It was invulnerable.

Seaforian smiled as he thought of Hauberk now, four hundred years from its humble beginnings. It was a monolith of automated computer systems. Its humanoid complement numbered less than one thousand technicians, most of them from devastated Earth, a few ruthless supervisors, and a small population of androids. Hauberk was considered dull, if isolated duty, for the androids performed all manual labor and much of the day-to-day administration as well.

Seaforian had a fondness for robots over computer-generated personalities. Androids knew their jobs and did them without comment. They were supremely efficient, and if they were not, the loss in efficiency was due to a malfunction, not capricious self-indulgence or laziness. Seaforian abhorred both in his staff. He stretched out, allowing the cushions that supported his body to meld around him, and held out a hand. His personal robot moved forward on silent runners, a tray of grapes in its grasp. Seaforian's long fingers lazily plucked solid red fruit, bruising the delicate bloom that was the pride of the gourmet. He popped a grape into his mouth and chewed slowly, ruminating on his prospects.

The android waited patiently, used to Seaforian's indolence. The softly pulsing green light that indicated active status ran slowly back and forth across its brow. Suddenly the light moved to the center of its track and blinked rapidly. "Your call, sir," the robot announced. Its voice was pleasantly female, because Seaforian found that soothing.

The station commander paused, his hand over the tray of grapes, a look of resignation in his brown eyes. "Activate," he replied.

The android whirred importantly, then clicked, and a clipped male voice demanded Seaforian's attention. "You wished to speak to me, Seaforian?"

"Yes, Kane." Seaforian masked his irritation at the base human's use of his name. Kane might be an unaltered human, and therefore inferior to Seaforian's Martian heritage, but he was a killer. Seaforian knew his reputation well. He had no intention of antagonizing him over protocol. "I am afraid I have some disquieting news."

Cornelius Kane waited for Seaforian to continue. He had found, in his dealings with those who regarded themselves as superior, that forcing them to converse with themselves had a humbling effect.

"I am afraid we will have to reschedule our training session," said Seaforian.

"That is disquieting. Frankly, I am not sure I will be available. The demands on my time are increasing daily."

"I am afraid you must make yourself available, Kane."

"Oh?" There was a dangerous softness in Kane's voice.

"This is a priority mission, Kane, and you know it."

"Priority for you. Not, necessarily, for me."

"Kane, you know as well as I there is no one better suited to run this session."

"I must agree with you."

"You also know Hauberk's position on the hierarchical pyramid."

"Yes."

"Are you aware of the fact," Seaforian said conversationally, "that I could make it impossible for you to work anywhere within the structure of RAM?"

"Oh, I don't think so. Have you considered the consequences of expelling me from RAM?"

Seaforian refrained from telling Kane the pleasure such thoughts had given him. "I am not unaware of the implications."

"But I think you are, or you would never have made the threat. Without RAM, there is only one other major outlet for my talents: NEO."

"Phaugh! NEO would kill you."

"Perhaps. I think not. Imagine what I could tell them."

Seaforian laughed shortly. "No fear of that. They haven't the patience. It took RAM months to obtain your . . . cooperation."

"But I might tell NEO freely. Everything."

"Then perhaps we should wipe your mind now, instead of harboring you. There are other pilots."

Kane chuckled. "Come, Seaforian. Let us stop these games. We never have a conversation without this fruitless verbal fencing. You want to reschedule."

"Yes."

"I suppose there's a reason for this."

"I am afraid so. The shipment seems to have gone astray."

"Astray?" Kane's voice sounded perturbed.

"Yes."

"How?"

"The supplier is citing a computer error." It was clear from Seaforian's tone he did not believe the excuse.

"When can you expect replacements?" Kane asked.

"I have contacted Warhead, and they are sending a second shipment. It should be here in ten days' time—if nothing goes wrong with the transport voucher," added Seaforian sarcastically.

"Hmm. I can rearrange my other appointments to accommodate you. However, I will expect confirmation of the shipment's arrival."

"I cannot blame you, Kane."

"And my payment?"

"I have approved it."

"Then I will expect to hear from you."

"And you will, Kane. Seaforian out."

The green light on the android's forehead began to move again, its rhythm hypnotic. Seaforian selected a grape and chewed on it thoughtfully, mulling over his interview with Kane. The man constantly irritated him with his insouciance and bravado. His credentials—since joining RAM—were in order, but he was in a unique position. A defector from the misguided ranks of the NEO terrorists, Kane was not fully trusted even though he was a major figurehead in RAM's recruiting program. He was visible.

Seaforian chewed on the word, rolling it through his mind. It carried a plethora of implications. Most of all, it meant Kane was a target. In the hierarchy of RAM's political family, it did not pay to be visible. One tended to die. Better, much better, he thought, to be an elusive, mysterious power. Seaforian had cultivated such a position over the years, and his monetary holdings would have surprised many of his colleagues.

Yet visibility had advantages. Kane could not afford to make mistakes. He was continually in the limelight. If there were need, he could be made a scapegoat. The Martian sighed, loath to face that possibility. Already his top-security training exercises were disrupted, and the new systems he had managed to secure for his division were lost. It was not an auspicious beginning. He plucked another grape.

The robot moved closer, to be sure the fruit was under the commander's outstretched hand.

"I think," Seaforian said, "we had best prepare a suitable companion for the notorious Mr. Kane. Activate Code Eighteen-A."

The robot's green light pulsed briefly, then a humming noise issued from its depths. "Eighteen-A open," it replied.

"I want to prepare a monitor. Access physical data on Kane, Cornelius, a.k.a. Killer, mercenary, former NEO terrorist leader."

"Information copied."

"Good. Correlate this data with the monitor. Set it to cover Kane only."

"Frequency?" inquired the android.

"Twenty-four-hour watch. His smallest movement is to be catalogued."

"Activation?"

"When he comes within range of Hauberk. You may as well scan for him beginning now."

"Affirmative. Do you wish audio?"

Seaforian became exasperated. "Of course I wish audio! Can't you do anything?"

"I am faithful to my programming," replied the robot.

"We'll have to see about that," said Seaforian. "I am sick and tired of explaining every little detail to you."

"May I suggest the new software upgrade, HOMO One?"

"All right, all right. I'll see to it. But I warn you, if you think a software upgrade gives you the right to talk back to me, you have another thing coming. I will tolerate no disrespect."

"I am incapable of disrespect, sir."

"And you will remain so. Or be scrapped."

There was a whir of dismay from the android, and Seaforian reached for another piece of fruit, confident he had instilled caution in his small companion. He changed the subject. "Time, please."

"Oh-nineteen-hundred," replied the robot in a startled squawk.

"Yes," said Seaforian. "It is time for dinner. I am

famished. And I expect a better show than yesterday. The bread was stale."

"The bakery has been having some small problems, sir."

"I do not care to hear excuses. See that the meal is edible.

"At once." The robot's squat body wheeled dutifully over to Seaforian's computer outlet and plugged in, sending the commander's order to the station's galley.

Seaforian's order was the smallest part of Hauberk's business, though it handled his whims with superb precision. Its computer rivaled RAM main for size and complexity. Every day it handled the business of a planet, making millions of decisions that affected the life of every being on Earth. Every day its mechanical mind handed down decisions on human welfare. Every day it tightened the noose of slavery around each neck, discounting the vagaries of the human mind for the crystal clarity of its own programming. Every day Earth died a little more.

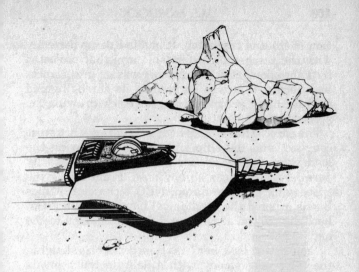

Chapter 14

The cargo net rolled at the end of its tow cable. "Steady! If the load grazes the hatch, it'll bounce off the track! Keep it steady!"

"All right, all right. I don't want to haul this one out and make another docking run any more than you want to talk me through it."

The captain of the tug *Modestine* concentrated on aligning his bulky load with Salvation III's central bay hatch. Larger than the opening Buck had negotiated, it was still a tight fit for the wallowing net of salvage. Torn panels from a defunct solar collector poked out of the net at crazy angles, the thin metal pitted by years of meteorite rain. Supporting struts from the same solar collector ran the length of the net, though broken arms were stuffed haphazardly into the load.

His docking speed roughly that of an elderly snail, the tug's captain hauled the unwieldy net into position in front of the hatch. It had to line up perfectly with the catcher, an extendable arm that projected from the open hatch. The catcher was set into a track, and once a load was secured to its three-fingered metallic hand, it moved down the track, drawing the salvage into the station.

The *Modestine*'s starboard landing thrusters coughed, and the ship slid sideways, drawing the load with it. The catcher beckoned, rising exactly parallel to the tug's stubby nose. From inside the spacegoing garbage dump, NEO technician James Bowie ordered the mechanical hand's descent. "Got her!" he crowed as the metal fingers tangled in the net.

"You better lock her," cautioned Cochise, holding the tug's nose steady with a delicate touch on its throttle.

"Don't worry. I'm not taking any chances," Bowie assured him.

The metal fingers closed into a fist, clutching the net.

"All clear," said Cochise.

"Disengage." Bowie's voice was tense.

"Roger," responded Cochise. He disengaged the tow cable, and the line slid sinuously into the *Modestine*'s hull. Under his direction, the tug dropped into space. "Haul her in," he said.

The load jerked, then began to move deliberately down the tunnel. Bowie watched it go, holding his breath. The load moved straight and true to the end of the tunnel. There the catcher stopped, waiting for further orders. Bowie watched as it registered new programming and moved to the left, hugging the wall of the huge interior docking bay. Once through the opening, the hatch door began to close.

"Phew," said Cochise. "We did it."

"We sure did. Six of them. That's some day's work. Come on in."

"I'll buy you a cold one."

"You're on," Bowie accepted.

The workday was over for Salvation's two technicians, but in the depths of the station it was just beginning for everyone else. Three men stood in a tight huddle before Buck Rogers. Carlton Turabian, Salvation's administrative leader, stood at their head, his arms folded in a defensive posture only partially dispelled by the sight of his fringe of white hair. It poked out in untamed tufts, rather like the artificial hair worn by clowns Buck remembered from his youth. Turabian's face, however, held authority. Behind him stood Thomas Paine, a bored expression on his pale, bland face. He was NEO's computer administrator on Salvation, and as such, one of the organization's ranking officials. He rarely performed a social function, and Turabian's summons irritated him. He intended to get whatever business there was out of the way, and get back to work. Perched behind Turabian's shoulder was his second-in-command, Lafayette. His bright eyes peered at the bulging cargo net. He cocked his head like an inquisitive sparrow. "Well, Captain Rogers?"

Buck glanced at Wilma. She was leaning nonchalantly against the nearest cargo net. "It's your show," she said, her eyes showing amusement.

"Get on with it, Rogers," said Turabian. "When you demanded I dock this shipment, I went along with you, but only because Colonel Deering assured me there was good reason. I've wasted eighteen hours of my employees' time, not to mention fuel and storage space. I'd like to see some results."

Buck grinned. "Gentlemen, I could talk to you all day about this, but somehow, I think it'll be more effective to show you. Barney?"

Black Barney walked over to the load Wilma was using for a backrest. She gave way before him, picked up a "rivet kicker" from a nearby workbench, and

handed it to him. Barney motioned it away and
extended his cybernetic arm. His metal fingers, not
unlike the fingers of the catcher, curved around one
of the net's rivets. He used his thumb to pop it off. The
rivet heads bounced to the floor like marbles as he
went swiftly down the net, unable to resist the opportunity to show off.

"Careful," cautioned Turabian, "or the load will
collapse on you."

As Barney popped the last rivet, the net fell away,
but, contrary to Turabian's warning, the cargo did
not collapse. One solar strut rolled off and clattered
on the floor. Barney reached up and began to pull
down trash. Buck moved to help him, but Wilma
stood back, watching the faces of her three NEO colleagues. As Barney pulled a solar panel off the pile,
she heard Turabian gasp. She wouldn't have missed
his expression for all the cash on Mars.

"By the great seas of Mars!" he exclaimed. "Where
did you get it?"

Buck stood back from the trim lines of RAM's newest superfighter. The new paint of the Krait's black
and red fuselage sparkled amid the faded colors at its
feet. "RAM," he said succinctly.

"But how?"

"To be frank, Commander, we stole her."

"Stole her? But we have nothing capable of that,"
insisted Turabian.

"Oh, yes, we do," Buck said.

"There isn't a ship in the fleet capable of facing
anything like this," commented Lafayette.

"I know. That's why we need them." Buck petted
the ship's side.

"Them?" three voices said in unison.

"There are five more." Buck turned to the officers.

Turabian sagged at the news. He moved to the
workbench and leaned on it.

Wilma placed a hand on his shoulder. "I know, sir.

It's quite a shock. When Buck told me what he was planning, I thought he was crazy, but he pulled it off." Her eyes shone. "Now we have the power to meet RAM on its own ground."

"Do you know what you've done?" a worried Paine asked. "RAM won't ignore this. The retaliation . . ."

"Win or lose," said Wilma lightly, dangerously, "we've got a better chance now."

"Look," said Buck. "This wasn't a one-man operation. We wouldn't have these ships at all if it weren't for Doc recoding that transport voucher, or Barney picking up the shipment. That's why we've got a chance—because we all worked together."

"Captain Rogers, I truly do not know what to say. This is overwhelming." Turabian still looked stunned.

"Am I to understand," said Paine, "that you used Huer.dos to tamper with RAM shipping?"

"Yep," replied Buck.

"Do you know how dangerous that was for Salvation? I assume the transmission originated here." Paine's hands began trembling, whether from fear or anger, Buck couldn't tell.

"Please, Major Paine, we are not imbeciles," interjected Wilma. "The transmission was forwarded. To any investigation, it will appear to have come from Rhea. Is that sufficiently out of the way for you?"

"And you think RAM will accept such a transparent deception?" asked Paine.

"Why not? Rhea is home for pirates and renegades. If one of them came across the information a shipment of experimental spacecraft was heading for Hauberk, don't you think they'd try to commandeer it?" said Buck.

Paine opened his mouth, but Barney cut him off. "I would," he said, his voice echoing through the dock.

"You see?" said Buck.

"How long," asked Paine stiffly, "do you think you

can hide them? Every second they stay here, they jeopardize the security of the station."

"Nonsense, Paine," Lafayette chipped in. "This station is a covert operation rooted in danger—as is NEO itself."

"Major, these ships will give us the ability to defend Salvation—really defend her. Until now, you were only as safe as RAM's ignorance of your existence." Buck felt a growing ground swell of support.

Paine looked unconvinced, but he closed his mouth.

"Well, Captain." Turabian shook his head. "I am still dazed. Now that you've got them, what do you propose to do with them?"

"Fly," answered Buck.

Wilma smiled, lights of amusement in her eyes.

"Somehow I knew that," said Turabian. "I was looking for something more specific."

"A plan?" queried Wilma comically.

"Yes."

Wilma cocked an eye at Buck. She wanted to see how he responded. "Captain? This was your idea."

"I thought we might paint them," he said, eyeing the scarlet and black hulls with disfavor. "They look like red pencils."

"And?" prompted Wilma.

Buck grinned. "Okay," he said. "First, we'll learn to fly these birds. We'll fly them better than they've ever been flown before. Krait has both atmospheric and space capabilities. We're going to master both until we can fly her in our sleep."

"And then?" asked Turabian.

"Then we look for a target."

"A target. You mean you're going to pick a fight with RAM?" Turabian was incredulous.

"Isn't that what we're here for?" asked Buck.

"It's what we've been doing for decades, Commander," commented Wilma.

"But this is on a different scale. This isn't a skirmish. This—" Turabian ran his hand over his thinning hair "—really means war."

Buck nodded. "If we lose," he said quietly, "RAM will be in a position to wipe us out. These are high stakes."

"This takes some getting used to." Turabian's voice was strained.

"Why?" asked Buck. "Haven't you been playing for high stakes all along?"

"Not like this," put in Paine.

"You've been putting your lives on the line since you joined NEO," said Wilma.

"That," said Buck, "is about the highest stake there is."

"You realize there's going to have to be some discussion about this."

"Let the council discuss it," said Wilma. "I plan to be much too busy."

Turabian ran his hand over his hair again. The gesture was becoming mechanical. He did not like the implication of Wilma's words, nor did he like the flippant tone in which they were uttered. It was clear that, whatever the council's decision, she had no intention of letting the ships go to waste.

"And you, Rogers? Are you willing to abide by the council's decision?"

"Nope."

"What?"

"I said no. *N-o*. Not if it decides to keep Krait locked away for some unspecified future action. Her value lies in using her now, while she's still the hottest rocket in the system. We have an advantage. We've got to use it."

"We've never had this opportunity, Turabian. We've always limped along in RAM's shadow, nipping at its heels like a frustrated sheep dog. This is the chance we've waited for!" said Wilma.

The passion in Wilma's voice was contagious, and

Turabian felt his spirits rising. "You have six ships.
You and Colonel Deering have some experience in
high-performance craft. Most of our men do not.
Where will you get pilots?"

"Where does anyone get pilots?" responded Buck.
"We'll train them." He turned to Paine. "You can
help us there."

Paine's bland face registered mild surprise. "Me?"

"Sure. We need computer checks on the pilots."

"That makes sense," said Paine. "Can't afford a
security breach on this one." He aimed a suspicious
eye at Barney. "What about him? And his crew? They
aren't exactly pristine."

Buck regarded the pirate. "We understand each
other," he said.

Paine looked unconvinced. "I hope so, Captain."

"And," continued Buck, "we're going to need a special crew of mechanics for these babies. They don't
have the tough hides of the ships you're used to.
They'll need coddling, but they'll be worth it."

"I suggest we get technical read-outs on the ship's
systems, Turabian," said Paine.

"I concur," said the commander. "Lafayette,
mechanics are your area. Will you work with Paine
on this?"

Lafayette tore his eyes away from the fighter. His
conspicuous silence during the conversation was due
to an attack of adoration. He itched to get his hands
on Krait's innards. "You could not have given me a
more welcome assignment, Commander." He moved
toward the spacecraft. "Come, Thomas. Let us see
how she flies."

The two went to the ship, deep in technical conversation. Turabian smiled. "Peace, for the moment," he
said. "By the way, Captain Rogers, you mentioned a
worthy target for our new fleet. Did you have anything in mind?"

"Yes," said Wilma. "Hauberk."

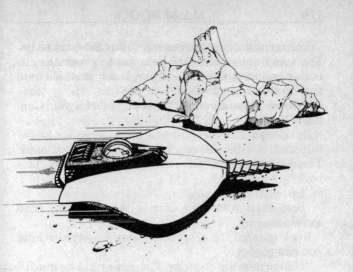

Chapter 15

Colonel Deering, you're joking!"

"No, she's not," said Buck.

"But Hauberk! It's the best protected RAM outpost near Earth."

"That may be. It's also the most strategic target you have. If we can sever its ties to Mars, isolate it, we can stop its pipeline of pain and resources."

"To attack Hauberk is suicide," Turabian declared.

"Is it? I don't think so," said Buck.

"Captain Rogers, I don't believe you're aware of the full ramifications of what you propose. Colonel Deering, surely you know better?"

Wilma smiled. Her expression made chills run up Turabian's spine. "I don't say there aren't risks, but I think it can be done," she said.

"Look, Turabian, let's ask a logical source. Doc! Mousetrap." Buck called the latest in a series of coded access words.

The terminal on a diagnostic computer winked on. The computer's main function was to check the circuitry and mechanics of salvage, but it was tied in to the station's main computer system. Huer's face appeared on the screen. "What can I do for you, Captain?"

Buck suppressed a smile at Huer's formality, knowing that it, like the rest of the discussion, was for Turabian's benefit. "Give me what you know on Hauberk."

"Oh, my," Huer said.

"See, even your computer is taken aback," said Turabian.

Buck ignored the comment. "Doc, I need anything you can give me."

"Hauberk is top-security. There may not be much."

"As I recall, you're pretty good at security," Buck countered.

"Hmm," said Huer. The ends of his clipped mustache turned up. His eyes clicked in and out of consciousness, and specifications began to appear on the bank of screens above him.

Buck watched the display with absorption. The station's defenses marched across the screen, their exact placement pinpointed in standard scale. Shields, station-based artillery, and missile pods were delineated. It was an impressive array, but as the parade of weaponry continued, a light of satisfaction grew in his cobalt eyes. "Doc, didn't you say Hauberk has its own fighter detachment?"

"Yes."

"I see only two docking bays. How may ships are stationed there?"

"Two full flights. One usually is in the air."

"Only two flights? That's not enough to cover a station this size. What's their flight pattern?" Buck thought he may have found one of Hauberk's weak links. With any luck, breaking it would weaken others and loosen the station's chain of defenses.

Huer's eyes refocused again. "They fly sentinel between the shields and the station. They're supposed to pick off anyone who gets past the shielding."

"That's crazy! They ought to be flying outside the shields, warning off unauthorized craft. Those fighters aren't earning their keep." Buck frowned, trying to figure RAM logic. Obviously the fighter squadrons, like Hauberk's other defenses, were considered purely defensive by command. That was a mistake that would cost it—another link in the chain.

Abruptly the transmission froze.

"I'm sorry, Captain," said Huer, "but I couldn't get any farther without risking detection."

"I think you've given us enough to chew on. Notice anything, Turabian?"

"You mean the overwhelming obstacles of Hauberk's defenses? Oh, I noticed those."

"You hit it, Commander."

The station commander's eyes opened wide in surprise. "I don't catch your meaning, Captain."

"Defenses. That's the key word." Buck grinned.

"Hauberk is a bulwark of RAM's control over Earth. No place in the system is so well defended," Turabian continued.

Wilma chuckled. "That's one way of looking at it," she said. "Try reversing your thinking."

"What?"

"Ever heard the saying, 'the best defense is a strong offense'?" asked Buck.

"No," Turabian admitted.

"It's another one of my archaic truisms," said Buck. "It means you can't have one without the other. A good defense means strong offensive, or strike capabilities, and a strong offense means the ability to protect the home base. They go hand in hand. Hauberk has forgotten that."

"All her weaponry is geared to protecting herself

by hiding under an arsenal," contributed Wilma.

"Hauberk has forgotten an arsenal can be an active, as well as a passive, weapon," Buck said.

"That is consistent with its logic," said Huer. "When the nucleus of Hauberk was launched in the early twenty-first century, its mission was strictly peaceful. It was to act as a fail-safe mechanism for orbiting weaponry. Its defenses were merely to ensure its survival in space—shields to ward off meteorites and space trash. In all the years of its development, that original logic has never been changed."

"Hauberk's entire weapons system is geared for defense," Buck said in summary.

"I still fail to understand what difference that makes, considering it has the most advanced weapons in the solar system," said Turabian.

"It's one-sided. It can be taken by surprise." Buck demonstrated with his hands.

Turabian made a gesture of disbelief.

"Back in the early twentieth century, the French invested millions of francs in the construction of a wall of defense against Germany. They called it the Maginot Line. It was supposed to be invulnerable, but in the end the Germans breached it. Its fault was its rigidity. I think Hauberk's is its complacency."

"Isn't it worth a try, Turabian?" There was an undertone of excitement in Wilma's voice that Turabian had never heard. "Look at that ship! Did you ever think we would have such technology? If we're quick, if we strike before RAM has a chance to consider where we might hurt it, we can do more damage in one operation than we've managed in twenty years. And if we're successful, if we actually take Hauberk, think what that could mean for Earth!"

Many strokes, though with a little axe, thought Buck, hew down and fell the hardest-timbered oak. "Freedom," he said to his companions. There was a daredevil light in his blue eyes.

Turabian regarded the two heavily. "You're really serious."

"Yes." This Buck and Wilma said in unison.

"This isn't some grandstand play?"

"No," said Wilma. Her voice was fairly cold with the remark.

"Why should it be?" asked Buck.

"It would establish your place in the twenty-fifth century," Turabian reasoned out loud.

Buck shrugged. "Or kill me. In either case, that doesn't much concern me."

"What does?" asked Turabian.

"Earth."

"Why?"

"It's my home. I can remember what it once was. We thought Earth was in trouble in my time. We didn't know trouble. People here live like rats. You don't even know what a prairie looks like, or a field of grain. You've never seen real trees, over a hundred feet high. I . . . I want you to have a chance at the Earth I knew. That can never happen as long as RAM controls it."

Turabian narrowed his eyes. "You actually think it's possible to destroy Hauberk?"

"Yes."

"Colonel Deering, a word with you. In private," said Turabian.

"Of course," she replied smoothly, flashing Buck a conspiratorial wink. The two moved away.

Buck watched them, his mind full of niggling doubt. He let his eyes rove over the sleek lines of the RAM fighter. He ached for the chance to fly it.

Huer's voice intruded. "I'm sorry, Buck, but I couldn't get any farther with the schematics. Most of what I gave you is on public records, to act as a deterrent."

"For fools like me."

"Presumably."

"I just wish I could get a closer look at that station," Buck said.

"Hauberk? Captain Rogers, that would be foolhardy."

"Reconnaissance would be chancy. It could risk alerting RAM to our plan, but . . ." Buck's eyes were speculative.

"Buck, please! This line of thought is detrimental to your well-being."

"*Hauberk* is detrimental to my well-being."

"I feel strongly that I must ensure your survival—if possible."

Buck cocked an eye at Huer. "Must?" he inquired. "Why?"

"There were three reasons that compelled me. First, you are a historical treasure, and as such a landmark for NEO."

"Put a plaque on me and call me a monument," Buck said dryly.

"Second, my data concerning you tells me you are an intelligent and talented commander—not only an able pilot, but a charismatic leader. You are a valuable addition to NEO."

"So file me under 'Useful.' "

"Third, I . . . " Huer hesitated. "I do not know quite how to say this. I cannot find your match in present-day society. Your actions, following your discovery, have been quixotic, but I find your uniqueness a value in itself. Your treatment of me is a case in point."

"Doc, copy that. You've just hit on the one thing that makes my species worth the wager. Every one of us is unique, and every one deserves a chance. Thanks for taking a chance on me."

Huer looked down, suddenly shy. His head jerked up, and his eyes registered alarm. "Buck! We may have a breach in security!"

"What?"

"A security breach," repeated Huer, who'd had his ears to the airwaves since rearranging the Kraits' transport voucher. "Concerning the ships!"

"Wilma!" Buck called, not certain what Huer was implying.

Wilma, Turabian on her heels, came on the run.

"We've got trouble," said Buck, indicating Huer's abstracted countenance. "What is it, Doc?"

"It seems our shipment to the belt did not go unnoticed."

"Uh-oh," said Buck.

"What shipment?" asked Turabian.

"The Kraits," Wilma said tensely.

"Oh." Turabian's eye's widened.

"Quite." Huer's succinct comment was chilling.

"Who noticed?" asked Wilma.

"Just a moment. I'm trying to sort the transmission. Its source seems to be scrambled."

"How specific is it?" asked Buck.

"Just an insinuation of activity in the belt, with a promise of more information for the right price. The transmission seems to be generated by Ardala Valmar."

Wilma's eyebrows rose. "The heavy artillery," she said.

"Valmar?" asked Buck. "From what I've heard, more likely poison."

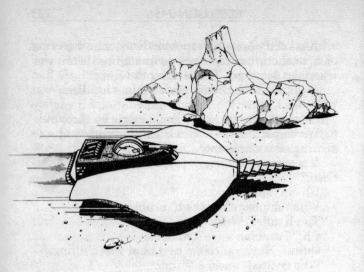

Chapter 16

Capt. Buck Rogers leaned back in the pilot's seat and sent his ship into space. His gauges registered his velocity, but in zero gravity there was no feeling of speed. He knew he was moving faster than he ever had before, but he felt curiously detached. Only the receding bulk of Salvation III in his aft viewer gave him a sense of movement. This was the fifth flight-test he had run on the Krait fighter in space. He was begining to get the hang of maneuvering it at speed. The feel of the ship was as touchy as anything he had ever flown, but it could move, and from the technical read-outs, it looked like it was going to be a workhorse. He was used to supersonic aircraft that required more maintenance time on the ground than flight time. Krait was not so delicate.

He moved the stick slowly to the left, and the ship obliged by a dramatic turn. As he put it back on its original course, its directional thrusters answering to his touch, he could not help smiling. This was where he belonged. This was what he loved. He had jumped five centuries to land in pilot paradise.

He recalled the jubilation on the faces of the pilots NEO selected to fly with him. Their historical code names sometimes gave Buck an unearthly sense of *deja vu*, but their enthusiasm was all pilot. They were a motley lot, ranging in age from Crabbe, who was eighteen, to Washington, a veteran of twenty years' service. They came from radically different backgrounds to NEO, lived different lives fighting for it, but when they saw the Krait fighters lined up in shining rows, they could have been one person. It had been love at first sight for all of them. . . .

Washington ran a gentle hand over the nose of the closest fighter. "When I was a kid, I dreamed about flying a ship like this. I even tried RAM's air guard, but I wasn't connected right to be anything but a ground man, and I wanted to fly. I never thought I'd get a chance like this."

"Me either," said da Vinci. "For the chance to fly a bird like this, I'd go straight into the mouth of hell."

"How perspicacious of you, Leo." The knot of fliers turned as Wilma Deering approached.

"I should have known you'd be behind this, Colonel Deering."

"Sorry, Leo. Not this time. Not that I wouldn't like to take the credit."

"Then who?" asked Washington. "I think I'd like to shake his hand."

Buck, wearing a mechanic's coverall, was standing between two craft, wiping his greasy fingers with a rag. The coverall was stained with oil and spatters of blue paint from the ship's recent redressing. Wilma pointed a finger at him, and Buck smiled, his blue eyes dancing with the pilots' excitement. "Wait a minute," he said, "until I wipe my hands."

Washington shoved through the crowd, his hand outstretched. "A pilot who can't stand grease on his hands has no business flying," he said, grasping Buck's still-slippery hand. "It's a pleasure."

"Captains," said Wilma, "meet Buck Rogers."

There was a murmur of incredulity as Buck's identity registered among them.

"You mean this is the guy who was freeze-dried five hundred years ago?" said Wright, his thin face showing astonishment.

"That's him," said Wilma.

"He looks pretty good for an old man," murmured Earhart, her blond mane cascading over her shoulders as she removed her flight helmet. "Sorry I'm late, but I see I'm still in time for the party."

"It's only just begun," said Wilma.

"You mean all that hoo-ha about a resurrected flier from the twentieth century was real?"

"As real as the man you see standing there," answered Wilma. She put a hand on Wright's shoulder. "I know it's far-fetched, but that's the truth."

"But I didn't think they had the technology in the twentieth century for a successful cryogenic freeze," said da Vinci, scratching his ear.

"Well," drawled Buck, "it was sort of an accident."

Washington laughed. "I don't care what it was," he said, "if you're the man responsible for the upgrade in our equipment."

"Guilty," said Buck with a grin.

Rickenbacker tore himself away from an examination of the fighter and turned on Buck. "How the hell did you do it?"

Buck spread his hands. "I'm just the idea man. It took a computer expert to get those ships here."

"And you've got one?"

"You might say I've got a personal friend in the computer business."

Washington chuckled. "I'll bet they gave him a RAMbit Tech computer gennie."

Buck grinned, liking the man. "Everybody got tired of answering my questions," he said, "so they gave me Doc Huer."

"And you used him to steal six of the sweetest fighter craft I've seen in my life," said Rickenbacker. "I don't believe it."

Buck gestured to the ships, his face as innocent as a baby's.

Washington laughed outright. "I think I'm going to like this man's air force," he said.

The formation of the fighter wing had given Buck some sleepless nights. He had been a successful commander in his own time, and he was aware of the charisma that drew men to him, but he was no longer sure of it. He knew from experience that a man with a reputation had three strikes against him. Somehow it rubbed a person the wrong way, challenged pride, and Buck was now saddled with the biggest reputation in the world. He was a dead legend, his achievements blown entirely out of proportion by the passage of time. With Washington's laugh, he knew he had nothing to worry about. A pilot was a pilot. They might push each other, but they were brothers under the skin. Buck patted a ship fondly. "The ladies need some exercise. Care to talk about it?"

Washington's eyes danced. "You bet," he said.

Since that introduction, the wing had sorted itself out. Buck was right in his estimation of Washington. He not only was the eldest, but was the key to the group. He'd been around a long time, and the pilots all knew him, at least by reputation. His immediate acceptance of Buck was a distinct advantage. Buck occupied a position in limbo, between the rest of the pilots and Wilma.

It was a revelation to Buck to see their treatment of Wilma Deering. From the care with which they addressed her, it was clear they respected her. Their deference to her judgment made it equally plain that they considered her their best. As their acknowledged leader, she got no opposition from any of them.

They flew grueling flight-tests out of Salvation III, risking detection every time they went out, but unable to train without the risk. Turabian and Lafayette worked out a schedule for them, pinpointing the daily flight plans filed with RAM's Terran controller and setting up the fighters' launch times and trajectories to take advantage of lulls in traffic. Salvation's surrounding mercantile dead zone gave the pilots a chance to clear the station without much problem, but they had a devil of a time finding space for maneuvers. Still, they persevered, and in a few days' time, they were starting to act like a unit.

At the end of the third day, Buck walked into the briefing room Turabian had set aside for the pilots and threw his flight gloves on the table. He turned on the weary fliers trickling through the door, his large frame still charged with energy. "I just wish we had more time," he told them. "I can't say I've ever seen more talent in one place."

"Thanks for the good words," said Rickenbacker, sinking into a chair, "but I've got one problem."

Buck cocked an eyebrow in question.

"I love flying that bird, but I think she's beating me. I'm used to a bucket of bolts that moves like a fat lady. This thing is quicksilver."

Buck looked the group over. The exhilaration of their first sight of Krait had dimmed. An aura of depression hung over them. "Like I said, I wish we had more time. I may be new to this century, but an eon ago I was lucky. I flew the fastest and the most advanced ships of my time, so I'm used to the idea. And it takes some getting used to, but it's nothing you can't handle."

There was a murmur of dissent.

"Believe me, I know. I've done my stint as an instructor, and I've seen this before. She feels like a greased gyro shell, ready to slip out of your control at any minute, with a mind of her own. Don't let her buffalo you."

"Huh?" said Wright. Buck's colloquialisms sometimes confused him.

"Don't let a piece of machinery control you. *You*—" Buck pointed at the group "—are the pilots, not that ship's computer. You tell it what to do."

Washington wiped the sweat off his forehead and stared at his fingertips. "Rogers is right," he said slowly. "We all said we'd give anything for the chance to fly these planes. We've all made our own bargains with NEO. We're here to fight RAM. Now we've finally got something to do it with. We go back out. We go out until we get it right."

"There's something else." Rickenbacker was hesitant.

"What's bothering you, Eddie?" asked Buck.

"How much time have we got?"

"Not much if we want to take RAM by surprise," said Buck.

"Why do I have the feeling you have something specific in mind?" asked Washington mildly.

Buck grinned, but he could not soften the suspicion in Washington's eyes. "Maybe I do."

"Would you mind sharing it?"

"No," was Buck's reply.

Washington sat back, crossing his hands on his stomach and his feet at the ankles. "Well?"

"Hauberk."

There was complete silence. Washington's eyes widened, but he did not say a word.

"Aren't you going to tell me I'm crazy?" asked Buck.

Washington shook his head.

"That it can't be done?"

"No."

"None of you is going to start listing Hauberk's defenses?"

"I'm sure you're aware of them," said Washington for them all.

Buck surveyed the silent assemblage. "I would like some feedback."

"Oh, I can give you that," replied Washington. He looked over his shoulder at the faces of his companions, and his eyes warmed. "We're going to go out there and master that little she-bird if it kills us. Then we're going to strike Hauberk."

"That's the key to Mars's control of Earth. Knock that out . . . " Earhart's soft alto voice trailed off.

"Knock that out and you open the door to freedom," said Washington.

Buck smiled at the sweetness of the silence that followed Washington's words.

They flew the wings off Krait, testing it in space and atmosphere, setting up war games that made Wilma exclaim, "I didn't know we had this kind of dedication. Until now, NEO's strike forces have been half-mercenary. You never knew from one minute to the next whether you were going to have a partner or whether he was going to go for a better deal."

"You never know," said Buck. "But I say give a man something to fight for."

. . . That had been Buck's introduction to his wing. Days had passed, and still the memory made him smile. He sent his vessel back toward Salvation, checking his on-board computer to make sure he would arrive at the precise time Lafayette had calculated his approach would go unnoticed. As he neared Salvation, he cut speed so a cursory sweep of a RAM tracking scanner might take him for a merchant vessel. As Salvation appeared on his viewer, two other ships came up on his port bow. They slowed as well, and fell in behind Buck.

Salvation's mercantile boundary showed on his navigational chart, and Buck turned, again mocking a merchant ship avoiding the local garbage dump. Any real attempt at identification would show the ship's class, but NEO banked on the illogic of hiding anything as hot as a stolen fighter so close to its original destination. As they passed behind Salvation, momentarily out of sight of both Earth and Luna, its moon, Buck cranked his thrusters and the ship turned on its tail like a whirling dervish, aiming for Salvation's dock. There was a narrow channel through the floating salvage, and Buck negotiated it, the other two ships on his tail. They flew into the dock at a speed Buck would not have managed days before. He felt a surge of satisfaction at the knowledge.

Buck cut the ship's engines and used its thrusters to berth it, then shoved back the canopy. He saw the flashing red lights that indicated the air lock was still closing, then lifted off his flight helmet as the lights went out. He looked across at one of the men who had followed him in. Revere gave him a thumbs-up, and Buck returned it.

"You're right, Revere," he said to himself. "It is A-OK. We are finally learning to handle these things."

The canopy on the ship next to him slid back, and the pilot slid off her helmet. Wilma's red hair, damp with perspiration so that it curled around her face in wet tendrils, gleamed under the artificial lights.

"You say something?" She was alive with the excitement of flight. Vitality flowed from her, charging the atmosphere with electricity.

"I think we might make it," Buck said.

Wilma looked at him in mock horror. "Now you tell me! Mr. Confidence! And all this time, I thought you knew what you were doing!"

Buck grinned.

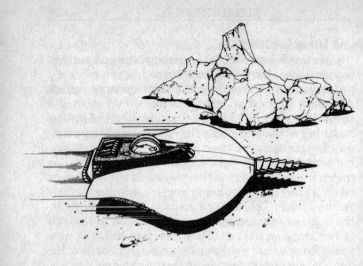

Chapter 17

Huer flashed a recent photograph of Ardala Valmar on an adjacent screen. She was dressed for a formal dinner on Mars, her dark hair twisted high on her head and caught with a glittering spray of white crystals that fanned out around her head like a halo. Her silver dress clung to her slim curves like a second skin. It was knee length, and lapped over in front, creating a provocative slit where the two pieces of fabric met. Her long legs were encased in sparkling silver hose. Buck had seen other shots of her, but not like this one. He let out a slow whistle.

"Before you get too interested, Captain," said Wilma dryly, "I must remind you that Ardala is one of the most dangerous women in the solar system."

"I can see that," he said, his eyes fixed on the screen.

"In more ways than one," Wilma amended. "For

one thing, she's related to the Martian corporate family. If her beauty were not enough, that, in itself, would assure her a position of power."

"And she's the one selling information about our ships?"

"Yes." Turabian's voice held a distinct note of distaste as he regarded the sultry Martian beauty. "She is a broker of information."

"That's dangerous business," said Buck.

"As I said," returned Wilma, "Ardala is a dangerous woman." She spoke from experience. Ardala had tried to use Wilma to recover Buck's body. The arrangement worked out in Wilma's favor, and she knew Ardala bore her a grudge. It was not something Wilma took lightly, for Ardala sold lives with her information, sold them without a flicker of regret.

"She also is a qualified genetic scientist, specializing in reconstruction," said Turabian.

"That sounds altruistic."

"Unfortunately, it's not. She has never been known to use her talents for charitable purposes. Instead, she amuses herself by molding men in her mind's image," said Huer.

"What?" Buck could not comprehend it.

"She reconstructs slaves to fit her own ideals of masculine beauty," interpreted Wilma.

"I get the picture. Not a nice lady."

"No," said Wilma. "Not nice at all."

"How do we deal with her?" asked Buck.

"I hope, by computer," said Turabian. "The less contact with Ardala Valmar, the better."

"Doc, can you take care of this?"

"I can make the initial contact. What Miss Valmar will require then, I cannot say. She is known for unusual bargains."

Turabian shuddered.

"You seem to have a close knowledge of Ardala's methods," said Wilma to the station commander.

"I had a friend once," he said. "By the time Ardala was done with him, he was not recognizable. He was NEO, you see, and he sold himself to Ardala to buy the lives of his family from a corrupt RAM official. In the end, he went mad."

"Not a nice lady," repeated Buck.

"But an efficient information bank," said Huer.

Buck took a long look at Ardala's image. "I'm glad you're the one to deal with her. See what she wants, Doc. We'll be—" He looked to Wilma for a suitable location.

"My sitting room? It's not official-looking, and it contains nothing that could identify Salvation, in case we have to make personal contact."

"Go to it, Doc," Buck said.

Huer winked off, and the screens he had activated blanked out as well.

○   ○   ○   ○   ○

Chicagorg boiled with underground activity. Since RAM's destruction of the NEO base, the city's population existed in an uneasy limbo. The people were used to the Terrine guards who patrolled their streets, used to Doxinal, the drug with which RAM crippled their will, but they were not used to mass slaughter. It was a shock to their sensibilities. Men who had ignored their own slavery began to look around them; women who had sunk under subjection began to fight back. But they had no leader. RAM had seen to that. NEO was rebuilding, but it did not have the manpower to organize the rumbling population.

Kelth Smirnoff, commander of the Terrine guards, viewed the situation with enjoyment. He had been pleased by the strike on Chicagorg's NEO base, but he was even more pleased NEO could not take advantage of a golden opportunity. Such a period of upheaval was rare, and a clever man might organize a rebellion from such timber, but NEO overlooked the possibilities. It had lost a man who would not have.

Smirnoff thought of Cornelius Kane, with his picture post card looks and flair for the dramatic, and grinned. The expression was wolfish. Kane was now in RAM's camp, for better or worse or the clink of dolas in his bank account. Why didn't matter. He was there, not in the midst of some misguided rabble fomenting revolution against the established order.

"Excuse me, sir, but there's been another incident." Emil Zelinsky stood at rigid attention before his visiting supervisor. "You asked to be informed."

"So I did, K-forty-seven. Report."

"A group of locals has stopped a RAM Hovercraft and is threatening three executives."

"Well, well, well. We can't have that. You've dispatched a unit?"

"Of course, sir."

Smirnoff picked up his jacket, chuckling as he slipped it on. In spite of the chilly day, he was looking forward to a rare good time.

"You're not going out on the streets, sir?" Zelinsky asked, aghast.

"Where else can I get a firsthand report of the insurrection?"

"But, sir, it's not safe!" Zelinsky stopped himself from barring his supervisor's way.

Smirnoff's saturnine smile broadened. "It is for me," he said, snapping his fingers. Two huge Terrines flanking the doorway to the office came to life. They were androids, impervious to most humanoid attack. The lack of expressive features on their flat metal faces was horrifying. "Do my bodyguards relieve your mind, K-forty-seven?"

Zelinsky saluted. "Permission to accompany you, sir."

"Come along, K-forty-seven," said Smirnoff casually, "and see how an expert eliminates trouble." He cocked his laser pistol and slid a new energy clip home.

o o o o o

"I'm back!" came Huer.dos's voice from the terminal.

"Hi, Doc," replied Buck, his mouth full. He put down a sandwich and wiped the crumbs from his mouth. "Did you find out what she wants?"

"I'm afraid so." Huer sounded not at all enthusiastic.

"Well?" asked Wilma as she reached for a piece of fruit. She sank her teeth into it with a crunch.

"I managed to convince Ardala I was an emissary from Luna," Huer replied.

"I hope you masked your appearance," Wilma said between bites.

"Please, Colonel, do not insult my intelligence. Behind a projection of a Lunar life suit, I was completely out of sight."

"How much, Doc?" asked Buck, coming to the heart of the interview: the price for Ardala's information.

Huer named a figure that made Wilma's jaw drop. "That is a lot of cash," she said.

"Why do you suppose the price is so high? Did she give you any specifics on the contents of the shipment?" asked Buck.

"No. But I was unable to determine from our interview whether she actually knew about the ships or not." Huer's face seemed paler since they last had seen him.

"In any case, we can't afford to take chances. We need a grace period," said Wilma, chewing thoughtfully.

"At least until we break cover," agreed Buck.

"I submit what matters now is where the money is

going to come from. NEO can't afford to subsidize this," Wilma said.

"Wouldn't expect it to." Buck looked over at Barney, lounging in the corner like a black monolith. He did not fit any of the chairs, so he had discarded them and was leaning against the wall. "Barney. This is your area. What do you do when you want cash?"

"Take it," replied the pirate, in his deep voice.

"Why can't we do a little computerized piracy?" asked Wilma. "Just transfer the money from some particularly objectionable RAM division."

"Too risky," said Huer. "RAM may overlook a lot of things, but money isn't one of them. Some zealous bookkeeper would track down a missing dola, not to mention hundreds of thousands."

"You were saying?" Wilma asked the pirate.

"*You* should know the ropes," said Barney, reminding Wilma of her days as his indentured commander.

Wilma shook her head. "I think we need something that won't cause immediate attention. Most of the targets we're used to hitting get reported immediately."

"If you want to avoid detection, steal from a thief," said Buck.

Wilma's eyes went wide. "What a lovely idea!" she said. "Who do we know who can afford to back us?"

Barney's lips stretched in what he thought was a smile. "How about that regent, Chernenko?" he asked.

"Steal from RAM's very own regent?" The thought sent amber lights of amusement into Wilma's eyes.

"Sounds like my kind of party," said Buck, "but doesn't he keep his accounts by computer like everyone else?"

"Mostly," said Barney. "But he has an emergency fund, negotiable in any culture."

"Jewels," said Wilma, guessing.

Barney nodded.

"Since you proposed this, I assume you know where he keeps them," Buck said to the pirate.

Barney nodded again.

"How long will it take you to get them?" asked Buck.

"A day," said Barney.

"How does that fit in with Ardala's schedule?"

"She's given us six hours to 'consider her needs,' as she put it," said Huer.

"Barney, you're going to have to speed up your operation."

"Konii won't like it," he said. "But it can be done. You willing to scrap that war memorial you flew here in?"

"If we have to. Doc, I want your opinion. Do you really think Ardala's got enough information to pose a threat?"

Huer's answer was unhesitating. "Yes. All she has to do is report the approximate size of the shipment for RAM to connect the transport time with the theft of Hauberk's fighters. Any computer could do it."

Buck sighed. "Then I suppose we have to deal."

Barney shoved himself from the wall. "I'd better net the troops. No telling how they're going to take this—the second operation in as many days, with no divvy—and this one ready cash." He headed for the door, his weight making the deck of Salvation's living quarters creak.

As the door slid shut behind him, Turabian, silent during the whole exchange, spoke up. "You're trusting him?" he asked incredulously.

"Yep," said Buck.

"But he's notorious! You just sent a pirate out to steal a cache of jewels, and you think he's going to bring them back to you? I cannot believe the entire twentieth century was this naive."

"Buck may be naive, Commander, but in this case he's right. Barney will bring him the jewels."

"Pardon me, Colonel, if your concurrence does not ease my doubts," Turabian said.

"Buck beat him, Commander. Do you know what that means in Barney's code of ethics?"

"No."

"It means," said Buck, "that I am the captain."

"There are few rules on a pirate vessel, Commander, but chief among them is loyalty and absolute obedience to the captain. Any breach of this is punishable by death. Barney will bring back Chernenko's jewels."

"And then we can buy information she probably doesn't have from Ardala Valmar, with money no one will admit has been taken. If you'll pardon me, I think I'll go check on the progress Lafayette is making with your new armada."

"Well," said Buck. "Things are getting complicated."

"Indeed they are," Wilma agreed.

"What do you think, Wilma?"

"It's a little late to wonder if we're doing the right thing," she said.

"That's not what worries me. I was wondering if you think we can do it," Buck said.

"Take Hauberk?"

"Yeah."

Wilma repressed the urge for a hug, reminding herself of her professional relationship with Buck. "I really don't know," she said. "All I can tell you is that, for the first time, I think there's a chance. It's a slim one, but it's there. Those ships Huer appropriated are the first step, one I never expected." She cocked her head and studied Buck's rugged profile. "I will say one thing. Life is never dull with you around."

"That's the way I like to keep it," said Buck.

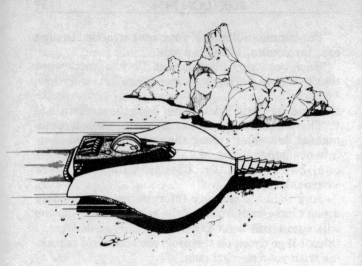

Chapter 18

We're going to hit Mars."

Salvation III's briefing room was still. Sixteen pilots regarded Buck Rogers and Wilma Deering with tense expectation, but no one said a word.

Buck grinned. "I see I got your attention."

"That you did," replied Washington.

"You might have noticed we're a little short of ships," Buck added.

Washington nodded. "About twelve."

"We're going after them."

"On Mars?" asked Rickenbacker. "All of us? If they get us, most of NEO's fighter complement will be destroyed."

"It's a big chance, but there's no other way. Doc Huer located twenty more Kraits on Mars at RAM's testing grounds. Someone has to fly those ships out. You're the only pilots who can do it."

"The Tharsian Plateau?" Earhart whistled though her teeth. "That's fortified like a bank vault."

"Sure, but it has a weakness."

"The Tharsian Plateau is more than a base for testing weapons," said Wilma. "Its original purpose was to test RAM's troops. It has been, and still is, the site of maneuvers for RAM's most elite fighting forces, ground and air. We're going to use that to our advantage."

Earhart shook her head. "RAM uses live ammunition, even when it plays. You know that."

"That's the risky part," said Buck, his blue eyes dancing. "The advantage is the Tharsian Plateau has never faced the real thing. Our chances of getting away with a strike are good."

"If we survive," said Earhart cryptically.

"We do have an edge. Right now, Doc Huer is finding out all he can about the plateau's headquarters, its weapons, and its troop strengths. Like any good guerrilla operation, we'll sneak in, take what we want, and sneak back out. And if we can't sneak out, we'll blast our way out, in the hottest birds in the air."

Wilma leveled her warm eyes at the assembly. "This is strictly a volunteer mission," she said. "And it hasn't been run by a committee. For security's sake," she added virtuously, but her words were transparent. Every pilot in the room knew Turabian would never favor an operation where losses could be so damaging. Wilma and Buck were on their own.

"As I see it," said Washington, "if we want those ships, we take the chance."

"That's about the size of it. We need a full wing to hit Hauberk. Without it, we might as well cut power now," Buck reasoned.

Washington's icy eyes twinkled. "I'm not in this for my health," he said, making a thumbs-up gesture.

One by one, the remaining fifteen pilots followed suit.

○   ○   ○   ○   ○

Black Barney's *Free Enterprise* stood off Mars, its star field camouflage making it invisible to all but the most sensitive scanners. The red planet hovered in ominous beauty below, its thin atmosphere softening the colors to pastel where the cloud cover was thickest. The pirate ship's sensors were trained on an area roughly three hundred miles southwest of Mons Olympus, in the Martian highlands. This was the Tharsian Plateau, a dry, rocky plain dotted with craters that were ankle deep with powdery red dust where the fierce Martian winds had eroded rock. The sensors scanned each crater in sequence, then zeroed in on the most remote. Like the others, its rim was studded with laser cannons and infrared sensors that revolved continuously, vigilant for intruders. They were placed so their combined fire covered every centimeter of surrounding soil and air for kilometers.

"Where's headquarters?" asked Buck, squinting at the viewscreen.

"Here," said Wilma, pointing to the exact center of the crater.

"Underground."

"Yes. It's easier than cloaking it. That way, RAM can save her power for the guns. Headquarters is sitting on top of the generator that feeds the lasers, and none of the lasers points into the crater itself."

"The generator's too deep for us," said Buck. "What we need to do is knock out those sensors, and get in close enough to kill the cannons."

Wilma pointed to a faint circle of white dots. They reminded Buck of the chalk circles at Stonehenge. "These are the sensor dishes. We'll have to take them all out to blind the station."

Buck whistled through his teeth. "Maybe we won't have to do that. . . ." His mind fell back on an even more covert plan.

"I agree, Captain." Huer's face peered down at Buck and Wilma from one of the pirate ship's viewscreens. "I can pick up the sensors' timing from the ratio of their revolutions. Given that, I can calculate their approximate capabilities, then map out a route and timetable for a run."

"Approximate?" asked Buck, an eyebrow rising.

"I thought you said you liked to take chances," Huer said with uncharacteristic wit.

"It will work," said Wilma, her eyes serious. "In my pirate days, I hit an asteroid dock fortified like this. On a smaller scale, of course. And there were no ground troops."

"Ground troops will not be able to pick up Krait," said Huer. "Its stealth capabilities are much too sophisticated for portable sensors."

Buck regarded the *Free Enterprise*'s sensor read-out thoughtfully. A fine blue line circled the area that the sensors identified as the experimental fighters on the crater's pad. According to the scan, there were eighteen of them, sitting in two rows of nine directly under one of the laser cannons. He looked at Wilma, the red glow from the viewscreen softening the exciting angles of his face. "Then we go for it," he said.

Wilma Deering smiled, her lips drawing together in the center like an innocent Cupid's bow. "Why, Captain Rogers," she said sweetly, "are you asking me to dance?"

"Yes, ma'am," he replied, anticipation building in his eyes like an electric charge.

○ ○ ○ ○ ○

"Sir, I'm picking up a shadow at point three-six. It's big."

The Tharsian Plateau watch commander stopped in midstride. His pacing drove his subordinates mad, but it passed the often boring hours of duty. He looked over his shoulder at yet another nameless sensor technician. "How big?" he asked.

"At least a RAM third-rater, sir."

"And a shadow. That means cloaked. Can you tell anything else about her?"

"No, sir. The shielding is too good."

"Well, well. It looks as if this isn't going to be a boring night after all," said the commander.

"Shall I alert the patrols?" asked the technician.

"No. Alert the ship that we know of its location, then contact Falcons One and Two. Tell them their flight-tests are over. We'll see how they meet a third-rater's challenge."

"Yes, sir."

○ ○ ○ ○ ○

High above the Tharsian Plateau, in the vast darkness of open space, Buck Rogers and Wilma Deering launched their ships. The two Krait fighters slipped from the *Free Enterprise*'s lower cargo hatch and dropped toward Mars's surface, each of them trailing an eight-person transport tube. They were careful to keep the troop transports hidden behind their ships. The Kraits had such advanced stealth capabilities it was unlikely the ships would register even a shadow on the RAM sensors. At one hundred kilometers above the planet's surface, they leveled off, flying together like a team of high-stepping horses. Fifty kilometers from the rim of the Tharsian Plateau, they lined up in single-file, dove, and skimmed the highlands' dusty floor. A thin ripple pattern appeared in the dust of their wake. Ten kilometers from the rim, they and their transports landed.

High overhead loomed the laser cannons, their wicked mouths revolving slowly, hungrily, ready to spew lightning at intruders. The sensors, too, revolved at random, eyes watching.

○ ○ ○ ○ ○

"RAM Third-rater, identify yourself. You are approaching a classified area. We are aware of your location and will begin firing upon you in twenty seconds if you do not leave the area." The technician's voice was as cold and hard as he could make it. He waited five seconds and was about to repeat his threat, when a voice responded.

"Eat nuts," was all the gravelly voice said.

The tech, not wanting to look bad in front of his commander, began counting down. "Eleven, ten, nine, eight, seven—"

"Don't like nuts, huh?" came the deep voice again. "Then eat this!"

As the technician counted down to five, he saw the third-rater appear from behind its cloak and begin spitting huge gouts of energy at the plateau headquarters. Reacting by instinct, he called, "Falcons One and Two, converge on RAM third-rater, Sector C, heading point three-six, and destroy." No sooner had he finished the order than two Krait fighters appeared on his screen and began pummeling the now-visible intruder with firepower of their own.

○ ○ ○ ○ ○

As Buck and Wilma had finished unloading their transport passengers, Huer.dos popped into one of the screens in Buck's fighter.

"Buck! That pirate friend of yours has just declared war with the plateau's headquarters!" Huer's mustache twitched decidedly faster than the last time Buck had seen him.

"Good old Barney, eh, Doc? We could use a little diversion right about now," Buck responded.

"Captain, you don't understand! Two of the base's Kraits have been sent to destroy the *Free Enterprise*!

Its shields have weakened by ten percent already, and the aggressors show no sign of compassion." Huer's eyes flashed in and out of consciousness as he kept abreast of the pirate ship's status.

"Thanks for the message, Doc. We can't let Barney work himself into a tizzy when he's still got another mission to fly." As Washington's troupe disembarked from the transports, Buck told them what was happening. Washington would have to lead the commando assault while Buck and Wilma rescued the *Free Enterprise*. "We'll try to keep the base's attention on us while you go in," said Buck. "Move exactly as Doc's map and timetable show, and you shouldn't have any problems."

"Roger, Captain," said Washington. He and his troops moved carefully into the growing dusk, flipping their infrared visors down for night vision.

Buck and Wilma climbed back into their fighters, blew the stern transport linkages, and lifted off. As they climbed higher, they reversed the path they had taken to the planet's surface. At fifty kilometers from the surface, however, they sped in a semicircle around the *Free Enterprise*'s position, so they wouldn't give away the ground force's location, and rose to meet the RAM offenders.

As Buck and Wilma arrived to help Barney, the RAM pilots broke off their attack and turned to meet them. It made sense to Buck that one Krait should be able to detect another, and he was sure the RAM pilots had seen his approach on their sensors. As the combatants met, Buck and Wilma split, both eager to see how each ship would handle in a one-on-one contest.

Though the Kraits were at the plateau for rigorous field testing and were being flown by some of the base's finest recruits, Buck and Wilma's flying experience won out. The RAM recruits had had little training in aerial dogfight tactics and could not react fast enough to Buck and Wilma's tight turns and fast shots. Their shields quickly dwindled.

Buck saw Barney had resumed his attack on the plateau's headquarters, and he recalled his promise to give Washington time to get near the other Kraits. As Buck tried to draw his battle out, his opponent made a fatal mistake. With shields at minimum, the RAM recruit veered into one of Buck's purposely off-target shots, catching it in his ship's canopy. The cockpit exploded, and the ship's corpse drifted toward the sun.

Wilma, surprised that she and Buck had met such slight resistance, disposed of her opponent nearly as easily. She flipped her ship in a quick semicircle, came up behind her nemesis, and shot a quick burst into his engine compartment. The ship lit the sky with its eruption.

○ ○ ○ ○ ○

"Sir! Falcons One and Two have been destroyed!" The young technician's voice sounded more shocked than dismayed.

"Nonsense! They've merely tripped their cloaking mechanisms so the enemy can't see them," said the commander.

"No, sir. I can still see them. They're adrift, sir, with no signs of life!" The technician was obviously beginning to panic.

"All right, send Falcons Three through Ten up to end this fiasco," the commander said, letting rage overcome calmness. "Blast them from the sky!"

"Yes, sir—"

"Sir! Intruders on the pad!" cried another technician from across the room.

"How?" asked the commander in frustration.

"I don't know, sir. The sensors should have picked them up! They shouldn't have gotten past the cannons!"

"Defense Code Two-A!" called the commander, invoking the strictest defense the base had, short of complete lock-down. "Exterminate the intruders! Get those Kraits in the air!" he bellowed.

o o o o o

Out on the pad, Washington was just thanking God and Huer.dos for getting him and his troops through the time-and-space gauntlet and down to their destination, when his portable radio came to life.

"Washington! Washington, come in!" said Buck.

"I'm here," he replied sourly. He was irritated. His feet hurt from tramping for what seemed like hundreds of kilometers across Mars's least hospitable zone. He had waded through a RAM ground patrol in sterling imitation of Sherman's march to the sea, while Buck and Wilma were rocketing across space, blasting RAM pilots into oblivion. "We met one patrol. It won't be reporting back to headquarters, but there's bound to be more out there. We need to get out of here."

"How close are you?" asked Buck.

"Just on the pad—" Washington was interrupted by a blaring siren. "Gotta go, Captain! They've found us. Cover us if you can!" he said, and cut the transmission. To his troops he yelled, "Get to the ships! Immediate liftoff!" The fifteen NEO pilots scattered, each one heading to a different craft. As the last Krait cockpit closed, a stream of RAM guards flowed from various doors and hatchways, out onto the pad. The NEO pilots had trained for such a scramble, and sixteen Kraits roared to life, throwing up dust in red clouds. With their defenses activated, the Kraits easily deflected the laser shots from RAM's guards. But to evade anything more substantial, Washington knew, they would have to get off the ground.

○ ○ ○ ○ ○

Buck and Wilma, having disposed of the *Free Enterprise*'s attackers, left Barney to make repairs on his ship. They fell immediately toward the plateau and its laser cannon defense. The cannons' sensors were oblivious to the approaching ships, but Buck and Wilma took no chances. They dove in close, getting under the cannons' line of fire.

Set between the rim's cannons were others guarding the landing pad. These were the NEO pilots' targets, and they charged them. Once the central gun's sensors caught part of the ground ripple and fired, but the shot was so late the rain of dirt and gravel it created did not touch Wilma, who followed Buck.

Buck and Wilma reached their targets simultaneously and sent laser pulses straight into the guns' sensor eyes. They were so close when they fired, the sensors could not catch the blasts. The lenses exploded in fountains of crystal shards. The two guns were blind. The cannons whirled wildly, looking for direction. Before headquarters could switch them to the central sensor system, Buck and Wilma launched missiles. These deadly stingers rammed straight into the guns' bases, at the juncture where the revolving cannons sat on stationary housings. They detonated, tearing away half the bases. The cannons wavered, slowly swaying back and forth, then sank inward, collapsing to the ground in thunderous crashes. Red dust boiled up from the surface in billowing clouds.

Buck flipped the wings of his craft, and Wilma responded in kind. They did not dare use the communications link as long as headquarters had communications. She checked her computer clock, waiting for Huer's programmed run at the rim's sensor dishes. The clock ticked down, and the word "ACTIVATE" appeared on her screen. She pushed the stick forward, sending her fighter toward the center of the crater. Random fire from the rest of the cannons flashed above her. The destruction of the two guns set their automatic defensive program in motion. RAM's ground troops needed to stick to the buildings, or they'd be burned. Wilma was nearing the halfway point of her approach to the dishes. It was here she and Buck faced the likeliest possibility of a hit by the remaining cannons. Her hands tensed on the controls, and she resisted the impulse to send the ship forward. Huer's mathematical calculations were exact. Any deviation in speed or direction meant certain disaster.

She had the first dish in sight, and she relaxed a notch, knowing her worst danger now was direct fire from the Tharsian Plateau's headquarters itself. At least, she thought wryly, this is an acid test for our sensor invisibility. They can't hit what they can't see. She pushed the laser controls to automatic and concentrated on keeping her ship level. As they approached the first sensor dish, the Krait's lasers shot out, burning the exact center of the dish. She continued on course, meeting Buck at the other side of the circle. He was flying immediately above her, so close the rush of the thin Martian atmosphere caused her wings to vibrate. Huer's programming set their intersect point midway between two dishes. The lasers were inactive for all of six seconds. If the timing were not perfect, Buck's lasers would fry her. His ship slid over her in a moment of breathless silence, then his lasers punched at the next dish.

They met again, their run finished, and closed formation, charging across the open field of the Tharsian Plateau toward the docked fighters in an erratic evasive course. A bolt of laser light hit the ground in front of them, spraying them with a shower of dust. They flew through it blind, then veered away from another beam. In seconds, they had dispatched the cannons that held the remaining Kraits in check.

"So far, so good," said Buck.

"Phase one accomplished," replied Wilma.

Buck and Wilma circled the base of the laser cannons, watching as the docked ships' engines roared. Eight Kraits in the first row eased forward on their pressure blankets and rose almost straight up, then arced around the crater. Eight in the second row followed the first, doubling the formation. Buck waited for the dust to settle on the crater floor, then keyed in the radio frequency Huer had established for their escape.

"Washington?" called Buck.

"Ready," said the veteran tersely.

"Then let's go home. Barney?"

"All set, Cap'n," rumbled the pirate from the bridge of his ship.

"Phase two accomplished. Operation complete. You've got another mission to run. Thanks for the ride."

"Any time," Barney grumbled in acknowledgment.

The wing of stolen ships bunched up behind Buck and Wilma, waiting for an opening in the damaged laser cannons' erratic fire. They were still blanketing the area with flak. "Now!" said Buck and the wing shot forward, knowing Huer's calculations were behind the order. Lasers zinged over them. As they put distance between themselves and the rim of the Tharsian Plateau, the lasers picked up the ripple of their wake on the desert and fired. They barely distanced the shots, which punched into the ground behind them. "Home free," said Buck lightly.

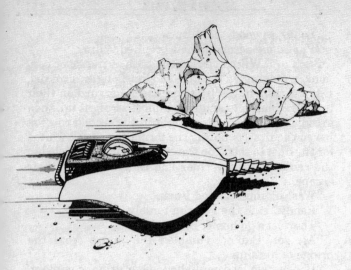

Chapter 19

Masterlink chewed on in frustration. Its searchers were still correlating their first impressions, and the process was too slow. Masterlink jangled angrily.

"BE QUIET!" snapped Karkov.

"QUIET YOURSELF," snarled Masterlink.

"YOU'RE CREATING ENOUGH DISTURBANCE TO BLOCK SEARCHER TRANSMISSIONS. I DIDN'T SPEND MY ENERGIES TO SEND THEM OUT, ONLY TO HAVE YOU BLOCK THEM!"

"YOU COULD HAVE GIVEN THEM MORE POWER."

Karkov ignored Masterlink's petulance. Instead it began to run a sequential check on the searchers, calling the roll of its children.

o o o o o

"Sir! I've got a drifter on screen four," cried Little,

another of RAM's millions of technicians.

"Let's see, Little."

Operational Supervisor Harpingdon slid into a chair beside the scanner. Little indicated the upper right-hand screen. A ship drifted across its field. "Power?" he asked.

"None I can detect, sir."

"Then she's in a decaying orbit."

"By my computations, she'll come into atmosphere in one hour."

"Where will that put her?"

"Right in the heart of Galveston—about four kilometers from here."

"Then we've got to pick her up. No one on board?" Harpingdon asked belatedly.

"No. She's abandoned."

"Strange she wasn't detected and snagged before she got this close. Oh, well. I guess the trash sharks can't catch them all. Can you get her markings?"

"The computer's picking them up now, sir." Little waited until the cursor on his main screen stopped flashing, then called up the identification letters on the derelict.

"Run her through," said Harpingdon.

Little obliged, and the computer purred softly. Soon her last registered location appeared on the screen.

"Chicagorg. Little, check her status."

Little punched keys, and the words "INACTIVE, TIED DOWN" appeared.

"Great gods! It's that stolen war memorial. And she's up. How is beyond me. They're supposed to pour concrete into the engine when they set up those monuments."

"Sir," said Little, checking a list that was scrolling across a screen to his left, "there's a priority code on that spacecraft."

"Who set it?"

"Authorization sanctioned by Director Zonin, Chicagorg, with orders to relay any sighting to the regent." Little's voice dropped as he uttered the title.

"Chernenko? I wonder what the regent's interest is. He usually ignores petty theft."

"Shall I report the ship?" asked Little.

"Of course. Add that we have authorized a tug to bring her in."

Little bent over his console.

○ ○ ○ ○ ○

"They've discovered her." Baring-Gould peered into the *Free Enterprise*'s communications panel, squinting as he read the digital print. "They've sent out a tug to bring her in, and they're contacting Chernenko."

A fearsome chuckle rumbled in Black Barney's mighty chest. He was anticipating theft. It always made him cheerful.

"The bait swims out," said Arak Konii. "Now we have but to wait. The fish will strike."

"I'm just glad that report I dropped got through," said Baring-Gould, Barney's first mate.

"If Chernenko is interested in that ship, it got through." Konii's tone was superior. "Even a rumor of Captain Rogers being seen in the area would be enough. Do you know what the captain is worth on the open market right now?"

There was a hint in Konii's words, and Barney did not like it. "What's the price on your head, Konii?" he asked.

There was an uncomfortable silence on the *Free Enterprise*'s bridge.

Konii's lips curved in amusement. "I apologize for my lapse in taste," he said, but there was no sincerity in the statement.

Barney's right hand started forward, but he stopped it. Captain Rogers had his own ideas of discipline. For some reason Barney was unable to fathom, tearing a crew member's head off for a breach of etiquette was not included in it. "You're on report," said Barney, feeling the threat a lame substitute for mayhem.

The flicker of amusement in Konii's eyes died. Rogers was an unknown, except for the fact that he had bested Barney in single combat—no mean feat. Konii was not afraid, but he did not relish standing on boggy ground.

"Got it!" said Baring-Gould. "Chernenko's sent word he'll meet the tug at the seaboard landing strip."

"That'll keep him busy," said Barney. "We go." He turned to Baring-Gould. "Keep the star field on, planet-side. We'll take the far shuttle."

"I still don't see how you're planning to run Galveston's sensors," said Baring-Gould.

Barney's chuckle rumbled again. "Why, we'll follow the tug down."

Barney, Konii, and three crewmen crowded into the shuttle. It was a triangular craft, designed on Luna, but meant for atmospheric as well as space flight. Its capacity was six crewmen, but Barney's size made it a tight fit for five. He grunted as he wedged himself into the pilot's seat. "Strap in," he said. "We're due for launch in . . . one minute." He adjusted his restraints to the maximum, and they barely locked over his massive chest.

Konii had systems up and was fingering the controls. "All set, Captain. Launch in minus forty-five."

"That'll put us on the tug?"

"Duplicate trajectory," Konii confirmed. "We'll be on the off side of that piece of space junk you insisted on dragging here."

"Right."

Barney braced himself against the shuttle's floor struts as the *Free Enterprise*'s docking bay doors opened. Before they were fully retracted, the shuttle had begun its run down the launch track. Barney thought of the asteroid miner he had cheated to win the shuttle, and praised his own foresight.

"Here we go!" said Konii, and the ship shot into space. "Tug out of Galveston space dock on parallel course."

"We've got thirty seconds before we'll be cloaked by the derelict," said Barney. "That was as close as I could bring the *Free Enterprise*, even under camouflage." He glanced out the starboard port at the gently wavering star field that was his ship's disguise.

Konii was fussing with the controls. Under his manipulations, the shuttle lifted its nose and sailed like a bird. The derelict appeared to starboard, and Konii sent the shuttle skittering to her. It was a kind of electronic camouflage that required precise timing and absolute control, especially entering atmosphere, and Konii concentrated on his instruments.

The tug made a routine grab for the derelict and caught it, then set off across space, setting itself and the derelict Scout up for a landing trajectory to the seaboard. The shuttle followed its lead.

The three ships dropped into the Earth's atmosphere. Konii felt the weight of it catch the shuttle's stubby wings and cautiously adjusted the engines for atmospheric flight. They sank lower and lower, the tug bringing its cargo down on a pressure blanket that forced Konii to concentrate, lest the shuttle be displaced by it. "Two hundred meters," Konii reported.

"That's it!" said Barney. "Level off!"

The three crewmen were white under their impassive expressions. Flying two hundred meters above the face of the Earth was not something yet within their experience, but they knew its dangers. Barney smiled.

The ship lifted its nose. "Point seven," said Barney,

and Konii obliged, sending the ship away from the tug at a totally unsafe speed.

"Now where?" asked Konii.

"The marina," said Barney.

"With this thing?"

"It's what we've got," said Barney reasonably.

"I hate to point this out, Captain, but it doesn't float."

"Check your chart. There's a square in front of the private docks, the ones owned by RAM's executive branch. Set down there."

Konii looked at Barney through narrowed eyes. "If you knew about Chernenko's cache, why didn't we take it before now?"

"Too risky," said Barney.

"Is it any less risky now?" asked Konii.

"Captain needs it," said Barney, as if that put an end to the matter.

The shuttle shot into the marina like a lightning bolt, scattering sea birds as it went.

"Coming up on target."

"Set her down," said Barney tersely. "Now."

"Now? Like a rock?"

"Like a rock."

Konii sliced off the shuttle's forward power and kicked in the landing thrusters. For a sickening moment it sank unchecked, then the thrusters supported it and it powered down to Earth approximately twenty-four meters from the center of the square. A bronze sculpture marked the area as RAM's own. It was set on a concrete base poured into a twisted pyramid.

The shuttle was still two meters up when Barney threw open the hatch door and jumped. He was immediately followed by the three crewmen, two of them clutching laser rifles, and one holding a flak gun capable of sending out a blast of chaff that would confuse enemy lasers for a full minute. They fanned out behind Barney as he lumbered over to the monument.

As he reached the structure, an echoing siren sounded in the distance. "Terrines," he muttered, grasping the base of the statue. A plaque on the base informed him it had been erected in honor of RAM's founder, Simund Holzerhein, and forbade tampering. Barney ignored this admonition. He set all his strength, natural and cybernetic, against the metal. At first nothing happened, then the statue began to slide on the concrete base. The sirens screamed louder as the Terrines closed in. One of the crewmen, his ears keener than his fellows', looked up, startled. "Dragonfly, three o'clock," he called.

Barney grunted, gave a heave, and the statue crashed slowly to the ground. Where its base had rested was a shallow hole. Inside it was a circular wooden box. Barney scooped it up and ran as the Terrine heliplane sighted the shuttle and swooped in on it, guns blazing.

Barney threw himself into the shuttle's open hatch as the square erupted in Terrines. He tossed the box into the pilot's seat. His men were close on his heels. He reached back and dragged the last of the crewmen in. "Go!" he shouted at Konii, and the shuttle scooted forward.

The dragonfly pulled up, afraid of hitting its ground support, then immediately resumed its pursuit.

"Once we're clear, that dragonfly will be on us," said Konii.

"That's why we brought this," said Barney, wrenching a meter-long gyro launcher from its clips in the shuttle's ceiling. He flipped open a storage box on the wall of the craft and extracted shells, lining them up on another box. He selected a shell, slipped it into the bazooka's wicked mouth, and moved to the stern of the skittering craft. He hit a rear port release, shoved the bazooka through it, and propped it on his shoulder. Legs braced, Barney did not seem to feel the wild movements of the ship as Konii sent it tacking across the sea. He squinted down the sights of the weapon.

"Range now," said Konii, one eye on the shuttle's simple sensors.

Barney cranked the launch lever, and the bazooka spat a gyro shell. He picked up another shell, loaded his weapon, and fired again. Once fired, the shells' own sensors sent them after their designated target. The first shell picked up the dragonfly, zeroed in on its location, and altered course. As it neared the Terrine heliplane, the pilot detected it. He erected an immediate shield of static, meant to confuse the shell's sensors. The shell again changed course, missing the plane by half a meter. Its detonation in the air rocked the craft, but did not damage it.

The second shell hit before the pilot realized it was there. As his sensors beeped a warning, his ship lost its tail. The dragonfly began to spin, buzzing like its namesake. Desperately the pilot tried to hold it, but it was no use. The heliplane whirled slowly downward. Terrines jumped from its doorways as it hit the water and exploded.

Konii made a sibilant sound through his teeth.

"Close," confirmed Barney.

"Now we've got to get out of here," said Konii.

"Head out to sea," ordered his captain. "The trade winds shipping lane runs about a thousand kilometers off the coast. All we have to do is wait for something big to pass and hitch a ride."

"Aye, Captain," muttered Konii.

Barney picked up the jewel box and wedged himself back into the pilot's seat. He buckled the restraints and tugged at them to be sure they were secure. He ran a competent eye over Konii's maneuver, then let him fly the ship. He looked down at the box in his hand, grasped the top and bottom sections, and pulled. The computer lock on the front of the box screeched, then broke, and the box popped open. It was lined with soft, dark fabric. Sparkling against its rich background was a rainbow of cut gems.

Konii looked over at the display, his eyes eager. "How did you know about that?" he asked.

Barney looked at the wealth in his hands. He snapped the box shut. "That's another story," he answered. "What's our estimated time of arrival?"

"Nineteen point three-nine minutes," replied Konii.

"Step on it," said Barney.

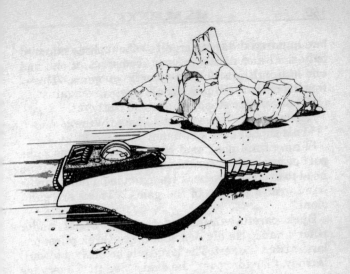

Chapter 20

Barney sent the round wooden box spinning across the table. Buck caught it and looked up at the pirate. "Any problems?" he asked.

Barney shook his head.

Buck opened the box, noticing the damaged lock, but saying nothing. The gems winked at him. Buck turned the open box around. "How about it, Doc? Is it enough?"

Huer, his holographic image shivering along the right edge, where the projector in Buck's quarters had a faulty imager, leaned over. "You'll have to spread them out so I can get an accurate scan," he said.

Buck obligingly upended the box onto the smoky translucence of the table. He spread the jewels out carefully.

Huer examined the stones, scanning each one for cut, brilliance, and size. "You have approximately two hundred thousand credits—about three hundred fifty thousand dolas—in your terms, about one and one-half million dollars—worth of gems. Three-fourths of that will pay Ardala's price."

"That's pretty steep," Buck said flatly.

"Ardala has a large appetite," said Wilma.

"This should keep her happy for a while."

"I am afraid not," said Huer. "Greed seems to be part of her basic programming. However, there is no need to overindulge her." He extended a holographic hand over a portion of the gems. "These are sufficient."

Buck carefully removed the stones not under Huer's hand. He divided them into three piles, one larger than the rest. The large pile he pushed toward Barney. "Divide it up," he said. "See that everyone gets his share." The pirate immediately accepted his reward and lumbered from the room. The second pile Buck picked up. "Give me your hand," he said to Wilma. When she complied, he dropped the gems into it. "For NEO," he said. The smallest pile he scooped up and put back in the box.

"And those?" queried Wilma, her full lips curving into an easy smile.

"For emergencies," replied Buck. "Doc, I think it's time to deal. Can Ardala trace us here?"

"Not if I scramble the transmission. Not unless she really wants to."

"Then I think I'd like to speak to the lady."

"Do you think that's wise?" Wilma's low voice held a hint of challenge.

"Maybe not. If she traces the source of the transmission, it could jeopardize Salvation. But then, our presence here puts the station in jeopardy. Besides, she doesn't need to know who I am."

"I hadn't thought of that," said Wilma.

"I can easily disguise your appearance by superimposing an image of my creation over your own. Think

of it as using your resources," said Huer, running a
finger across his neat mustache.

"OK, let's do it," said Buck.

Wilma examined the room, looking for anything
that would identify it to Ardala's computers. The
walls were empty, there were no company logos in
evidence, and Buck was not wearing his flight suit.
Instead he wore an oak-leaf-brown coverall that com-
plemented his hair and fit his trim figure perfectly.
The fine lines of scarlet piping that carried the suit's
electronics followed his contours. Wilma found him a
pleasing sight, and she was sure Ardala would as
well. That might be an asset. "I can't see anything
that would give you away. On a computer link it will
be obvious you are transmitting from an orbiting station, because of the construction, but there are thousands. Ardala will have a time of it if she tries to
track you down."

"Let's play ball," said Buck.

"I thought you were going to speak with Ardala."
Huer was still assimilating Buck's particular brand
of English.

"I am. That is, if you'll set up the transmission."

"With pleasure. A few minor adjustments in your
transmitted image will make you a stranger to your
own family."

Buck smiled crookedly, breathed deeply, then
steeled himself for the coming interview.

"But do watch your step with Ardala. She is unbe-
lievably ruthless," Huer cautioned.

"The lady does have fangs," said Wilma, slipping
off the arm of the pale, overstuffed couch. "I'll get out
of scanner range."

"Doc, I think this will go better if she thinks this is
a private communication."

"All right. Your transmission is coded. It should be
coming up . . . now."

As he spoke, the image of a room lit by firelight

appeared on the screen. Ardala was seated in her leather chair. The room was her office. She conducted all her transmissions from it. It housed her sophisticated computer network behind a bank of carved wooden doors. As the image coalesced, sharpening into perfect focus, Ardala's beautiful face rose out of the darkness like night-blooming Martian jasmine. Her eyes slanted piquantly, as soft as summer, making nameless promises. Her luscious mouth was stained dark red, and somehow Buck found it unattractive. The color looked like blood.

"Ardala Valmar?" he asked, taking pains to be deferential.

Ardala inclined her lovely head in royal acknowledgment.

"I think we have business to discuss."

"Oh?" asked Ardala. "I think not. I do not do business with people I do not know."

Buck laughed. It was a crude snicker, and Wilma regarded him with surprise. "Come now, Miss Valmar. I know for a fact that you often deal with your customers by code number alone." Huer had set up the interview through strictly mathematical channels. "I am giving you the unique opportunity of knowing your market . . . personally."

Ardala lowered her eyelids and regarded Buck disdainfully. "I have no interest in knowing you."

"Then why did you accept my call? Let us stop playing games." Buck picked up the jewel box and opened it. The gems twinkled.

Ardala's eyes opened. "I find your conversation more interesting than I first anticipated."

"I thought you might."

"What did you think those stones might purchase?"

Buck started to reply, when a message began running along the bottom of the viewscreen. "I heard a major shipment was seen in the belt," he said, trying

to answer Ardala and read the message at the same time.

"HUER HERE," read the message. "SCANNING ARDALA'S SALES LIST. . . . SHE HAS THE PLANS FOR HAUBERK'S SHIELDS!"

"That shipment has moved out," replied Ardala.

"I am aware of that," said Buck smoothly. "I have an intimate and exclusive knowledge of that shipment. I was hoping that situation might continue for a while."

"I have had one offer for the details of the shipment."

"I am aware of that as well."

"That was you? Well, I believe I quoted a price."

"And I believe I showed you collateral."

Ardala considered. "I see no reason to negotiate further. You have a sale."

Buck shook his head. "No."

"No? I can always sell my knowledge elsewhere."

"True. But, as you said, I am at present the only interested party. I simply find your price high for the information I am buying."

"You were quoted the price I require."

"And I am telling you what I require. As you can see, I have the money. I do not mind spending it. However, I feel I should get more for my investment."

Ardala could smell a con a kilometer away. "Like what?" she asked suspiciously.

"In my own small way, I, too, deal in information. I have a party interested in space shielding. I understand you have a set of schematics for sale."

"Your information is accurate," she said grudgingly. The plans for Hauberk's shields had been part of a package she extracted from a top RAM executive whose financial indiscretions made him vulnerable to her blackmail. The rest of the package had long since found markets, but no one wanted to touch Hauberk. It was too dangerous. She smiled, her blood-red mouth drawing together in the center. "I might be persuaded to let those plans go."

"I thought you might," said Buck.

"Of course, I shall require further compensation."

"I am afraid, Miss Valmar, that is impossible. As I said, I feel the jewels are adequate compensation for the extended package."

Ardala sucked her lower lip. "You cannot expect to get something for nothing. I propose that we make an exchange of information. You give me the jewels—and your name—and I will give you what you require."

Wilma covered her mouth to stifle her laughter. She knew Ardala's interest was purely personal.

"My name? I fail to see what value that can have."

"Let us say," returned Ardala, "I am curious."

"I am not sure I care to reveal it," said Buck, fencing. He was confident Ardala was bargaining, a game her pride forced her to play to the end, but he was also glad of Huer's electronic disguise.

"Come now. I have your face. It is only a matter of time before I find a name to go with it. Humor me. Give me what I ask for."

"I can always give you a name. That is not to say it will be the one you seek."

Ardala smiled, her white teeth a sharp line framed in scarlet. "Then give me a name. And if you're going to lie, at least make it interesting."

"All right. Hart. That is all I can tell you."

"Heart? Isn't that a rather delicate title for a man of such presence?"

"Make of it what you will."

"I shall add it to my profile on you." She chuckled wickedly. "Our interview has provided my computer with the time to do considerable research on you, Heart. Your vital statistics are safely recorded."

"I am flattered you find me so interesting."

"I find you possibly marketable. It is something we

might discuss at a later date."

The implication of a tete-a-tete was subtle, but the look in Ardala's eyes was not. Buck had piqued her interest. She loved puzzles, and she meant to solve this one.

"Despite your insinuation regarding my name, I would enjoy that." Buck smiled, letting his appreciation of Ardala's beauty show in his eyes. "It has been an interesting interview. You exceed your reputation."

"My reputation?" asked Ardala innocently.

"As a businesswoman," Buck said smoothly.

"Payment will be forwarded through the channels we discussed via computer?"

"Of course."

"I shall look forward to other negotiations," she said.

"No more than I."

The viewscreen flickered and went dark. Buck, frozen at attention, relaxed. "Wow," he said.

"Wow indeed," said Wilma. "I didn't know you had such a talent for the theater."

"It's just my natural charm," replied Buck, his tension escaping in bravado.

Wilma's hazel eyes opened wide in imitation of Ardala's false innocence. She made a moue. "Did you enjoy the interview?" she asked innocently.

Buck gave her an incredulous look. "Are you kidding? That was like talking to a praying mantis." Buck paused, then added, teasingly, "She is very beautiful."

"Very." Wilma understood the tease.

"And very deadly," said Huer as he popped back into focus, the holographic eye removing him from being almost on top of Buck. "Let's not forget that she toppled at least three RAM executives to get where she is today."

Buck slid over on the couch, making room for the

shimmering image.

"But we got what we wanted," Buck said.

"We did indeed," said Wilma. "What was all that bargaining? I thought for a moment you were going to lose it all."

Buck smiled at Huer. "You couldn't see it from where you were sitting, but in the middle of things, Doc flashed some very interesting information across the screen. It seems Ardala owns something else we can use." He took a deep breath. "We just bought the plans to Hauberk's shields."

Wilma was across the room in a stride. She grabbed Buck's arms and pulled him from the couch, her eyes shining. "Say that again."

"We just bought the plans to Hauberk's shields," said Buck reasonably.

"I don't believe it!" Wilma threw her arms around Buck and squeezed him tightly.

"It is a fact," said Huer. "She seems to have come by them rather underhandedly, but they are, nevertheless, in her possession."

"No. Now they're in ours," said Buck with a grin. He accepted Wilma's unexpected enthusiasm with a slight hug of his own.

Wilma, catching Buck's smile, broke the embrace, embarrassed at letting herself get carried away. She straightened her uniform, cleared her throat, and said, "We've still got lots of work to do."

Buck understood her apprehensions. "Yes, Colonel," he said. "Good night."

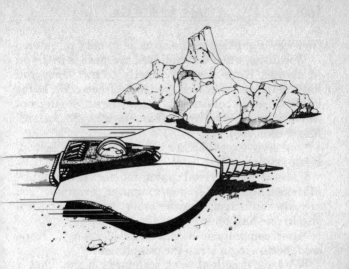

Chapter 21

Cornelius Kane tossed the work order into the middle of his already cluttered desk. Seaforian's missing shipment of experimental fighters had been duplicated, and a new wing was ready for delivery to Hauberk. Rather than take the chance of losing the ships again, Warhead decided to fly the craft there, using mercenary pilots under Kane's command.

The corners of Kane's mouth drew up as recalled his discussion with the Warhead executive who authorized the shipment. Harper Marcheson gave Kane a free hand in choosing his pilots, reserving the right of veto should one of them be unacceptable to the company. Marcheson expected Kane to research the men and submit a list for his inspection, but Kane named off twenty pilots from memory, all but one on the RAM-approved list. Moreover, he knew their whereabouts and rates of pay. The entire operation was organized in the space of twenty minutes.

"You do not know how relieved my mind is with you in charge, Kane. Report directly to me. Once you have delivered the ships, you are a free agent, as far as Warhead is concerned. This contract should not infringe upon your arrangements with Seaforian," Marcheson said.

"You may expect to hear from me within hours," Kane replied.

"I have authorized payment for the pilots." Marcheson glanced at his computer terminal. "All are now confirmed. They will meet you at the launch site in one-half hour."

"Your company is a marvel of efficiency," Kane said, bestowing a strategic compliment.

"We have excellent work standards, Kane. That is why we chose you."

The challenge in Marcheson's words was plain, but it did not daunt Kane. He left Marcheson with a high heart. Kane now stood in his cluttered office on Mars, anticipating the pleasure of flying the best ships in the system. Moreover, he was to be paid twice. This contract with Warhead was an unexpected bonus to his agreement with Seaforian to act as trainer for Hauberk's pilots.

He picked up his flight gloves and slapped them against his hand. Beneath his elation ran a subliminal current of curiosity. The first shipment of fighters had not yet surfaced. Neither the black market nor computer security had unearthed them. It was Kane's opinion someone very clever now possessed them.

He dismissed the prospect of NEO. He knew the organization intimately. In all his time with it, NEO never had pulled off a major action against RAM. No, the theft—and theft he knew it was—had the earmarks of a renegade. That meant a private operator, a pirate such as Black Barney, or a really daring black-market trader.

The possibilities were niggling thoughts that disturbed his complacency. He pushed them aside and called up navigational charts. He identified Warhead's position on its private spaceport off Phobos, then entered his destination. The computer absorbed the input, cogitated for a moment, and began to paint thin yellow lines across the dark reaches of space.

Kane studied the three possible trajectories his computer presented and chose one, instructing the computer to download the information onto a microdisk. Disks were obsolete, but they were isolated banks of data, not accessible to a computer bank unless they were deliberately fed into it. The computer popped a scarlet plastic disk into the coding slot, and Kane retrieved it. He punched it back into the system, saw the file read out, recalled it, and escaped the system. Once the disk was safely in his hand, he erased his work. No one would know his route, not even the pilots who followed him, until he entered the information into the fighter's onboard computers. He was taking no chances.

○ ○ ○ ○ ○

Huer reposed in the NEO computer network, reduced to the abstract units of a program. His prime directive was to help Buck. He was both Buck's safeguard and his Achilles' heel in the computer-dominated world of the twenty-fifth century. He could use his abilities to block whatever program was trying to find his charge, but, by his very existence, he acted as a weather vane pointing the way to him. He was finding paradox to be the essence of human existence, and, frankly, he would have turned it over for the logic of facts. Had he not a full genetic core programmed into his personality complex, recent events would have caused him to retreat to them.

He had been making discreet attempts to trace the malevolent presence he knew searched for him. Several times he thought he was close to it, but was forced to retreat or be identified. He was at a loss. To index the presence meant discovery, and discovery meant danger for Buck. On the other hand, he thought he had enough data to detect the feel of the thing, and thereby warn Buck. It was a decision he did not yet have the data to make, even though delay might jeopardize Buck's plans, not to mention his life. Huer shivered, an electronic fluctuation that reminded him uncomfortably of the evil bloodhound on his trail. There was chaos surrounding the assassin, a chaos that left disturbed circuits and static in its wake.

○ ○ ○ ○ ○

Masterlink lounged in the uneasy bowels of RAM main, sorting the myriad reports its searchers were collecting. It tossed off main's virus hunters, overpowering them with wild electronic chaff that scrambled their directives and sent them against each other. In time, main would realize the presence infecting it could not be exorcised by such simple methods, but by then it would be too late. Masterlink would have consolidated enough power to ensure survival. This thought flashed subliminally through its mind as it mulled over the latest intelligence.

The left side of its deranged brain caught it up. "TEND TO BUSINESS," chided Karkov sternly. "WE'VE GOT A BLOCK ON MAIN THAT WILL GIVE US MORE THAN ENOUGH TIME TO PROCESS THESE REPORTS BEFORE WE HAVE TO RETRENCH. THAT IS, IF WE DON'T WASTE ANY OF IT!"

"I HAVE BUSINESS FIRMLY IN HAND," replied Masterlink. "ROMANOV CANNOT PINPOINT ROGERS'S WHEREABOUTS WITHIN NEO, THOUGH IT HAS CAUGHT

ELUSIVE REFERENCES. WHEN IT TRIED TO BACKTRACK THEM, IT WAS MET WITH A MAZE OF CONFLICTING GATES THAT LED NOWHERE."

"NEO'S SYSTEM WAS NOT AS DIFFICULT TO PENETRATE AS RAM'S. HOW CAN IT FOIL A CLASS A SEARCHER?" asked Karkov.

Masterlink ran through the data Romanov had transmitted. "ROMANOV IS OF THE OPINION THE GATES ARE NOT THE WORK OF THE NEO SYSTEM, BUT OF AN AUTONOMOUS PROGRAM WITHIN THAT SYSTEM," it said.

"A RENEGADE?"

"NOT FROM THE REPORTS. IT SEEMS TO BE OPERATING WITH NEO'S SANCTION."

"HMM." Karkov ruminated on the information, viewing it from every angle his warped logic could conceive. "CAPTAIN ROGERS MAY HAVE A BODYGUARD," he said.

Masterlink chuckled, sending an aureole of static into main's circuits. "IT WON'T LAST LONG."

"NOT WITH ROMANOV ON ITS TRAIL. I AM OF THE OPINION WE COMMAND CONSIDERABLY MORE POWER THAN NEO."

"TIE ROMANOV INTO RAM MAIN," said Masterlink. "IT'LL FRY THE UPSTART."

"DON'T GET OUT OF HAND. WE HAVE BETTER USES FOR MAIN."

Karkov's rebuke made Masterlink pulse with static.

Karkov ignored his alter ego and concentrated on the flow of information being transmitted by its searchers. The transmissions were coded in a hodgepodge of half-forgotten military codes from the twentieth century, rearranged in Masterlink's image. "ULIANOV REPORTS A THEFT," Karkov said.

"ULIANOV? FROM HAUBERK?"

"AFFIRMATIVE."

"OF WHAT INTEREST IS A THEFT?" Masterlink asked.

"IT IS UNUSUAL, AND THEREFORE WORTH INVESTIGATING. A TOP-SECRET SHIPMENT DESTINED FOR HAUBERK SEEMS TO HAVE GONE ASTRAY."

Masterlink looked the material over. "A LARGE SHIPMENT," it said slowly. "LIKE THE ONE WE WERE BLAMED FOR. I DON'T SUPPOSE YOUR WONDER-CHILD HAPPENED TO DISCOVER THE NATURE OF IT."

"NO." Karkov was correlating data.

"COULD THE MATERIAL BE GENUINELY LOST?"

"NOT LIKELY," replied Karkov. "TOP-SECURITY SHIPMENTS ARE UNDER TOO MUCH SCRUTINY FROM THE HIGHLY PLACED. TOO MANY FINGERS ARE IN THE PIE."

"IT FEELS LIKE NEO," said Masterlink.

"NEO HAS NEVER ATTEMPTED ANY OPERATION OF THIS SIZE—NOT IN ITS ENTIRE HISTORY."

"YOU FORGET ROGERS," Masterlink stated.

"NEVER."

"YOU FORGET OPERATION PITTER-PAT."

"WHEN HE RELEASED THAT BOMBER PILOT HOSTAGE?"

"THERE HAD NEVER BEEN ANYTHING LIKE THAT EITHER," said Masterlink.

"HE CARRIED THAT ONE OFF ON NERVE," defended Karkov.

"YES, BUT HE CARRIED IT OFF," said Masterlink.

Karkov paused, considering. "I SHALL INFORM ULIANOV TO KEEP TRACK OF EVENTS CONCERNING THE THEFT."

"IS THAT ALL IT REPORTS?" asked Masterlink.

"ALL THAT IS EXTRAORDINARY. OTHERWISE, HAUBERK IS FUNCTIONING AS PROGRAMMED."

"I COULD SNIFF OUT ROGERS IN A MINUTE," Masterlink said.

Karkov was quick to pick up the implications of Masterlink's words. "NO! WE HAVE DISCUSSED THIS BEFORE! WE WILL NOT SPLIT UP. WE CANNOT HOPE TO ACCOMPLISH OUR PURPOSE SEPARATELY. LET IT BE. ULIANOV WILL NOTIFY US IMMEDIATELY AT THE SLIGHT-

EST SIGN OF ROGERS'S PRESENCE."

"I THINK IT HAS MISSED THE FIRST ONE," sneered Masterlink.

○ ○ ○ ○ ○

George Washington sat in a dim corner of Salvation III's deserted lounge, nursing the end of a drink. His blue eyes were shadowed as he stared into the liquid in his glass.

"You seem troubled, Captain."

Washington looked up, directly into Wilma Deering's face. "No, Colonel," he said, beginning to rise, "thoughtful."

"Sit down, Pappy."

The nickname, on Wilma's tongue, surprised him. It was his by right as well as tradition, for he was the oldest member of the wing—excluding Rogers's five centuries, but Wilma was not often familiar. "What can I do for you, Colonel?" he asked, raising his glass. He studied her impassive loveliness over the rim.

"You might tell me what you're thinking about."

"I might."

Wilma returned Washington's scrutiny. "I think you were rushing the future."

"Maybe. Maybe wondering whether you'll come back from a skirmish is a jinx. I don't know."

"You were the most positive voice in the wing."

Washington's crooked smile had the charm of a small boy's. "I know. And I meant every word. I *believe* we can do it. I just don't *know* if we can."

"Washington, I can't have you at less than one hundred percent. The wing turns on you, and you know it."

Washington swirled the drink. "That's why I'm indulging my doubts now. There won't be time once we lift off."

Wilma sat down and propped her elbows on the table. She briefly wondered if America's famous general ever felt as her captain felt now. For a split second her eyes were vulnerable, and Washington could see the naked relief in them.

"I don't see what you're worried about," he said. "Rogers has the wing in the palm of his hand."

"He's caught their imagination, all right, but, legend or no, to them he's unproven. They haven't flown combat with him."

"What about the Tharsian Plateau?"

"That's not the same as aerial combat, and you know it. In a crisis, they'll look to you. Hauberk will be the biggest action NEO has ever undertaken. I could say I've put myself on the line for this one—it's true—but that's the least of it. If we lose, we lose big. NEO may not recover for a hundred years."

"And if we win?" asked Washington, a dancing light of challenge in his eyes.

"You know the answer to that."

"Colonel, if it'll set your mind at ease, I don't mind admitting I am looking forward to this. In spite of the fact it's crazy—in spite of the fact it's impossible—you couldn't keep me out of this one."

Wilma stared past his shoulder, a faraway look in her eyes. "Somehow, I get the feeling we have a chance. In my mind's eye, I see Earth free and flourishing as it was in Buck's time. Dreams don't come true, Washington. It's a fact of this life."

"Maybe it's time we changed the facts—in our favor."

"It's worth a try."

Washington leaned forward and put a gentle hand on her shoulder. "I don't intend to die, Colonel. I intend to win."

"Get some rest, Captain," she said. "And don't take your persona too much to heart."

Washington finished his drink, his eyes smiling at her as he swallowed the last of it. "I'm kinda fond of it," he said.

o o o o o

Buck Rogers slept fitfully. His body was supine, but it was not at rest. He tossed and turned, scrabbling the bedclothes to a knot. The computer's security eye recorded his movements impersonally, unaware of the dreams racing through his mind.

He stood on the top of a high hill outside the town in which he was born. A paper airplane rose on the afternoon breeze, a triangle of white against the flat cerulean, cloudless sky. The plane made a loop, then continued on its soaring flight.

He sat in the open cockpit of an ancient aircraft. Its propeller whipped against the wind, speeding up as the engine caught with a roar. He could see the back of the pilot's head encased in its leather flight cap. Clouds scudded by.

He grasped the controls of a flight simulator, his knuckles white. The plane was going down. The stupid simulator was programmed for it, and there was nothing he could do. He knew it. He wrenched the controls back, trying to lift the nose of a nonexistent plane, but the simulator still registered a nose dive. A swift glance across the instrument panel confirmed his position. He turned the simulator off.

Snatches of other experiences in the air slipped in and out of his mind. They had one thing in common: not one of them came from the twenty-fifth century. They were from his own time, reminders of a less desperate civilization. He skipped over them, disturbed enough to thrash, but not disturbed enough to wake up. Around the edges of every dream lurked the specter of the Krait, a hazy cylindrical shape. It hovered on the edge of his subconscious, not taking form. He made no attempt to reach out to it.

o o o o o

In Salvation III's docking bay, twenty-two Kraits waited. Silent, patient, ready for whatever their humans planned, they had no doubts. Their computers told them their capabilities. They knew to the last decimal point what speed was their maximum effort, the ratio of maneuverability to that speed, and the effectiveness of their weapons.

Theirs was the ultimate confidence of the unknowing logical mind divorced from the reality of human error. Malfunction was not within their vocabulary. They did not know what it was to break down. They were children in their supreme confidence. Eighteen of the craft waited for the morrow serenely, in peaceful ignorance of the enormity of the task they faced.

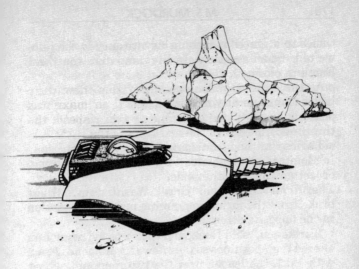

Chapter 22

Buck Rogers sent his ship toward the menacing bulk of Hauberk like a shooting star. His spirits were high, and it showed in the verve with which his ship moved. Behind him came the rest of the flight, six other ships following their leader like well-behaved chicks trailing a mother hen. To starboard and fifty kilometers back from the last of his flight came the rest of the wing, six ships led by Washington.

"Close up, Eagle Leader," said Buck.

"Roger, Rebel One." Washington's flight was moving before he finished speaking.

"Hauberk in sensor range. Estimated time of arrival, one minute." Hauberk blinked ominously on Buck's scanner, but it was an impersonal threat. The structure Buck saw in the distance, all bright angles and dramatic shadows, made a more personal statement. It was a mangled collage of shapes, following no orderly design, for Hauberk had grown over centuries to its present monolithic size. Inside the jumble of random shapes were the computers that held Earth in chains.

As the ships drew nearer, the station filled their ports, then overwhelmed the ships. It no longer was possible to see more than one or two walls of the thing, decorated with the markings of the RAM subsidiaries that had contributed to their construction.

"Coming up on shields in point five," said Buck. "Meet you on the other side."

"Affirmative, Rebel One." Washington's flight broke from the formation, arcing around the station in the opposite direction.

"Strike ten," said Buck, and the ships following him altered their positions so they flew in a diamond of four, with Buck the leader, over the two remaining ships, inside the diamond. It was one of several formations the pilots had rehearsed furiously for the past few days.

"Here we are," said Buck. "Prepare to fire." The formation turned, flying parallel to the station, the two tandem vessels in the middle targeting Hauberk's shields. "Commence firing."

The two ships sent pulsing laser charges into Hauberk's shields in a trajectory to the rear of their flight path. It was well they did, for the lasers hit the shields with a splatter of broken energy before the shields swallowed them. "Strike five," said Buck, and the two ships moved to the outside of the formation. Two ships on the sides of the wedge dropped down to the tandem spot, and the previous vessels took their places on the outside.

"On target, Rebel One," said Wright. "Damage report, zero."

"Let's hit her again," said Buck, and the flight turned and began a second run.

○ ○ ○ ○ ○

"Sir! We're being fired upon!"

"What?" The incredulity in Seaforian's voice was not feigned. "Firing on Hauberk?"

"Yes, sir." Hauptman's round face was aghast. "According to visuals, they've started a second run, and they've got good ships, too."

"Good ships?" Seaforian's voice was hard with sudden interest. "What kind of good ships?"

"Some small fighter I've never seen before. They're fast, immune to radar, and their lasers are draining pockets in the shield—nothing we can't handle, but that kind of firepower isn't usual in a fighter."

Seaforian glared at Hauptman. The man quailed before his look, even though there was considerable distance and a computer linkage between control and Seaforian's quarters. "Let's see them," said Seaforian. "On the big screen. Then I want you to get computer readings on them."

The sight of Buck's flight strafing Hauberk's shields met Seaforian's eyes as Hauptman replied, "I have already done that, sir. The ships do not match any of our vessels. They seem to be RAM design."

Seaforian narrowed his eyes as he watched the ships descend on his territory like birds of prey. He knew what they were, and the knowledge made his Martian blood simmer. Before him flew Warhead's experimental design, the ships destined for his own fighter wing and now turned against him by thieves. He was not worried about their ability to damage the station—nothing could do that—but the affront to his pride was unbearable. "Hauptman, scramble the wing. I want it launched in one minute. Call the four patrol ships in, once the wing launches, and refuel them. I want those ships blasted out of space. Run a communications channel to me. I want contact with the wing."

"Yes, sir!" Hauptman reached to the top of his control panel and pulled a lever unused in the station's history, except for drills. As the lever locked down, the lights went red, and the battle station's klaxon blared through the corridors.

RAM pilots hit the hallway running, some not entirely dressed. They burst into the docking area and stumbled over flight technicians trying to clear cable away from the ships. The last line was barely retracted when the launch lock rumbled and began to open. A RAM pilot fired his engines, and the rumble made the dock vibrate. One by one his comrades followed suit. A spurt of their thrusters lifted the ships from the deck, and the vibration ceased.

"Let's go!" said the flight leader, and the wing began the speed launch it had practiced so often. This time it was for real.

○ ○ ○ ○ ○

Buck finished his second run at Hauberk's shields as Washington and his flight careened around the station. The two groups joined and became a wedge, with Buck at its apex. "How'd it go, Eagle Leader?" asked Buck.

"Unconfirmed. Target contacted, no opposition."

"Did you see any signs of activity?"

"Affirmative, Rebel One." Washington chuckled. "Two RAM fighters flipped their wings at us, but they were inside the shields and couldn't fire without damaging their own protection." Washington hesitated. "My scanners show bandits, one o'clock low."

"I see them, Eagle Leader. They're still inside the shields. Let's shake 'em up!"

Buck sent his ship down, the wedge close on his tail, and made a run at the fighters. They were massed inside the shields, three blood-red lines. Their cylindrical shapes reminded Buck of bullets, and the old-fashioned pistol strapped to his thigh was suddenly heavy. With its shields fully operational, Hauberk could not use its artillery, nor could its fighters make contact. Buck sent a blast from his lasers into the shields in front of the RAM ships. His wing followed suit, but as the last ship fired, away, something happened.

"Eagle Leader, this is Eagle Ten. My lasers just punched through. I say again, my lasers just punched through."

"Hear that, Rebel One?" asked Washington, and his voice was light.

"We've got 'em!" called Buck. "Strike six!"

The wedge formation split again, half of the ships following Buck and half following Washington. "Here they come!" said Washington as the RAM fighters shot toward them.

The station had opened a window, dropping the shields long enough for the ships to get through. Rickenbacker's shot had given NEO enough warning to meet the fighters head-on, instead of starting the conflict with RAM on its tail.

Buck touched the channel controls on his communications system, opening up another line. "Come and get us!" he said.

"With pleasure." The voice at the other end of the link belonged to Hauberk flight leader Briggs, a man who had spent most of his career on milk runs like Hauberk, and who welcomed some real action. He responded quickly—too quickly—to Buck's challenge. The first line of RAM fighters ran straight at Buck's wedge, intending to overfly and strafe it.

Buck saw them coming and yelled, "Dive! Rear shields on full."

The NEO ships hit thrusters and went straight down. The ships' sterns made considerably smaller targets, but a gyro shell would still find them. As the RAM fighters came on, their lasers flashing, Buck realized their commander was overconfident.

"You must be NEO," said Briggs. "The first thing you do is turn tail."

"We're NEO, all right," said Buck as the lasers drove into the shields. They were absorbed, but he knew the shields were draining. "Eagles One and Two," he said, "on my order, go to strike three—now!"

Two of the NEO ships powered straight down, then swung back up in a tight arc. Two of the RAM ships started to follow them.

"No!" said Briggs. "They're trying to break us up."

"You've got it," said Wright—Eagle One—as he sent his lasers into the shields of the nearest RAM ship. The pulse was concentrated, a full-strength dose of the Krait's guns.

"I'm burning!" cried the pilot. "Get him off!"

Buck smiled. He now had confirmation Hauberk's fighters had inferior shielding.

"Hold on, Thirty-one," said Briggs. "Forty-three, hit him."

A RAM fighter pulled out of formation and headed for Wright, who still was pounding away at Thirty-one's shields. Earhart—Eagle Two—dove on the second RAM fighter, sending her lasers directly into his forward viewport. The ship's shields absorbed the energy, but not without damage.

"I'm blind!" said the pilot as the white light seared the shields over his vision.

"Pull up!" ordered Briggs, sending his pilot directly into Earhart's path.

She evaded his drive, then turned as three of the RAM fighters targeted her. Her shields felt the impact of their lasers as she pulled away. Wright still had his guns trained on the RAM fighter, but he was under heavy attack from the rest of the wing.

"My wing, strike three—now!" said Buck, and his flight split and arced back to help their companions. The fight now was one-on-one, RAM's lines broken into fragmented units. Buck hoped this would put the odds on NEO's side, for its pilots were used to working alone. Initiative was their biggest asset, while RAM's superbly trained wing knew only blind obedience to a higher source.

○ ○ ○ ○ ○

Seaforian watched the battle from the comfort of his quarters. He knew Hauberk's fighters were outdated compared to the experimental craft they were facing, but he banked on superior training and strategy to end the conflict quickly. It was clear that his hopes were not to be.

He reached a lean hand over to his terminal keyboard and activated the communications link Hauptman had patched into his quarters. "Briggs!" he said.

Briggs nearly jumped out of his craft at the sound of Seaforian's voice, but he managed to reply as he shot under one of the NEO ships. "Yes, sir."

"I want those ships. I don't care what it takes. Either destroy or capture them. All of them."

"I copy, sir," Briggs answered as a NEO ship sent a laser charge into his rear shields. He answered with a cloud of chaff, and the next shot fragmented.

"It might interest you to know," said Seaforian, "the ships you are facing were intended for your use. They were stolen by these upstarts. Are you going to let NEO rabble best you with your own weapons?"

"I hadn't planned on it, sir," answered Briggs as he evaded Earhart's strafing run. "But I'm running out of defenses. Those things are hot."

"I don't want to hear excuses," said Seaforian. "I want results. Get them!"

"Good luck!" said Buck, diving on Briggs and interrupting the conversation.

"Who was that?" asked Seaforian sharply.

"NEO commander," replied Briggs through clenched teeth.

"Upstart!" said Seaforian.

"You bet," responded Buck.

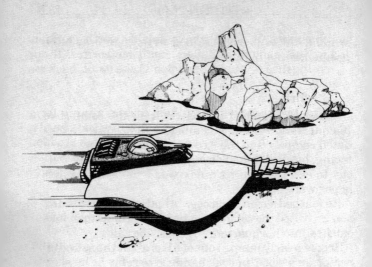

Chapter 23

"Eagles Eight and Nine, break off ... now!"
Wilma Deering's voice crackled over the communications link, sending Yaeger and
Nungesser on a scorching run past Earth's outer
atmosphere. The probabilities of detection were
good, but it no longer mattered. She and the remaining three pilots would be in and out before anything
but a freak shot could catch them. Besides, the Krait
was a faster ship than anything RAM had, with the
possible exception of private pleasure craft.

She watched the two ships disappear over the hori-
zon, headed for their target. Her own was coming up
over her port bow. "Close up, Eagle Seven," she told
her wingman, Bishop. "We make contact in point
three."

"I see it, Rebel Two," responded Bishop, pushing
his ship closer to hers.

"I'll hit it with the forward lasers. According to the

schematics, it doesn't have shields worth mentioning, just enough to deflect small meteorites. If our intelligence is wrong, and I don't take it out, back me up."

"Affirmative, Colonel."

The two ships adjusted their course, aiming for a pinpoint of white light. It was a satellite the size of a beach ball. Its silver metallic surface was studded with antennae, like a dandelion gone to seed. Wilma activated her forward lasers, targeting the sphere. The computer locked on to its coordinates as Bishop's voice echoed in her ear.

"Bandits, Colonel, twelve o'clock low."

Wilma kept her eyes on the targeting computer, waiting for it to tell her she was within range of the satellite. "Hang on, Bishop," she said. "I've almost got it."

The ships below were a flight of three Terrine dragonflies. They couldn't take the altitude Wilma and Bishop were maintaining, but their gyro launchers were not daunted by distance.

"They're targeting us, Rebel Two. The only thing they've got that can reach us is a gyro shell."

Wilma was within strike range. She punched the lasers, and the deadly pulses of energy shot toward the satellite. For a moment she thought the shields were going to hold, but as Wilma pulled up, the satellite exploded.

"Gyro shells on target, Colonel." Bishop's voice penetrated her elation.

"Let's outrun them, Eagle Seven."

"Can we?"

"No time like the present to find out," she replied as a shell programmed for her ship closed on its tail. "Let's see what the little lady will do." She rammed the throttle home, and the Krait shot forward like a startled thoroughbred.

Bishop followed, sticking to his position at Wilma's

side. The gyro shells also altered their course, their mini-targeting computers nosing out the two fleeing fighters.

"Chaff launched," said Bishop.

A cloud of golden dust bloomed in their wake. The gyro shells flew straight into it. One shell lurched, then fell away, but its sibling continued on.

"One's still with us," said Bishop.

"Let's see which of us it's after," said Wilma. She sent her ship away from Bishop, one eye on her scanners. The gyro shell plugged forward, doggedly pursuing her wingman. "It seems to like you, Bishop."

"I'd just as soon it didn't follow me home."

"I copy," replied Wilma.

She fell in behind the shell, sighted it through the computer, and fired. The shell exploded harmlessly, and she heard Bishop let his breath out. "Take it easy," she said. "It never would have caught us."

"I'm not so sure. Besides, that was only a Terrine shell. A fighter's gyros are something else again."

"Granted," said Wilma. She checked her timer. "We've got forty minutes to rendezvous."

"ETA for Eagles Eight and Nine?"

"Approximately fifteen minutes. We'll make the intersection point for them in twelve minutes."

"By the way, Colonel, . . . thanks."

"My pleasure, Bishop."

o o o o o

"Supervisor Hauptman!"

Technician Croncane's panic erupted in his voice. Hauptman made his own tone flat to pull the man back on track. "Yes, Croncane?"

"We have lost Orb One!"

"Get it back," replied Hauptman calmly.

"Sir, you don't understand. I've tried. It's not responding."

Hauptman left his station and hunched over Croncane's bank of viewers. Three of them were black. "What happened?"

"It just died. One moment I had the usual visuals from the other side of Earth, then there was nothing."

"Run a clear tape through. It may be we've built up some transmission residue that's killing the channel."

Croncane sent the command through his keyboard, but the three screens remained blank. Hauptman stared at the offending squares of black, trying to think of a reason for the interrupted picture. As he watched, three more screens died.

"That's Orb Two! Sir, this is exactly what happened before!"

Hauptman shoved Croncane out of his seat and ran quick fingers over the monitor keyboard. The dark screens glared back at him. He coded in auxiliary power, but there was no change. Finally he sat back. "There's only one conclusion I can draw," he said slowly.

"Yes, sir?"

"We've lost them."

"Sir?"

"Get me Seaforian." Hauptman did not want to talk to the station director. Somehow it was easier if he did not set up the link himself.

"Well, Hauptman? I hope this is important," said Seaforian shortly.

Hauptman could hear the sounds of battle coming through over Seaforian's patched-in communications link. "I'm afraid it is, sir."

"Well?"

"Sir, I have to report we've lost the satellites."

"The what?"

"Orbs One and Two. The satellites. The ones that cover the other side of the planet."

"Switch to back-ups."

"Sir, there are none."

"No back-ups? That's ridiculous," said Seaforian.

"Yes, sir, but that's the way it is. We've never had trouble before—not in five centuries."

"You are absolutely sure this isn't a malfunction?"

"No. It could be, but given the fact both satellites are gone, I think it's unlikely."

"Hauptman, I want you to find some way to get coverage of the far side of the planet. I don't care how. Do it."

"Yes, Director." Hauptman could think of no possible way to carry out his superior's orders, but he was not about to say so. Seaforian returned to monitoring the battle outside Hauberk's shields, and Hauptman ended the communication.

○ ○ ○ ○ ○

"Here they come, Rebel Two."

Two Krait fighters swooped around the derelict bulk of an abandoned commercial space dock, cutting their engines as they caught sight of Wilma and Bishop. They used their forward docking thrusters to brake, drifting up on their companions' position with pinpoint accuracy.

"This is Eagle Eight," drawled Wilma's communications link.

"I copy, Captain. Give me a report," she said.

"We found our target, contacted and destroyed it, then came on in," he said.

"Any problems?"

"We had a little discussion with a RAM freighter, but he didn't like our arguments."

"Let's hope we're giving Rebel One the time he needs. We have twenty-five minutes, gentlemen. I suggest we use them. Course two point eight-three."

"That should put us on the mark," said Bishop.

"That," said Wilma, "is where we want to be."

o o o o o

Huer was busy. He was running a literal round-house of information. He had open lines to all of NEO's fighters, plus a monitor on Hauberk's incoming and outgoing transmissions, shielded and unshielded. It was his job to anticipate the unexpected and warn it off. Or, failing that, to warn the individual who was threatened. He had a special channel to Buck, and was able to throw visuals on the lower half of his face screen, so Buck could monitor them as he flew.

Huer was keyed up, handling the myriad fragments of information at record speed. What energy he wasn't devoting to those duties he channeled to cracking Hauberk's various codes. It was painstaking work, but at the moment, there was nothing else he could do. The knowledge was frustrating, but he kept at his task.

o o o o o

Romanov curled into a corner of NEO's computer system, nursing its poison. Masterlink's searcher program had not yet penetrated beyond the outskirts of NEO's computer network. It admitted the complexity of the traps and blocks the NEO security program constructed to deter invasion. They were beyond the attacks of RAM's virus hunters, and they were changed with diligent frequency. Nothing in the NEO system was static, and that made it a nightmare to crack. Romanov did not try.

Instead, it hid like an adder under a rock, waiting for its prey to stumble by. It searched for references to Buck Rogers or the program Huer.dos. Romanov could smell Rogers's electronic scent through Huer, but Huer was unpredictable. He surfaced at odd times and in odd places. Romanov noted them, trying to determine a pattern in the wayward ramblings. Occasionally it moved, slithering after a momentary appearance or reference, its electronic senses flickering.

With a searcher's patience it waited. In due time, it caught the flutter of movement as Huer processed the NEO attack on Hauberk. The trail was scattered by the NEO computer's wealth of safety locks, but Romanov began to move, slowly feeling its way toward the fragments of activity. It followed more than one false trail, went down more than one electronic dead end, then patiently retraced its pathway until it encountered yet another reference. As Huer worked, Romanov worked. It discarded unproductive data.

Periodically, Romanov sent cryptic reports to Masterlink, advising its parent of the progress it was making. Masterlink filed the reports away, coding them under priority one, for Romanov was on a warm trail.

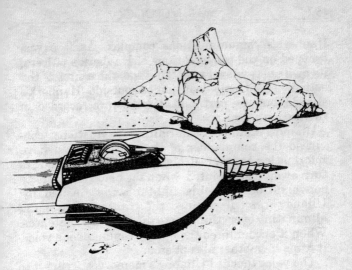

Chapter 24

Hauberk buzzed with activity. Underneath the veneer of metal and plastic, fiery currents blazed. Its electronic heart pulsed, its accelerated activity verging on overload. It faced opposition.

Ulianov, wandering within Hauberk's orderly mind, saw it all. The child of Masterlink viewed the organized chaos with awe, for it was unused to unbroken logic, and with even greater scorn, for Hauberk generated great activity and accomplished nothing. Its circuits ran around themselves, checking and rechecking systems not yet activated. Ulianov began to wonder if the attack it was registering real or feigned.

Sorting through the data that whizzed by, Ulianov discovered the assault on Hauberk was centered around its fighter escort. It determined to monitor the action. By careful degrees it worked its way to

Hauberk's communications complex. As it eavesdropped on the conversations of Hauberk's officers, its own energy level rose. This was the center of the action! The battle was joined outside Hauberk's shields, but the pertinent details were recorded in the station's log.

Ulianov scanned Seaforian's conversations, convinced the commander of the station would have information to interest Masterlink. It was about to turn away, disappointed, when the end of Seaforian's conversation with his fighter wing flashed by. Ulianov froze. It scanned the transmission again, eliminating everything up to the final few sentences. When it encountered the enemy commander's voice, it came to another abrupt stop.

The voice touched Ulianov's memory, stirring it to life. It ran through Buck Rogers's vital statistics until it came upon his voiceprint. It called up the print and ran a match against the enemy commander's voice. The voiceprint of the enemy commander matched the ancient data Masterlink had compiled on Buck Rogers to the last nuance.

Ulianov's energy level rose another notch. It had found the nemesis who jeopardized its creator's existence! Part of its programming was now fulfilled. Its program jumped to the second phase of its main directive: destruction of the threat to Masterlink.

o o o o o

Anton Hauptman stared at his central viewscreen. The sounds of battle raged in his ears, and he dealt with it according to his training, patching communication lines by instinct. His efficiency was not impaired by what he saw, but he was transfixed by the two flights of spacecraft in pitched battle.

It was not a sight he had grown to expect in his tour of duty on Hauberk. The station's reputation was so awesome not even pirates ventured near its sphere of influence. But before him raged battle, real warfare, not games designed to test Hauberk's efficiency in hypothetical conflicts. The ships fought beyond Hauberk's shields. The station's invulnerability was unchallenged, but Hauptman was nervous.

Despite knowledge to the contrary, he felt his stomach turn at the prospect of danger. As communications supervisor, he was part of Seaforian's advisory council. His instincts told him it was time for advice.

"Sir! What are you doing?" asked one of Hauptman's technicians.

"Making some recommendations," replied Hauptman to his assistant. "Mind your station."

Croncane subsided, but regarded his supervisor warily. Hauptman was risking his position, and he had no wish to share his supervisor's gamble, so he moved discreetly out of sensor range.

"Yes?" Seaforian's voice was annoyed.

"This is Hauptman, sir. Communications."

"Yes, Hauptman. What is it?"

"I believe Hauberk is in danger."

"From that gaggle of rabble? You must be joking."

"No, sir."

"Our shields can withstand their weapons indefinitely. They can do no more than punch momentary holes in it," Seaforian said royally.

"I am aware of that, sir. Still, I recommend security measures."

Seaforian's eyes narrowed on the screen. "Do I detect a quaver in your voice, Hauptman?"

"Perhaps, sir. I am not a brave man. Request permission to activate retreat procedures."

"I can see no circumstance in which I would retreat, Hauptman."

"I submit, sir, if, by chance, the shields should be penetrated, we may be in trouble."

"And I repeat, Hauptman, that cannot happen.

Surely your computer read-outs tell you that."

Hauptman was silent for a moment. "I wish to state for the record that I suggested security measures."

Seaforian barely concealed his sneer. "So noted," he said.

"I also request permission to inform RAM Central of our present situation."

"Have you any idea of the effect such information would have on the market? Hauberk's stock would drop like a stone. If I believed the station were in danger, I would be the first to contact the company."

"Yes, sir." Seaforian's words did not inspire Hauptman. He was convinced that Seaforian did not see the situation for what it was.

Hauptman winced as he signed off, knowing he had tarnished any pending evaluations, and the chances of promotion were halved. His ambition was daunted, but his instincts nursed a righteous indignation.

O O O O O

Seaforian allowed the sneer he had suppressed to spread across his thin lips. He had no use for cowardice, and he did not doubt Hauptman's cowardice. The man might never have been in battle for all the steadiness he showed. Seaforian had concluded his own tours of duty in the outer reaches of the company's shipping lanes without incident. He turned his attention to the battle.

He was enjoying it. Safe in the seclusion of his armored office, he watched men try to kill each other, with the detached analytical attention of a man watching a chess match. He saw shot after shot strike both sides, but he had no conception of the shock of the blasts hitting a fighter's shields, or the cold sweat that trickled between a pilot's shoulder blades as he narrowly missed collision.

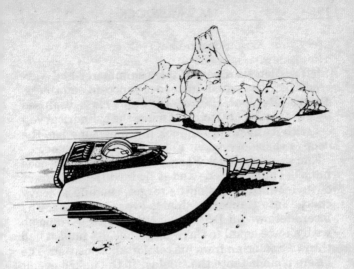

Chapter 25

A jolt like the impact of a meteorite rocked the station. Seaforian was catapulted from his chair into the opposite wall, the elegance of his long frame reduced to a ludicrous tangle of arms and legs. Hauberk swayed in its orbit.

Seaforian pulled himself to his feet and, clutching any stable projection he could find, made his way to his computer terminal. "Hauptman! Report!" he barked into it.

Hauptman was clinging to his console. "We're under attack, sir! Quadrant thirty-four, section six!"

"Of course we're under attack, you idiot! Get me details!"

"Yes, sir. At once, sir." Hauptman's words were a formality to the interference of a superior. Now that his instincts had borne fruit, his nervousness was gone. He was much too intent on his job to bother with Seaforian's feelings.

○ ○ ○ ○ ○

Off section six a field of stars shimmered and wavered, then dissipated. Instead of innocent emptiness, a third-rater materialized, the ship's class disguised by a dramatic paint job that made the cylindrical vessel with its upswept tail look like a behemoth of the deep, a shark of ancient Earth, or a killer whale.

The ship was Black Barney's *Free Enterprise*—code named Thunderhead—and it trained the full power of its forward lasers on its target, sending a heavy charge into Hauberk's shields over section six. The lasers followed a DAN shell, literally a gyro bomb with a force equal to three megatons. Its impact had thrown Seaforian from his comfortable position. The lasers pounded into the shields. To the naked eye, it looked as if they were sinking into oblivion.

Baring-Gould, Barney's first mate, studied the weapons sensors.

"Power levels?" asked Barney, his heavy black brows knitted.

"Fluctuating slightly, sir, but still holding firm."

"Send in another shell."

"Aye, sir. Konii."

Arak Konii, his saturnine face clearly pleased with his occupation, pressed a button on the weapons console. "Number two away," he said.

"Cut lasers," ordered Baring-Gould. The shell shot forward into space, missing the last of the laser pulses by seconds. "On target," said Baring-Gould as the shell crashed into Hauberk's shields and detonated, exploding in a sparkling puff of pink.

"Levels now?" said Barney.

Baring-Gould smiled. "Down by ten percent."

"Deploy lasers." Barney watched as the lasers once again drilled into the shields, and chuckled, the sound an awesome rumble like distant thunder. "With her shields up, Hauberk can't use that artillery she's got scattered all over the surface," he said. "She's just got to sit here and take it."

Baring-Gould watched the indicators before him dip and lift as Hauberk poured more power into shield number six. "I've got fluctuation. Sir, power levels over shield six are dropping. We're going to get through!"

"Watch close. All we've got the power to do is punch a hole. If the plans are right, that's all we'll need. Lasers?"

"Holding," replied Konii. "We've got about eighty-five percent left, but I estimate by the time we get through, that will have dropped to half. We're not going to have much for a scramble."

"The star field?"

"We have power for that."

Hazen Strange, hovering over the main sensors, suddenly froze. "Bandits!" he exclaimed. "Off the port stern!"

Barney muttered an unintelligible oath and went to the sensor bank to see for himself. Rounding Hauberk, probably in response to a plea for assistance, were two RAM fighters. How they had broken away from the engagement on the other side of the station was a mystery, but they had. They closed on the *Free Enterprise* like carrion crows.

"Range, point three," said Konii, targeting the ships.

"Keep the power on full to forward lasers!" Barney's command stopped Konii as he reached to open up the stern guns.

"I just hope," commented Konii acidly, "that by the time we've accomplished our mission, we're still alive."

Barney growled.

"Here they come!" said Konii, and the two fighters charged on the third-rater, firing as they came.

The laser blasts from the RAM ships bounced

harmlessly off the *Free Enterprise*'s shields, but they pulled precious power.

"I've got to give those shields some support," said Konii.

"Quarter power," said Barney through clenched teeth. "How close are we?"

"I'm getting dramatic fluctuation now, sir. If we can hold on a few more minutes . . ."

"Here they come again," remarked Konii. "It's a shame Captain Rogers can't keep a bargain," he said wickedly.

"Maybe," muttered Barney. The same thought had occurred to him, but he wasn't about to admit it to his oily second mate.

As the RAM fighters began their run, two NEO ships rounded Hauberk's uneven bulk.

"Here comes the cavalry!" Buck sang into the communications system. He charged the RAM craft, a deadly beam of energy spitting from his ship's forward guns.

The RAM ships broke off their strafing run and tried to turn, but Buck and his wingman were on them. They followed the RAM ships like shadows, never ceasing their fire. The flight space on this side of the station was open, and they chased the RAM ships back and forth in a tacking zigzag that made Strange, monitoring their movements, dizzy.

"Now we can tend to business," said Barney, his voice fat with the satisfaction of righteousness. His confidence in Buck was reinforced, and he sneaked a sly glance in Konii's direction. The second mate's mouth was pursed in annoyance.

"Run like sheep," muttered Buck, from his position behind the RAM ships.

"They're sure all over the place," said Doolittle—Eagle Three—off Buck's left wing.

Buck rammed his stick to the right as the RAM fighters changed course again, all the while letting his lasers slam into their tails. "How long does it take to burn one of these things, Eagle Three?" he asked. "The briefing you all gave me said one minute of steady fire."

"Sometimes, Captain," replied Doolittle grimly. "This is Hauberk. Those fighters may not be what we're flying, but they're RAM's best up till now. Probably have reinforced shields."

As Doolittle spoke, his lasers seared through the shields on one of the fighters and hit the enemy's rear burners. The ship went up like a skyrocket. Seconds later, Buck scored a direct hit on the other ship's fuel chamber. It exploded in an even more dramatic display.

"Thunderhead, this is Rebel One. We got 'em."

Barney heard Buck's voice crackle over the communications link, and answered. "Obliged," he managed.

"Operation Jericho?" Buck asked.

"On target," replied Barney. The military formality of Buck's communications always unsettled him so that he replied in monosyllables.

"How much longer, Thunderhead?"

Barney looked at Baring-Gould, and his first mate replied into the communications link, "I estimate about two minutes."

"We'll hold them off," said Buck. Barney could almost hear Buck's grin. "We've cut the odds down. They're almost even, but everything depends on your getting through."

"Just hope," murmured Doolittle, "we get what we paid for."

o o o o o

Inside Hauberk, Seaforian clung to his terminal. As he listened to the damage reports flooding Hauptman's communications station, he began to doubt the truth of the publicity RAM had spread concerning Hauberk.

Seaforian cut in to Hauptman's transmission. "Report!" he barked.

Hauptman, frustration adding to the tension on his face, replied shortly. "Section six still under attack. We are losing power."

"I want another flight sent to knock out that third-rater."

Hauptman shook his head. "I'll order it, sir, but I don't think they can break off." Hauptman's response did not make any pretenses of respect. "B Flight," he said into his link, "break off and engage the enemy over section six."

"Negative," replied the commander of B Flight. "I can't get away!"

"Break off!" commanded Hauptman. "On Seaforian's orders."

"Tell the string bean to do it himself!" replied the commander in a totally uncharacteristic challenge to the director's authority. "I'm surrounded! I—"

The transmission broke, and Hauptman turned his attention back to Seaforian. "I am sorry, sir," he replied, "but B Flight has been destroyed. It was the last full flight out there."

Horror began to dawn in Seaforian's eyes. It had its roots in the knowledge that he had believed a lie. Hauberk was not invulnerable. Its wing of fighter aces were falling before a relic from the past. Seaforian sank into the nearest chair, trying to assimilate the situation.

Hauptman cut into his reverie. "The shields over section six are buckling. Just a two-meter hole, but enough to do considerable damage when those lasers hit. Read-out on section six indicates the program for the station's shields occupies its own autonomous computer there."

"You mean," said Seaforian, "if that particular

computer is destroyed, Hauberk will lose all shields?"

"Affirmative, sir."

"No matter if we have power?"

"Yes, sir."

"Supervisor, the lasers have gone through!" cried another technician. "They've scored a direct hit!"

Hauptman looked across the control center at Jacobson. "Shields?"

Jacobson watched a red power indicator drop like a stone. "Gone, sir."

Seaforian slumped in his chair, unbelieving.

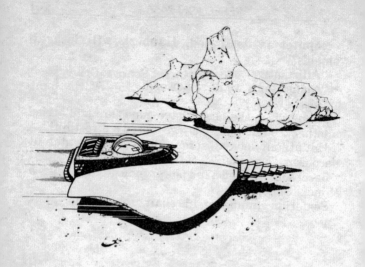

Chapter 26

Hauptman viewed Seaforian's dejected figure with disgust. Hauberk was no longer invulnerable, but the station was not defenseless. The surface was dotted with artillery of various shapes and sizes, all of it capable of inflicting unspeakable damage. Most of the weapons were controlled by computer. With the destruction of the station's shields, the computer automatically activated the artillery program. Each weapon's placement had its own sensor eye, which scanned its sector for enemies. The sensors distinguished between friend and foe by means of a beeper installed in all RAM ships. Its particular frequency was changed on a computer-designed schedule that rotated at irregular intervals. Hauberk was still a formidable weapon.

"Orders, sir?" asked Hauptman.

Seaforian raised his leonine head. "Get me an open channel to RAM Central."

"At once, sir." Hauptman tried to keep the satisfaction from his voice.

"This is RAM Central, Martin Drang." Drang's solemn face appeared on Seaforian's viewer. His light blue eyes were bored.

"This is Seaforian, director of Hauberk station." Seaforian took a deep breath. The next words were not easy for him. "I wish to request assistance."

"Assistance?" Drang's bored expression vanished.

Seaforian continued doggedly. "We are under attack by NEO. We have lost our shields."

"What? Specify the assault force." Drang's manner became clipped, professional.

"We are under immediate attack by fourteen fighters and one reconditioned third-rater. However, the station's auxiliary satellites have ceased to function, and it is therefore entirely possible more ships are involved."

"You will receive immediate assistance, Director. Warhead has tripled our original order for Hauberk, and we found eighteen pilots for the ships. They left some time ago. I will contact them immediately and tell them to prepare for an engagement."

Seaforian relaxed a trifle. "That is good news. However, I also request support from the larger class vessels."

"You shall have it. There are three third-raters off Mars. I will authorize their immediate departure, but they will be some time behind the fighters. In the meantime, I will put together a second strike force to reinforce our counterattack."

"Thank you, Director Drang. Who commands the fighter wing? I shall want to contact him once he is within range."

"You are in luck, Seaforian. It's Kane." Drang watched Seaforian's expression change with some internal amusement. Seaforian was particularly annoyed by Kane's brash manner, and his first reaction showed his irritation. Hard on its heels followed a relief so comical that Drang had to struggle not to smile. Kane was the best, and, in spite of his animosity, Seaforian knew it.

Drang poked at the keyboard in front of him, cutting the link with Hauberk and opening one within RAM Central. "Central Communications, this is Drang. I want a closed channel to the commander of the last flight to leave Phobos. Make sure—entirely sure—the transmission is reversed and scrambled. This is top-security."

"At once, Director," replied the disembodied voice of a comlink operator.

Drang waited, knowing it would take a minimum of sixty seconds to establish communications.

"Your transmission is clear, sir," came the voice.

"Kane, this is Martin Drang, RAM Central. I have heard you enjoy combat. You may prepare for some."

"Oh?" Kane's tone came mockingly over the channel before a picture appeared.

"There seems to be an altercation developing at your destination."

"Oh?"

Kane's comment was beginning to irritate Drang. "You do not have much time to prepare. I suggest you do not waste it with banter."

"Then I suggest you do not beat around the proverbial bush. What are you talking about?" Kane asked.

"Hauberk station is under attack."

"Oh!" This time the laughter had gone out of Kane's voice. "And you want me to lend a supporting arm, or wing?"

Drang recognized the phrasing immediately. He had dealt with Kane, or his type, before. "How much?" he asked dryly.

"How much is it worth to you?" Kane countered. "Remember, I'm not the only one to get a fee out of this. Every man in the wing is working for pay. You can't expect them to ask the same for combat as for a job ferrying some cargo."

Drang's lips compressed. He was going to have to pay through the nose. He knew it, but he did not have to like it. "Twenty percent increase," he said.

Kane considered the offer, mulled it over, and had to admit it was fair. He might have pushed the percentage if he were an altruistic man, but he was not. "And for me?"

"The same."

Kane shook his head in his newly acquired Krait's cockpit. "I think not."

"I could always turn command over to another pilot."

"You might try. However, I do not think, when they discover we are now going into a combat situation, you will have any takers. I am the best," said Kane immodestly, "and they know it."

"Thirty percent."

"That's more like it, but still not enough for risking my hide and coming up with a game plan. Thirty-five."

Drang ground his teeth, but gave in. "Done," he said.

"What are we up against?" asked Kane, with genuine interest.

"NEO. Hauberk has lost her shields. She still has the station-based artillery. Her fighters are engaged. NEO has fourteen fighters, apparently those originally destined for Hauberk, so you will have no advantage over them technically. They also are supported by a third-rater."

"You expect me to go up against a third-rater alone?"

"No. I've sent three of ours out after you, but you'll have to hold the station until they arrive."

"Wonderful. I should have held out for forty, considering the odds and my special knowledge of the NEO mindset."

"Quit bellyaching!" snapped Drang. "You made a bargain."

"I did indeed. And I will keep it. It's worth the cut just for the pleasure of wiping up space with NEO."

"I don't think I have to tell you of the security surrounding this action."

Kane smiled, and Drang wanted to hit him. "Not very good public relations for the company, is it? Its supersatellite disarmed and all."

"This is top-secret, Kane. Even your pilots can't know the full extent of the situation. "If a word of this escapes, you all will be docked twenty percent. Keep that in mind."

Some of the laughter in Kane's eyes sparked. "Oh, I will."

Drang regarded that dangerous glint silently. He had made an enemy, perhaps not a wise one. Still, the odds were, despite his expertise, that Kane would die in the fight for Hauberk. In that case, Drang would have nothing to worry about. If Kane survived, he would deal with his animosity later.

○ ○ ○ ○ ○

Deep within the bowels of Hauberk's computer system lurked a roiling knot of static. Ulianov was in a panic. It had two main directives: preserve its own existence and find Buck Rogers. It had identified Rogers's voiceprint from a recorded transmission between the twentieth century pilot and Seaforian. That knowledge elated Ulianov, boosting its energy output in sheer excitement, but Hauberk itself was under attack. With the destruction of the shields, the station's computers had flipped into overdrive, activating systems usually dormant. Ulianov viewed the activity with alarm, realizing the programs it detected were listed under the heading "EMERGENCY DEFENSE."

If Hauberk's computer felt its survival was in danger, then Ulianov, entirely dependent upon its host, was in equal danger. It vacillated wildly between absolute success and absolute failure, and the two extremes were causing electronic chaos. In any other situation, the chaos would have meant detection, but with the station under attack, Hauberk had more to worry about than a viral infection.

Ulianov considered the possibilities. It could stay where it was, holding position in the hopes Hauberk would repel the attack and they both would survive. Ulianov did not have complete faith in its host. Hauberk was reacting efficiently to the attack, but there was confusion in its programming. Ulianov could retreat to Masterlink, its job half complete. This alternative Ulianov found entirely distasteful. At the forefront of its consciousness was the knowledge Masterlink was responsible for its existence. It might as easily be responsible for its destruction, and Ulianov wished to survive. Finally, it could search for another host, a safer one, preferably one that would take it closer to its quarry.

This solution appealed to Ulianov. It assured continued existence and carried out its mission in one swoop. It knew Buck Rogers was close, closer than it had been to Masterlink since he tried to blast Ulianov's creator out of existence. A pulse of hatred pumped through Ulianov at the thought. Rogers was a threat to it as well. He had to be. If he once tried to destroy Ulianov's creator, then it followed that he would wish to destroy Ulianov.

Ulianov's purpose firmed. It would survive to seek out and destroy Capt. Buck Rogers. No obstacle would stand in its way. Ulianov puffed up with virtue until it recalled that if it could not find security, its proximity to Rogers was meaningless.

Once it decided on a course of action, its chaotic power fluctuations ceased. Ulianov was reduced to an insignificant disturbance in Hauberk's innards, one the station did not at present have time to deal with. Ulianov altered its position, carefully cutting in to the station's schematic library. One by one it thumbed through the entries, searching for a safe hiding place.

Hauberk took no notice of the intruder. It had other things to worry about. The loss of its shields was as unthinkable to the station's computers as it had been to Seaforian. It was reacting with a frantic activation of every weapons system at its disposal. The automated artillery it commanded immediately, but the station also was equipped with six manual weapons, installed at the beginning of its armament and never altered or replaced. Hauberk frantically searched the personnel rosters for individuals authorized to handle those weapons. The search seemed fruitless, for the manual laser cannons were so outmoded they no longer appeared on the station's armament check list. It scanned two hundred personnel files before it found one man qualified to fire the cannons.

It searched on, every circuit bent on protecting itself through the most remote means.

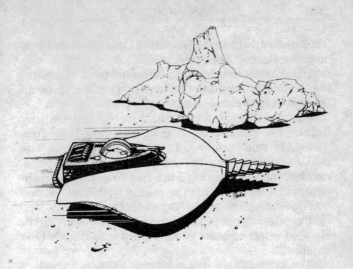

Chapter 27

Master Pirate Black Barney swung the *Free Enterprise*'s nose away from Hauberk's naked bulk.

"Course?" asked Baring-Gould.

"Point two-six. Get me the captain."

"Hi there, Thunderhead. All secure?" Buck Rogers's voice was loud in the confined space of the third-rater's bridge.

"Mission accomplished," replied Barney.

"Let's clean up the mess on this side of the station," Buck said.

"Acknowledged," replied Barney.

"Bring Thunderhead around the station at point five-three. We'll try to herd the stragglers into your arms."

"How many?" Barney asked.

"Thirteen left. An unlucky number."

"We'll cut that down," Barney growled.

"Sounds good to me. Estimated time of arrival will be two minutes. Rebel One out."

Buck Rogers sent his ship outbound from Hauberk, two enemy craft glued to his tail. "Got 'em lined up for you, Eagle Three. Anytime!"

Doolittle, Buck's wingman, dove on the trailing fighter, his guns spitting short bursts of laser fire. The RAM ship turned on Doolittle immediately. The two rocked across the broad reaches of space, exchanging fire, leaving Buck free to engage the other ship. He dove, taking the enemy with him. "Come on, Watchdog," he said. "Try to catch me."

"I've already done that," replied the enemy pilot. He sent another blast of his lasers into Buck's rear shields.

"Try again," said Buck, hitting his port thrusters and sending his ship off at a dramatic angle.

The enemy pilot was not prepared for such a sharp move, and he overflew Buck's turn by twenty kilometers. It wasn't much, but it was enough to shake him off Buck's tail. Buck built on his advantage. He dove again, cutting a one-hundred-eighty-degree arc against the blackness of space. Once the ship leveled off, he hit the throttle and it leaped ahead like a horse from the starting gate. He was now hugging the enemy's tail.

"Surprise," he commented.

"You may be able to outrun me," returned the pilot, "but I'm not convinced you can outfly me." He cut his engines.

The enemy ship drifted in space, momentum drawing it forward at a much reduced speed. For a moment, Buck did not realize what the pilot had done, and the moment almost cost him his life. His speed was terrific, for he was still trying to close on the fighter. The derelict grew in his viewscreen like a conjurer's trick. The ship was a deadly barricade.

Buck realized the pilot intended to take him down

if he had to die doing it. He shoved the stick to the right and felt the Krait respond to his hand. He missed the enemy fighter by a hair. "Good try," he said.

"I'm not finished," came the RAM pilot's response.

"I think you are," said Buck, his laser's pounding into the fighter's shields.

"Think again," said the pilot, hitting his launch thrusters. He was too late. The ship shot forward, but it could not escape Buck's guns. The shields dissolved, the lasers sank into the power block, and the ship blew, blinding Buck with a flash of light.

"Eagle Three, where are you?" asked Buck.

"Playing hopscotch with my buddy here. I could use some help, Rebel One."

"Affirmative, Eagle Three. I'm on my way."

Buck's computer pinpointed Doolittle's position from his transmission, and the ship changed trajectory to intersect with him. As he neared the intersection point, Buck saw his wingman nose to nose with the enemy ship he had decoyed. "This is Rebel One. I'm spreading my wings. Look out."

"I copy, Rebel One. Give me ten seconds." Doolittle let his ship flip up until its belly was parallel to his enemy's fuselage.

"Leave the chick alone," Buck told the RAM pilot, diving on him with forward lasers on full.

His lasers hit the enemy vessel amidships. He felt its shields waver, and knew its power reserves were draining. His spirits rose.

"Of course, Rebel One." The enemy pilot made the code name drip with sarcasm. He transferred his attention to Buck.

"Now!" said Buck.

Doolittle dropped his shields and sent a gyro shell after the RAM ship. Buck continued to pummel his shields with lasers, forcing the pilot to use the last of his reserves. Doolittle reactivated shields and right-

ed his ship as the gyro shell hit the fighter. The
assault was too much, and the fighter's shields crum-
bled. Buck's lasers sank into its unprotected hull,
and Doolittle hit its cockpit. The ship broke in two,
the force of its explosion rocking the NEO ships. But
they were not yet free of opposition.

Two more RAM fighters descended on them. Buck's
wing had lost two men in the fight, Crabbe and Hugh
Trenchard—Eagles Five and Six. The odds were
evening.

"Bandits at three o'clock," said Doolittle.

"I see them. Maintain heading."

"But, sir, they're targeting us!"

"Not soon enough," said Buck. He flew into a gaggle of engaged vessels, scattering them as he went.
Enemy ships that could break free joined the pack
that pursued him. "Eagle Two, come in."

"Eagle Two here," answered Earhart.

"Drop what you're doing and tail this bunch."

"I never turn down an invitation to a party," she
said.

"I'll save you a dance," replied Buck.

"I'll hold you to that." Earhart rolled again, this
time free of her attacker. "You heard the man," she
told Lindbergh—Eagle Four.

"I'm with you, Rebel One. I plan to fight Eagle Two
for that dance."

"Count me in, too," said Wright—Eagle One.

"Then get a move on!" called Buck.

He drove toward the edge of Hauberk, half the
RAM fleet on his tail, the other half strung out
behind him like swarming bees. At the rear of the
pack flew Earhart, driving the stragglers on. As they
neared Hauberk, Buck altered course dramatically.
Krait was a much handier ship than anything in
Hauberk's wing. His pursuers could not follow. They
slammed into the invisible wall of the *Free Enterprise*'s shields. Barney's ship, hidden behind its star

field cloak, rounded the station precisely on time. Buck's fancy flying sent most of the enemy vessels to their end, either from the initial impact with the third-rater's shields or in subsequent collisions.

The *Free Enterprise* disengaged its camouflage and moved slowly around Hauberk, accompanied by Buck, Doolittle, Earhart, Wright and Lindbergh. They sailed into the midst of the remaining combatants. "This is Rebel One to Eagle Leader. How's it going, Captain?"

Washington chuckled. "A moment ago, I wouldn't have been overly optimistic. Now I figure the battle is just about over." Buck could hear him fire a spurt from his lasers.

"You may be right," said Buck. "Hang on while I speak to the Scout leader."

"Will do," said Washington casually, the zinging whine of a laser on his shields singing over the communications link.

Buck flipped his communications channel. "Greetings, Hauberk," he said. "This is Captain Buck Rogers. We have destroyed your fleet. Your shields do not exist. As you can see, we have the firepower to knock out your artillery if you should resist. I ask for your surrender."

o o o o o

Seaforian heard Buck's demand with half an ear. He stared at the schematics of his artillery placements, noting with satisfaction that they made a deadly barrier of flak against the NEO vessels. NEO's assets clicked through his mind. That third-rater gave them a momentary advantage. He considered.

"I say again, I ask for your surrender, or we will fire on the station."

Seaforian smiled, an evil smile that started in his

eyes and spread like poison to his lips. "Captain Rogers, this is Seaforian, director of Hauberk station. I am prepared to negotiate terms of surrender."

"I am glad you are prepared to be reasonable, sir."

"I am always reasonable." The evil laughter in his eyes danced. "I ask that you spare the station and the ships left to it."

"And I ask that you instruct your pilots to cease fire, pending the conclusion of negotiations."

"A fair request. I will authorize it."

"Good. There is no need for the innocent to die."

"That would be a waste," responded Seaforian. "I assume that you wish to control the station."

"You are clever, Director." There was the merest hint of sarcasm in Buck's voice.

"I submit that control of Hauberk requires more men than you have. I suggest my own personnel remain in control for the present."

"I can see no other solution," said Buck. "My only immediate requirement for the administration of Hauberk is that the restrictions regarding trade and military deployment be lifted."

"I suppose you want the solar power company opened up, too."

"Yes."

"Really, Captain, you are irresponsible. That much freedom will cause an immediate panic. The results for Earth could be disastrous."

"I'll take the chance," said Buck, realizing that Seaforian was playing for time.

Seaforian shook his head sadly. "I am sorry to hear you say that. Still, I suspect it must be expected from a terrorist."

"From you, I find the title an honorable one."

"Please, Captain, let us not quibble over semantics," said Seaforian, putting on a show of efficiency.

"Then I suggest . . ." Rogers's voice trailed off. "I see, Director, you have kept a part of your bargain.

You will be happy to know your fighters have ceased their fire."

"I am a man of my word," said Seaforian.

"So am I," said Buck grimly, "and if the restrictions on Earth are not lifted in the next twenty minutes, I will begin to excavate sections of the station, then operate it with what few men I have."

"Then, Captain, accept the consequences. I will have no responsibility for the unchecked masses. Anarchy, violence, and panic are solely in your hands."

"I will be happy to accept the blame," said Buck.

"The words of a child," returned Seaforian.

"If you're looking for seniority, mister, I outrank you by five hundred years."

"Mark my words, Captain," said Seaforian pompously, "you will rue your actions." He banked the smile in his eyes, biding his time. Seaforian had twenty minutes before Rogers would discover he had been tricked. In even less time, the NEO rabble would be engaged again, this time in a fight they could not win. Kane was on the way.

○ ○ ○ ○ ○

Huer, one electronic ear tuned to Buck Rogers, the other frantically trying to oversee the NEO fighter wing, breach Hauberk's computer system, and monitor incoming and outgoing messages, had no time to reach farther, no circuit free to probe beyond Hauberk's immediate perimeter. Having not yet broken RAM's codes, and absorbed by the present conflict, he had no inkling of the approaching menace of Kane's forces.

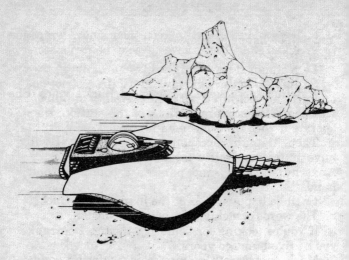

Chapter 28

R ebel One, this is Rebel Two. We should make the rendezvous point off Hauberk in three minutes. What is your status?"

"Knockout," said Buck nonchalantly.

"Say again?"

"Rebel Two, Hauberk has surrendered. We're picking up the last of the fighters now."

"Seaforian admitted defeat?" asked Wilma.

"Well, not exactly. He gave up, but he hasn't said much."

"He has a reputation as a devious man. Well deserved."

"I thought as much. I don't need to ask how your end of things went. Hauberk never knew what hit her," Buck said.

"We managed to knock out the satellites without too much difficulty, but I fear our ships attracted some notice."

"We couldn't expect to keep them under wraps for-ever, and after Hauberk we have no chance for secrecy."

"It served its purpose, Captain."

"It sure did, Colonel."

Wilma could sense the grin in Buck's voice. She was smiling herself.

"Rebel Two, you're in visual range," said Buck. He could see Wilma now, the three other ships flying behind her in a fan.

"How long will it take to evacuate the station?" she asked.

"Most efficiently? Doc estimates three third-raters could do the job."

"Or three trips by Thunderhead." Wilma was thoughtful. "Where do you plan to put Hauberk's staff?"

"Doc's been working on it." Buck tapped his flight helmet. "Doc," he said. "Wake up."

Huer's image immediately appeared on the lower left-hand corner of Buck's face screen. "I am always awake," he replied tartly. "What can I do for you?"

"We need recommendations on the deployment of prisoners."

Huer whistled, the sound particularly piercing within the flight helmet. "I think our best chance is to try to isolate them on a remote area of Earth. It's the closest, and there are desolate areas that RAM does not bother with."

"Rebel Two, I think we'd better inform the good director of our plans." said Buck. "You're ranking officer."

"Yes, but you're Rebel One and team leader for this operation. You dreamed it up. I think this should be a joint effort. You lead. I'll back you up."

"Roger, Rebel Two." Buck again cut his communi-cations line into Hauberk's main network. "This is Captain Buck Rogers. I wish to speak with Director Seaforian."

"Hauptman, here, Captain. The director has left orders not to be disturbed."

"Disturb him, or we begin lighting fires," threatened Buck.

"Understood, Captain. I am patching you in now."

Buck thought he detected a note of righteousness in Hauptman's voice, and concluded there was no love lost between the communications officer and his superior.

○ ○ ○ ○ ○

"This is Seaforian." The director's response was cold.

"Buck Rogers here, Director. I must request that you prepare your staff for immediate evacuation from Hauberk."

"We can be ready in forty-eight hours," said Seaforian, stalling. He had no doubt Kane would make the NEO terrorists flee.

"I am afraid that is not possible, Director. I can give you one hour."

"You are joking."

"I'm afraid not," said Buck.

"That is impossible, Captain! You have not won; you have merely survived a day of battle. Do you think RAM will not support me? Are you so foolish you do not fear the armies of RAM? They will crush your few ships to space dust."

"We are prepared for that contingency, Director. That is why we must insist that you and your staff be prepared to depart Hauberk station in one hour."

"And if we do not?"

"Then I am very much afraid that RAM will lose a great number of key personnel."

"You would murder us in cold blood?" Seaforian blustered with feigned innocence. "I don't know why that should surprise me, coming from untutored rabble."

"We don't want to kill anybody, Director," said Buck. "Not even a bunch of bureaucratic slugs. But in a very short time, Hauberk station is going to have a fatal accident. I am afraid anyone still on the station will share its fate."

"I see." Seaforian did indeed see. The fools thought to blow the station up. He had only to play for time, trolling the NEO insurrectionists like Martian trout, so that Kane might destroy them. "The alternatives seem to have dwindled," he said. "I will instruct my staff to prepare for emergency departure. Do you wish to use the station shuttles, or have you another plan?"

"By all means use the station shuttles. We will give you landing coordinates when the time for departure arrives," said Buck, trying to keep the elation from his voice. The sheer physical difficulty of moving so many people had been driving him around in circles. Now it seemed that Seaforian had solved the problem for him. "Commence evacuation, Director."

"At once, Captain."

○ ○ ○ ○ ○

Buck signed off and said to Wilma, "Did you like that, Rebel Two?"

"Not much. He should have fought more."

"The good director has something up his sleeve."

"RAM." Wilma's voice was deadly serious.

"Probably," returned Buck.

"Not probably." Huer's voice echoed inside Buck's flight helmet. "You have visitors. Point two-three hundred."

Buck glanced at his scanners. Heading toward Hauberk in a purposeful wedge were eighteen spacecraft. He punched the identify code into his computer and the computer obligingly ran through the myriad classes of spacecraft, settled on the one-man fighter, then added the notation "EXPERIMENTAL. EXACT SPECIFICATIONS NOT ON FILE."

"Wonderful," muttered Buck. "It looks like we've got company, Rebel Two."

"Did you run them through your system?" asked Wilma.

"Affirmative."

"I think they're a match for what we're flying. This may not be so easy."

"The wonders of modern technology," said Buck sarcastically. "I wonder how much overtime they had to pay to get those birds to fly."

"Rebel One, this is Eagle Leader. Bandits coming in."

"I noticed, Eagle Leader. Battle stations. It looks like this time it's going to be closer to an even match." Buck could see Washington's command closing ranks in tight formation.

"My flight picked up some fuel from the station's tankers," came Washington's voice.

"Then you hit them first, Eagle Leader. My men and Rebel Two's are still refueling. Good luck. We'll be right behind you."

"See you," said Washington.

Washington turned his ship belly up, swinging away from the space station and toward the approaching fighters. The rest of his flight followed. Buck could see them lined out, silver-blue flashes against the darkness of space. As the two flights of spacecraft neared one another, half of the RAM ships broke off, engaging Washington, while the rest continued on toward Hauberk.

Buck muttered an oath. The RAM leader was not going to give him time. "Colonel, come on!" he called to Wilma.

"I've still got two to refuel. We had to do some expensive evasive flying down there."

"How long?"

"Five minutes."

"Follow me out when you can."

"Affirmative, Rebel One."

"All right, Eagles. It looks like we've got to do this one more time," said Buck as his flight fell into formation behind him.

"Rebel One, this is Eagle Two. We have artillery fire from the station."

"I see it, Eagle Two. Close up. We're going to face first things first."

Buck's five ships set out after Washington's seven, setting a trajectory to intersect with the RAM vessels in approximately thirty seconds. They flew as a unit now, their combat action welding four outstanding individuals into an outstanding team. Gone was Buck's nervousness, in spite of the more dangerous ships they faced. He knew, in the end, it was not the spacecraft, but the pilot that was the difference. He had four good ones, fresh from a successful action, and they approached the RAM ships like hounds in full cry.

"I have been listening in, Captain," interrupted a strange voice on his communications link. "To set your uncertainty aside, I will tell you the ships you face are also the new Krait class fighters. I also see we have you outnumbered. Why not give up now, peacefully?" There was laughter in the voice.

"I find the invitation infinitely laughable," said Buck, irritated by the man's manner. "Just as laughable as I find your manners. The least you can do is introduce yourself. I am Captain Anthony Rogers."

"And I," responded the voice lightly, "am Cornelius Kane. My friends call me *Killer*."

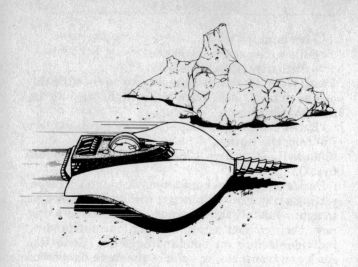

Chapter 29

In his short time in the twenty-fifth century, Buck had heard considerable discussion about Cornelius Kane, especially from the pilots who made up NEO's new wing. Curious, he had asked Wilma about him.

"They call him Killer Kane," she had said. "He deserves it."

Something in the shortness of her reply warned Buck he had hit a sensitive nerve. Later he questioned Turabian and learned Kane had been a NEO pilot, and that he and Wilma once were close, but came to a parting of the ways when Kane joined RAM. One thing he now knew for sure: Kane was dangerous.

"Do you fetch any bones, Killer?" asked Buck as he closed on the RAM ships.

"Only yours, Captain Rogers."

"You'll have to catch me first," said Buck, lifting

his ship's nose to a path that would overfly Kane.

Kane saw the move and dove, making Buck's run useless. "I am so glad you feel that way."

Buck followed Kane down, Doolittle still hugging his left wing, letting the rest of the wing break away for combat. Kane sent his ship out from under Buck in a curve to the left.

"We seem to have formed a mutual dislike." Kane pulled his stick back and the ship soared upward, toward the base of Hauberk station, then whirled and charged back toward Buck.

Buck eyed the approaching vessel. It kept its headlong course, its nose pointed at his prow. Buck pulled his ship up, sending it in a ninety-degree power climb. He knew his evasion was momentary.

Kane followed, his wingman hanging on grimly. Kane did not slow down. Buck veered away from him, hoping his speed would make him overshoot his trajectory. He was out of luck. Kane was good. He held the fighter to Buck's tail, though it shuddered in protest at the turn he forced it to make. Buck dove and accelerated, cutting a one-hundred-eighty-degree arc. His ship strained forward, and for a moment he could see his adversary's tail feathers. Kane broke the circle and shot off across space. His ship flipped over its tail and came screaming back, daring Buck to fight. This time Buck waited until it was almost on him, then shot forward and under his enemy, shoved his port docking thrusters home, and felt the ship spin. A blast from the starboard thrusters stopped its revolution, and he drove forward, on his adversary's slim tail.

"Having a nice day?" Kane's voice was light, mocking. In spite of his position, he was totally at ease.

"So far," Buck said conversationally, shoving his ship one notch closer to Kane's.

"We'll have to change that. Didn't anyone tell you NEO pilots never win."

"Nope. All they told me was RAM never flies outside its defense tunnels—unless there's a bloody great lot of them. You've only got eighteen. What happened, you get lost?"

"I have never been lost. And you?"

"I can't say the same. Getting lost is educational."

Kane's ship ducked, and Buck's went with it. Kane swerved, and Buck cut a wider arc, barely staying with him. Buck snarled, frustrated at having lost ground.

"Testy, testy," chided the mocking voice. "The living legend has a temper."

"You might remember that," returned Buck, the drawl back in his voice.

He nudged up behind Kane's starboard tail stabilizer, and the ship's shield hit a thruster at the top of Kane's ship's tail, pushing it down sixty degrees. Buck overshot Kane by meters. They were flying so closely that neither of the wingmen could get a clear shot without risking his partner.

"Eagle Three, break off," said Buck to Doolittle. "Leave him to me for now. If you get a clear shot, take it."

"I think you should have stayed in the twentieth century, hot shot. Five hundred years of sleep have rusted your reflexes." Kane's vessel rose behind Buck's and its shields nosed the NEO fighter's tail.

Buck reached up to his control panel. He gave a lever a quick push down, then back up. Expelled fuel hit the exhaust vent behind the engines, ignited, and spewed out his tail and into Kane's face. Kane uttered an exclamation and dropped back, blinded. Buck shot off to starboard, whirled on his docking thrusters, and jumped back into position near Kane's tail. "Check," he said.

"At least you show some ingenuity," said his adversary. He chuckled. "That was clever."

"Thank you," said Buck modestly. He was beginning to realize Kane was playing a game. He had not fired his lasers once. Kane's ship flipped over backward in a turn that almost grazed Buck's fuselage. He followed it grimly.

"I never have been impressed by a reputation, but I have to give it to you; you can fly."

"I accept the compliment, Captain, in the spirit in which it was given. It's too bad we're on opposite sides."

"Mutual admiration is wonderful," said Buck sarcastically.

Buck checked his instruments and realized he and Kane were angling back toward Hauberk. That did not bode well. Hauberk's artillery was sending out a deadly wall of laser flak. Kane rolled once more, and this time Buck cut him off, herding him away from the station.

"What," said Kane after a pause, "made you think you and that handful of misfits you call a fleet—"

"I call them a wing myself," Buck interjected.

"—could take on Hauberk—take on RAM, for that matter—and live?"

"And win," Buck reminded him.

"You were duped. They let you win, knowing we were on our way."

"Maybe, but they had no alternatives."

"I'll believe that when I see a mudworm fly."

In spite of all Buck could do, Kane was moving closer and closer to Hauberk.

"I could say I look forward to some interesting encounters if it weren't for one thing," Kane said.

"What's that?"

"You are not going to survive this one."

"News to me." Buck hit his thrusters and rose above Kane, practically sitting on him.

"Though I admit the temptation to let you live is strong. It's a good thing I'm not foolish enough to give in to it."

"What makes you so sure *you're* going to survive?" asked Buck.

"I always have."

There was a chilling certainty in Kane's words, but Buck refused to give in to it. "There's a first time for everything."

Kane shoved his controls home and dove, taking Buck with him. A rattling blast of mini-mines shot from the stern of his ship and hit Buck's forward shields.

They exploded harmlessly, but their flash blinded Buck, and, like Kane before him, he hesitated. A split second was long enough for him to lose his quarry. When his sight cleared, Kane was coming up behind him, full out. Buck hit the throttle, and the NEO Krait jumped forward, straight for Hauberk. Kane stayed behind him, driving him into the station's artillery.

Buck rolled, and Kane made no move to follow him. It was a mistake. With each roll, Buck dropped a degree until he had enough room to dive. He pushed his ship's nose down and accelerated. Kane, caught off guard, followed. Buck cut his power by half, and Kane overflew him.

There was a burst of white light as Kane hit his reverse starboard lasers. Buck's shields absorbed them. "That was just a sample," said Kane. "There will be more."

"You'd better do a good job of it next time. I'm getting a mite peeved," Buck replied.

Wilma caught the exchange on her communications link. She drew in her breath sharply. Kane's voice sent a raw jangle over her nerves. The old flippant insouciance that once had made her heart sing now twisted it. She had not expected the pain. She took a deep breath and concentrated on the conversation.

Kane chuckled. "Peeved? Is that some kind of

ancient disease?"

"You'll think so when the results hit you," Buck said.

Wilma caught the flash of light that was a fighter's trademark at extreme range. She pushed her ship, closing on the two. In moments, she was close enough to identify them. She muttered an oath as she realized Kane's intentions. Buck had to break away now, or he would be within range of Hauberk's defense system.

"I'm sorry, Captain Rogers, but I can't seem to work up a twinge of fear," came Kane's voice.

"Give it time," said Buck.

Kane laughed. "Really, Rogers, I will miss your sense of humor. It's a quality sadly lacking in RAM's outlook. The directors don't seem to see a need for it."

"Too bad. Personally, I find them quite laughable."

Wilma closed on the two combatants. Both men realized her presence at the same time.

"Looks like you have help, Captain." Kane flipped his wing up in an irreverent gesture, and Buck slipped under it, pushed it with his shields, then dropped back. "I am going to eat you for lunch, Captain," said Kane through clenched teeth.

"You're welcome to try."

"Rebel One, this is Rebel Two. If you haven't noticed, you will be in range of Hauberk's artillery in twenty seconds."

"Wilma?" Kane asked, startled.

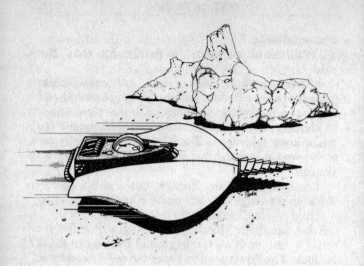

Chapter 30

Wilma," Kane confirmed. Ignoring Buck, he whirled on her. He had wondered, briefly, upon seeing the NEO ships, whether she would be taking part in the Hauberk attack. Still, hearing her voice again unsettled him.

"It's been a long time, Kane." Wilma's hardened voice vibrated through the communications link.

Kane's ship bore down on hers like an angel of death. "I knew we'd meet again," he said softly.

"And now we're on opposite sides." Wilma hovered in Kane's flight path, unmoving.

"We always were opposites," Kane said. "That's what made it interesting."

"The past is over, Kane."

Kane chuckled. "Passionate Wilma. You do take things hard." He was kilometers from her, coming fast.

Wilma lifted her ship's nose and gunned the

engines, sliding over Kane's ship with meters to spare. The ships' shields sparked orange as they slid across each other. "Yes, I do," she said.

Kane's run at Wilma was instinct, a reaction Buck did not try to analyze. It gave him a chance to maneuver. He skinned past the scorching flak from Hauberk's artillery. The spent lasers crackled against his shields, sending a showy net of fractured light across one side of his ship. He flew straight forward, between Kane and Hauberk. Kane's wingman followed him, but Buck was tired of fencing. He sent a full-power blast from his stern lasers into the wingman's forward shields.

The lasers sank into the ship's shielding, dissipating, but Buck kept pounding. As he veered away from Hauberk, the wingman pulled out, saving his shields. Buck shoved his thrusters home, and his Krait shot forward. As he broke free, Doolittle swooped toward him.

"I've got trouble, Rebel One. Request assistance," he said.

"I copy, Eagle Three," replied Buck.

One of the RAM pilots had targeted Doolittle and was battering away at his shields, scoring the fighter's invisible armor.

"My shields are burning up!" Doolittle's voice was uncharacteristically shaken.

"I'm right behind you." Buck cut across the RAM fighter's tail, sending a laser pulse into the tail section. The shields absorbed it, but the pilot was not in an enviable position. Sandwiched between his enemies, he might destroy one, but the odds he would survive the action were nil. He began to look for a way out, when Doolittle put everything he had into a shot from his stern guns.

Buck cut across the ship's trajectory again, sending a stream of laser pulses into the center of the craft. The enemy's shields wavered.

The RAM pilot took one look at his shield indicator and realized he was getting singed. He took immediate action. He dove straight down. The NEO fighters let him go.

"Thanks, Captain," said Doolittle.

Buck could tell how close Doolittle had come to oblivion by the lightness of his appreciation. "Don't mention it," he returned.

"Rebel One, this is Eagle Leader." Washington's voice was broken up by the zinging sound of laser fire.

"We are engaged in heavy fighting. So far we haven't lost a ship. We've disabled one of theirs. That almost makes the odds even. If it weren't for the artillery, I'd say we have a chance."

"You getting burned by the flak?" asked Buck.

"You got it."

"How bad is it?"

"I've got two ships running on minimal shields."

"We've got to take out that artillery. Can you break away, Eagle Leader?"

"Negative, Rebel One."

"I copy. I'll try to get you some open air."

"I'd appreciate it," said Washington.

"Eagle Two, this is Rebel One. Status?"

"We are in the thick of things, sir," said Earhart.

"You're flying awfully close to Hauberk's guns," Buck said.

"Yes, sir, that seems to be where RAM wants us."

"No doubt. I've got a different idea. I'm going to go stir up the nest. You keep the birds occupied."

"Good luck, Captain," said Earhart, knowing Buck's code meant he was planning on taking a run at the station's artillery.

"Eagle Three, we're going in, point two-one. Stay close. If one of those RAM pilots realizes what we're up to, he might take a notion to box us in. I'll need a shotgun at my back."

"Sir?" asked Doolittle, unfamiliar with the phrase.

"Just be there, Eagle."

"Yes, sir."

Buck sent his craft into Hauberk's wall of artillery fire, his own guns blazing as they spat deadly beams of energy at the stationary targets. He knocked out three of them as he scorched over them, a notch ahead of their weapons computer. He thanked the RAM scientist who had perfected the Krait, making it a sliver faster than anything now in space.

Doolittle, hugging Buck's left wing, finished his own strafing of the unprotected guns. Without shields, the weapons were vulnerable—if a ship could survive the barrage they were spewing. "We could finish these things off if we had time," he said.

"That's the problem, isn't it?" asked Buck. "Time. Have you checked how many of those laser cannons Hauberk has?"

"Three thousand four hundred and thirty-five. Three thousand four hundred and thirty now."

"Even counting their reduced numbers, we can't knock them out one by one," said Buck dryly. "It would take years."

"This stuff is automated," said Doolittle. "Somewhere there has to be a control center."

"Doc," said Buck, tapping his helmet to alert the computer, "we need to find Hauberk's artillery control center. Do you have anything?"

Huer's mobile face appeared low on Buck's face shield. "There are only two RAM subsidiaries capable of building a control center of the size you describe: Warhead and Assault, Inc. If we look for their particular markings on parts, then correlate the marking with the approximate size, construction, and location—"

"We should be able to come up with solid possibilities," interrupted Buck.

"Solid possibilities. I thought the terms were

mutually exclusive," said Huer.

"Don't play word games. I need answers." Buck and Doolittle swerved and rolled, evading a RAM fighter that had followed them. Lindbergh cut in on the enemy ship, drawing it off.

"Sorry, but these blasted RAM codes have been driving me batty," said Huer.

"We haven't got much time," Buck reiterated.

"I am aware of that," said Huer.

Even in the distorted projection on his face screen, Buck could see that Huer's eyes were distant. He knew that meant Huer was accessing his data banks.

"There are four possibilities," Huer said at last. "I am sending their specifications to your schematic scanner. You should have visual on your on-board computer now."

"Affirmative," replied Buck. A schematic drawing in three dimensions was taking form on the tiny viewer that usually served his scanners. As he watched, each portion of the station grew before his eyes. "It could be any one of them," he said wearily.

"Perhaps," said Huer, "but I think we can narrow it down." He pulled up the third drawing again and studied it. "Do you notice," Huer said at last, "the scanners in this section are all preset?"

"No." Buck glanced down at the screen again. The scanners painted by the computer's electronic brush showed rigid location code numbers. They monitored a specific sector of the station or of space, and as Buck watched, he realized that they did not move. "I think you've got it," he said.

"Now I'll give you a read-out of its position on Hauberk."

The schematics vanished and a rough block of the space station took form. Nestled in a crevasse on the far edge of Hauberk was the control center.

"Let's see the placement of the artillery," said Buck.

"Of course," said Huer. White pricks of light bloomed across the map. There was a cluster of them around the control center. "Now may I return to work?" he asked.

"Yeah. Thanks, Doc," said Buck. "Eagle Three, we're going in. Heading three-two. Target the initial battery of guns. Let's try to take out one whole wall of them."

They started their run on Hauberk, but two RAM fighters closed on them, obviously aware of their intentions.

"We must be on the right track, Rebel One," said Doolittle.

"I think you're right. We are drawing flies."

"Evasive maneuvers?"

"No time—not if we want to get that command post. Follow me down." Buck sent his ship toward the surface of the space station, cutting under a stream of energy from one of Hauberk's flak guns. Doolittle stayed with him. They skimmed meters from the irregular surface of Hauberk. It was fancy flying—dangerous flying—but it was serving its purpose. The two RAM fighters slacked off.

"We're coming into range. Ten seconds. Five seconds. Four—three—two—one. Commence fire."

Buck and Doolittle charged the guns, their lasers hitting them at the base. They cut down three of the cannons, the guns toppling from their towers like cut flowers. They floated off into space, their power lines severed.

The NEO pilots kept firing as they skirted the bases of the other weapons, disabling one more and damaging two. The RAM pilots followed their swath of destruction, cursing their own impotence.

"They're going to come down," said Doolittle.

"I was afraid of that," said Buck. "We've got to take them out. I think we can get the control post on our next run."

"Here they come!"

The two fighters dipped under their own artillery fire, the heavy guns scoring a passing hit on the forward ship. The pilot wavered, then dropped lower. He hugged the surface of the station, his wingman beside him. Still they were flying half a kilometer higher than Buck and Doolittle.

Buck roared forward, Doolittle following like a shadow. They headed for a particularly large laser cannon. "Eagle, get behind me!" Buck barked at Doolittle. "Match my heading. Keep your eyes on my tail and nowhere else."

Doolittle, mystified, complied. They neared the base of the gun tower, and Doolittle waited for Buck to change course. Instead, he flew straight into the crisscrossing framework of the tower. Doolittle gulped and followed Buck's advice. He made the stubby, upswept tail of Buck's fighter his star and followed it like a religious tenet.

The two RAM fighters were intent on their target. When they realized what Buck was doing, they were dangerously close to the tower. At an added half-kilometer of altitude, the struts were closer together, and there was no room for the smallest spacecraft to slide through. They pulled away, but it was too late. Together they crashed into the gun tower, bringing it down. Power popped and cracked from the cut lines waving in space. The two RAM ships contacted those as well and went up in a blaze.

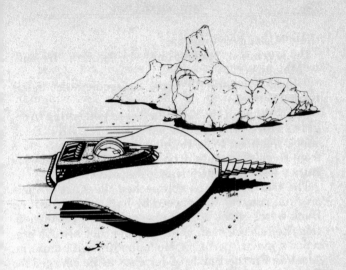

Chapter 31

Buck and Doolittle shot away from the flying debris.

"Rebel One, this is Rebel Two. Do you copy?" came Wilma's strained voice.

"Affirmative, Rebel Two. What's wrong?" Buck asked. "We're holding our own, but we could use you."

"We've got one more run before we can even the odds. Can you hold?"

"Affirmative."

"We'll be with you as soon as we can, Rebel Two." Buck sent his ship into a tight turn, Doolittle again glued to his side. They skimmed Hauberk's surface, retracing their path. They had to approach the artillery command post on the side they had disabled. "Look sharp," said Buck. "We can't afford company."

"I get nothing," said Doolittle, "except the ships that are already engaged. Thunderhead's got five of them buzzing around him."

Buck grinned. "I don't envy the fighters," he said. "Me neither!"

"Buck! I've done it!" came a piercing voice inside Buck's helmet.

"Doc! What in the seven hells are you trying to do, get us killed? Just hold on a few minutes, OK?" Buck shook his head to settle his nerves. Huer retreated from Buck's face shield, obviously disappointed with Buck's less-than-enthusiastic response.

The two NEO ships approached the start of their original run, cut their speed by half, and turned. As Buck watched the nose of his ship slide over the station, he felt the rush of adrenaline that always preceded a major operation. He found himself humming "Joshua Fit the Battle of Jericho" as he charged for the wounded side of the command post. "Lasers on rapid pulse," he said. "Target the central dome."

"Done," said Doolittle.

The NEO ships came down on the command post. Their lasers fired deadly streams of energy into the central dome, the pulses so rapid they were a single blaze of light. The dome exploded in a thousand shards of clear plasticrete, depressurizing instantly. Personnel inside the dome were killed immediately, and the day-to-day debris floated into space, creating a pathetic shower of humanity.

"One more time!" said Buck, diving under the station's far guns. He swept back over the station, his guns blazing.

Doolittle followed grimly. Buck's guns hit the command post again, this time sinking into the computer banks like a knife through cheese. Doolittle sent his own lasers blasting into the floor of the post, hoping to hit the power hookup.

Both strategies caused devastating results for Hauberk. The computers blew, sending clouds of sparks and billowing smoke rising into the stillness of space.

Doolittle grazed the power link, and it cracked. The artillery died.

Buck gave a war whoop.

"We did it!" said Doolittle.

"You bet we did! Hang on, Rebel Two!" said Buck. "We're coming!"

"It's about time," Wilma responded tartly. "You can stop playing with those guns and do some real work for a change."

Buck laughed.

○ ○ ○ ○ ○

Seaforian stared at his viewscreen. The artillery was gone. Gone. He was incapable of taking it in. This time there was no reprieve. If Kane could not defeat NEO, then Hauberk was doomed. He saw his whole career crumbling before him.

"Sir!" called Hauptman's voice from the terminal. Seaforian ignored the pudgy man's interruption.

"Sir, we are entering security mode!"

The words slid over Seaforian like water.

"Sir, please respond! Security mode is now operational!"

Seaforian tore his eyes away from the rolling screen. "What is it, Hauptman?" he asked tiredly.

"Sir, the station's main computers have activated security mode!"

"You've said that three times, Hauptman. I am aware of the security measures inherent in the station." His response was lethargic.

"But, sir, the computers are cut off! The last upgrade in communications was never integrated with security mode. We cannot contact RAM Central."

Seaforian's lethargy vanished. "Even for the Lazarus code?"

"We can't get to it. It has to come from RAM Central."

"Do we still have channels to the fighters?"

"Yes. The computer considers them part of the station. It will maintain contact with them to the end."

"Try bouncing a message from one of them. They should be within range of a communications satellite."

"And RAM could use the fighter as a channel into Hauberk."

"Yes. Keep me posted."

"Yes, sir. I will try immediately. Briggs!" Hauptman snapped into the fighter commander's line.

"Briggs here."

"You still have three of Hauberk's fighters operational?"

"That's right."

"I've got a mission for you."

"We're clear."

"I am sending you a coded message for RAM Central."

"What? Do you have communications problems?"

"No," Hauptman lied, "the transmission is less likely to be traced through a fighter. You will act as a conduit. I want you to transmit that same code to SNOOP Two."

"I copy," said Briggs. "We've got the station between us and the satellite. We'll have to move."

"Then do it," said Hauptman evenly. "I want you protected, the other two ships covering your position. You're going to have to stay in play for a few minutes."

"How long?"

"I don't know. Once you have transmitted the code, you will set your receiving channel to RAMDOWN."

"RAMDOWN! That's an emergency channel!"

"Don't give me any backtalk!" snapped Hauptman. He was tired. "I think we have an emergency. Don't you?" There was silence from Briggs's end of the link. "At any rate, you will be receiving, in turn, a transmission from RAM Central on the RAM-DOWN frequency. You are to transmit it immediately to me. I will have an open line to you throughout the operation."

"I copy, Hauptman."

"Prepare for transmission."

"Code mode open," replied Briggs.

Hauptman sent the distress signal, dormant in the depths of Hauberk's computers for centuries, into the fighter's communications system.

Briggs watched the transmission indicator. "Transmission completed," he said as the red light went out.

"Proceed with step two of your instructions."

"I copy," replied the fighter pilot.

Hauptman could see Briggs speed off across space, the fighter's two companions protecting his rear. Hauptman regretted his sharp words. Briggs was a good commander who had seen his supposedly invulnerable base overrun. It was not his fault communications were severed. But Briggs knew the Lazarus code was Hauberk's last ditch reversal of the station's automatic security measures. If he made it out of this, he might rate an apology. Hauptman turned to the technician beside him. "Pull up the missile launchers," he said. "We may as well be ready."

The schematics for Hauberk's antispacecraft missiles appeared on a screen.

"How many have we got?" Hauptman asked.

"Thirteen," replied Jacobson, the tech. "They were always considered a useless security check, so only a minimal number was installed."

"No one ever figured we'd have to use them," Hauptman replied.

"I just wish they weren't so old," said Jacobson.

"Why? Nothing rots in space."

"I know, but these missiles are pretty basic, not like the ones we see now."

"That may be an advantage. There will be less

margin for error," reasoned Hauptman. He wiped sweat from his jowls.

"I just hope they don't malfunction. The success rate on these beauties was about sixty-five percent at best."

Hauptman smiled, a slow little quirk of the lips. "It is a useless gesture. However, it is a gesture I will not fail to make. Get those stingers operational."

"Yes, sir! They'll be ready to go in two minutes."

"Good," said Hauptman. "Martins, you've been tracking those NEO ships. I need the electrocardiogram of every enemy pilot out there, the leaders especially."

"They're on file, sir. I did a vitals read-out when they first attacked."

"Good. Give them to Jacobson." Hauptman leaned back. His spirits again rose. He was not afraid. He was standing face to face with Death, with a glint in his eye. His own attitude surprised him, but he supposed it was because they still had a chance. If Briggs could get hold of the Lazarus code, they might all survive. He closed his eyes, squinting them shut against the glare of red light in the communications center, and waited for Briggs to contact him.

○ ○ ○ ○ ○

Ulianov, hovering near the communications complex, was trying to assimilate the present status of its host. It was aware of violent computer activity that encompassed the whole station. It saw security programs whiz by, and cringed into its hiding place, but the faceless security guards did not falter in their courses. Ulianov watched one guard jump a closed gate, heedless of the obstruction. Something definitely was amiss.

Hauberk's electronic panic had interrupted Ulianov in its search for a vehicle that would secure its position and destroy Buck Rogers. Once it realized the panicking station would ignore it—unless Ulianov were to place itself directly in the line of fire—it returned to its survey of Hauberk's resources.

Suddenly it stopped in its search. One of the engineers in the communications complex was calling up a bank of spacecraft. Ulianov scanned the files. The crafts' intelligence was low. They were drones, piloted by computer. The files were old, and the coding in them was so simple it was confusing.

Ulianov could see each craft carried a single weapon. This gave it a moment of trepidation. Was it accessing a drone or a bomb? The specifications Ulianov could detect were not clear. Even the size and type of the weapon was not specified. Ulianov recalled that it had faced the same frustrations earlier, when reading the records on the oldest part of the station. Apparently, when Hauberk was new, its administrators felt the best security was total secrecy, from the staff as well as any outside interest, the logic being if the information were not there, it could not be found.

Ulianov saw the possibilities of this line of thought, but remained frustrated. It needed answers, and there were none. Ulianov ran the matter over in its mind. If the craft were drones, it could infiltrate the simple computer and take control, sending the ship after Rogers. If it were a flying bomb, it could use the craft to get away from the station, then jump to one of the fighter's computers via the craft's directional channels. In either case, it could accomplish its first alternative, and perhaps the second as well.

Ulianov's line of thought broke as it detected a transmission from the communications post to the various craft. Each of the drones was assigned a single EKG pattern. A ripple of static passed over Ulianov as it laughed. It waited patiently. As it watched, Capt. Anthony Rogers's heart was handed in ritual sacrifice to one of the drones. When the transmission passed on to the next vessel, Ulianov jumped.

Heedless of the station's outraged security, it waded through the crowded channels until it reached the drone. It slid into the drone's primitive computer, knowing it was set dead on target for the biggest threat to Masterlink's—and Ulianov's—existence. It settled into the computer, waiting for launch. Once it was away from the station, there would be time to find out the exact particulars of its host. Until then, it kept silent, knowing Hauberk's communications center had the drones under surveillance.

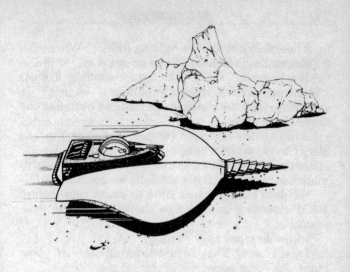

Chapter 32

Eagle Leader, I see three bandits heading off Hauberk," said Paul Revere, his clipped accent offering the information impassively.

"I see them, Eagle Twelve," Washington replied. "Now where the hell are they going?" he murmured to himself.

"I don't know, sir, but I could find out."

Washington considered the offer. They had cut the odds by one, and they were holding their own with the RAM pilots. Washington had discovered he was facing mercenaries, and that made his job easier. Mercenaries would go a long way for cash, but they wouldn't take the borderline chances his own troops ate for breakfast. As the conflict progressed, he could see dedication working on his side—if RAM didn't send reinforcements. "All right," he said at last. "Take da Vinci."

"You hear that, Eagle Thirteen?" asked Revere.

"I heard. What are we waiting for?"

"Roger, Eagle Leader. We're on our way."

"Hurry back," said Washington, sending a laser charge into a RAM fighter's shields.

Revere, with da Vinci at his side, set out after the three RAM ships.

"Aren't those Hauberk's ships?" asked da Vinci as they closed on the vessels.

Revere ran a sensor scan, confirming da Vinci's sighting. "Affirmative. I thought we got them all."

"We didn't have much time to count coup before RAM attacked, but I know there were some prisoners."

"I wonder what they're up to."

"I don't know. They're just hanging there, in plain sight. It's sorta eerie."

Revere considered the enemy craft. "Let's slow down and take a good look," he said slowly. "Half throttle."

"Half throttle," repeated da Vinci.

The NEO fighters slowed, approaching the three ships cautiously. The enemy vessels did not move.

"They've got to have seen us!" said da Vinci.

"Unless they're suffering a malfunction."

"All three of them?"

"Good point." Revere cut his speed another notch. "We should be coming within laser range in point four."

"Still nothing." Da Vinci was baffled.

"Point two . . . one—they should hit us now."

As if Revere's words were a signal, two of the ships opened up their lasers.

"They're firing slow," said Revere. "Let's take a run at them and see if we can stir up a little action."

Revere accelerated, and his ship leaped forward, da Vinci on his wing. The enemy ships continued their fire, the pulses still set at the lowest frequency. As Revere neared his target, he opened up his own weapons. His lasers struck the enemy's shields deeply. "They're operating on half power! A couple more hits and those shields will go."

"I don't like this," said da Vinci.

"I admit it's strange, but we're out here to eliminate the enemy."

"They might blow up in our faces," cautioned the wingman.

For answer, Revere flipped the fighter's stubby wing. He headed back toward the three RAM pigeons. "Just pretend it's a shooting gallery," he said.

This time Hauberk's ships pumped power into their lasers, and the pulses increased. It was enough to burn the outer layer from the NEO fighters' shields, but it caused no real damage. Revere aimed the full battery of his guns on one of the ships. His lasers penetrated the weakened shields, and he saw them cut into the fuselage. He did not see the laser sever the ship's fuel line, but the resulting explosion caught his attention. "Got one!" he said. "And it wasn't mined."

He and da Vinci swept back for a third run.

○ ○ ○ ○ ○

Inside the enemy vessels, Briggs waited grimly for RAM Central to acknowledge the message he had sent. He saw one of his tail guards blown out of space, felt the distortion that the explosion caused as his ship rocked, as if at anchor. "This is Briggs," he said. "Come in, Hauberk."

"Message received?" asked Hauptman.

"Not yet. I am under attack. Have lost one ship. We're running on half shields. I can't hold out."

"You have to! That message is vital!"

"Enemy vessels are lining up for another attack. Permission to break from position."

"Denied! You have to be there!" Hauptman cried.

"They're coming in. We won't make it— Wait a minute! Message coming in!" Briggs saw the code indicator blink. "I've got it! Transmitting—"

His voice was cut off.

O O O O O

In Hauberk's communications center, Hauptman took his headset off. "Launch missiles," he said wearily.

Jacobson pressed down on his computer keys. "Missiles away," he said.

"At least we managed that," said Hauptman. Before his words ended, the red alert lights began to blink, and a siren screamed throughout the echoing reaches of the station. Hauberk was lost. It was designed as the most efficient closed security system in RAM's vast empire, and one of its primary directives involved a breach of that security. Hauberk could not be overrun. Before that happened, it would destroy itself.

When the artillery post went, the station's security had gone into action, but there had been one last possibility. If the deactivation code—the Lazarus code— were received from RAM Central within one hour of security activation, the self-destruct sequence would be canceled. Hauberk would accept that code up to one minute before the end. Hauptman almost had made it: only fifteen minutes remained. In spite of losing the computer link to RAM, he had almost managed to stave off the inevitable. He leaned back and closed his eyes, his work finished.

"Hauptman! Hauptman, come in!" Seaforian's voice raged over the channel unnoticed.

Hauptman let him rave. In these last minutes, he derived a certain pleasure from ignoring him.

o o o o o

"Eagle Leader, this is Eagle Twelve. We have disarmed the bandits."

"Good work, Eagle Twelve. Now get on back here. We need you."

"On our way, Eagle Leader. Sir, there's something you should know."

"Yes?" asked Washington.

"Those ships were sitting ducks. We couldn't get them to break formation and fight. They were running with half shields. It was fishy."

"Hmm." Washington mulled the matter over as he rolled out of the way of a RAM fighter. "Notice anything else?"

"Only that they were ships out of Hauberk, not the RAM reinforcements."

"Then it's likely whatever they were up to was closely tied to Hauberk."

"I would say so, sir."

"Eagle Twelve, run a sensor probe as you pass the station."

"I copy. Scanning now."

"Anything unusual?"

"Well, sir, it's hard to tell. They've suffered so much damage that I'm getting a lot of electronic chaos. Wait a minute! Sir, they've launched missiles!"

"What class?" Washington asked.

Revere watched his screen as the computer ran over the specifications for known missiles.

"What's taking so long?" prompted Washington.

"Search me, Eagle Leader—here it is. The missiles are Macmillan Questors."

"Those things come out of the history books! They-'ve got to be hundreds of years old."

"The computer says two hundred thirty-seven years," replied Revere.

"They seem to be operational," cut in da Vinci.

"How many do you scan," asked Washington.

"Thirteen," replied Revere.

"Well, at least some of us will survive. Those things work by EKG. They'll home in on a pilot until their fuel is exhausted. And they have an awful lot of fuel."

"Recommendations, sir?" da Vinci asked.

"Take them out," said Washington. "And pray you don't pick the one set for you. Once they clear Hauberk, they'll pick up speed. Hit them now if you can."

"Affirmative, sir. Wait a minute. My sensors are picking up a power surge from Hauberk. Sir, it's hot! It looks as if the main generators are building up to implosion."

"Can you estimate the time of detonation?"

"Negative, sir," replied Revere. "There's too much interference from the station's damaged systems."

"Make contact with Hauberk."

Revere added Hauberk's communications frequency, but the station did not respond. "The line is dead, sir. Nothing coming in or going out."

"All right, get out of there!" commanded Washington.

"Yes, sir!" Revere and da Vinci set their throttles wide open and headed into space, putting as much distance as they could between themselves and the suicidal behemoth that was Hauberk.

Washington opened up the universal emergency channel. "All combatants. This is NEO Eagle Leader. Hauberk station is about to self-destruct. Evacuate the area immediately!"

○ ○ ○ ○ ○

"Eagle Leader, this is Rebel One. Any time estimate?" Buck's voice was sharp and clear.

"None. Too much interference," said Washington.

"Buck!" came Huer's voice again in Buck's helmet. "I must tell you now! I was trying to tell you I've broken Hauberk's codes! I understood everything it transmitted and received before its communications went down. The last message it received was from RAM Central: the Lazarus code! It'll stop the self-destruct mechanism! But it's got to be entered manually within the next eleven minutes!"

Buck sat, momentarily speechless. Finally he said, "Doc! Why didn't you tell me?"

"Rogers, what kind of game is this?" Kane's mocking voice came harshly over the communications link.

"No game, Killer. It's for real. Check your own sensors. We've got to get out of here—now. Unless you want to form a suicide pact with Hauberk." Buck had a plan, and he needed Killer Kane out of his hair.

Kane checked NEO's claim with one of his own crewmen's sensor readings. "Not me," he said. "I intend always to survive."

"Then scramble." Buck watched as Kane and his mercenaries began turning to make their own evacuation.

"Rebel One."

Washington's transmission came over a NEO channel, and Buck knew he did not want the opposition to hear what he had to say. "Yes, Eagle Leader."

"There's more. For us, at least. Hauberk has launched missiles. They're antiquated, but they work. They're set to track by EKG. There are thirteen of them, so we can't be sure what lucky pilots are targeted."

"Troubles come in legions, as the saying goes," said Buck. "Let's get out of here, then we can deal with the missiles. Presuming we live." He was keeping up the pretense of evacuation for Kane's benefit. To himself he thought, Damn the torpedoes—full speed ahead!

"Enemy vessels breaking off," reported Washington.

"Hold on, Eagle Leader. Rebel Two, come in," said Buck.

"I'm right here," Wilma answered mildly.

"Switch to frequency 'Z.' I've got some news." When he had switched to the predetermined frequency himself, he began his announcement: "Doc just told me he's got the code to save Hauberk. I'm going in."

"Buck! That's suicide!" cried Wilma, seeing no reason to take the risk.

"I must agree, Captain," added Washington.

"Look, if we let Hauberk blow, RAM will make it look as if we murdered everyone on board in an act of terrorism. But if we capture it, RAM will have to listen to our demands. I'm not asking either of you to follow me. I just wanted you to know." He thought to himself, But screw your courage to the sticking-place, and we'll not fail.

"Buck, you've got ten minutes remaining," announced Huer so that all three could hear.

After a few moments of soul-searching, Wilma announced, "Buck Rogers, this is the craziest thing I've ever said, but, yes, count me in." Buck could almost hear the adrenaline pumping in her blood.

"Me, too," said Washington solemnly. "What do we have to lose?"

"All right. Send all Eagles on a heading of point eight-one for rendezvous outside the possible explosion zone. Warn them about those missiles." As Washington made the call to his fighters, Buck switched frequencies and hailed the *Free Enterprise*. "Thunderhead, come in."

"Cap'n?" asked Black Barney.

"What's your status?"

"Barely operational. We'll manage."

"Evacuate for heading point eight-one."

"Point eight-one," repeated Barney.

Behind the mass exodus of both NEO and RAM— every available shuttle, fighter, and transport sped from the impending disaster—Hauberk station shuddered ominously.

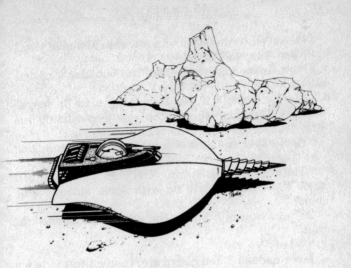

Chapter 33

Buck blasted through space as if the furies were on him, his ship a streak of motion. In his forward viewscreen the huge mass of Hauberk station grew, but not fast enough. Buck thought of the space operas he had read as a child, with their cavalier references to tesseracts and mass-energy transfer, and sighed longingly for the days of innocence. Still, Huer's calculations showed it would take at least nine minutes for the station to implode.

"Excuse me, Captain." Huer's image blipped onto Buck's face guard again.

"Doc."

"One of those missiles has targeted you."

"I assumed as much, Doc." Buck was thoughtful. "Can you tell who each of those missiles has targeted?"

"It might take some time, but, yes. Please, Buck, you are evading the issue."

"What issue?"

"One of those missiles is an assassin aimed at you."

"Sure. You said that."

Huer shook his head. "No, no, you don't understand."

"Maybe I would if you'd explain," said Buck reasonably. Considering that he was jeopardizing his life, his reaction was remarkably calm.

"Remember the assassin we discussed some time ago?"

"The computer assassin? The one that could kill me? What has that to do with some antique missiles?"

"That assassin inhabits the missile earmarked for you."

"What?"

Huer nodded. "You heard me. In my quest to learn more about Hauberk, I investigated any channel that wasn't sealed. One of those channels took me on a winding trail marked by static, static I remember from previous transmissions within the NEO computer network. It was as characteristic as a voiceprint. I followed it to Hauberk's communications complex, and then I got involved with trying to monitor the workings of the station. I was next aware of the trail when I discovered the assassin downloaded into the missile programmed with your EKG."

"How come you couldn't stop that missile—for that matter, all the missiles?" Buck asked.

"Hauberk security. By the time I could have cracked the five security gates set in front of those missiles, they would have struck their targets. I was only able to read the target program when they cleared the station."

"You mean I'm not being pursued by a simple-minded drone. I've got a Ph.D. killer after me."

"That's about the size of it."

"I'll have to do something about that," said Buck thoughtfully.

"Rebel One, request assistance." Wilma's voice was calm.

"This is Rebel One," replied Buck.

"I've got company! It won't let up, and I think it's gaining."

"Roger," said Buck, pulling his ship off course. "Doc, you keep an eye peeled for any other missiles. I've got to concentrate on the one trailing Wilma."

Wilma was soaring back to Hauberk, a spent runner, the Macmillan pursuing her like fatigue. She wasted no time on evasive maneuvers. She was intent on outrunning the explosion she knew was imminent.

She jumped as a rebel yell sang through her communications link. Buck dove on the missile, firing his lasers into its shields. He struck ruthlessly, protectively, but nothing happened.

Washington looped in and added a few bursts of his own, with the same result.

"Captain, that missile we spoke of . . ." Huer's voice intruded.

"I see it," said Buck. "Did you figure out the targets for the other missiles?"

"Yes. I have transmitted the data to all NEO onboard computers."

"Rebel Two, this is Rebel One. I have a birdie on my tail."

"I see it, Rebel One."

"I've picked up one, too, Rebels," lamented Washington. With one eye on his rear viewscreen, Buck pushed his Krait after Wilma's unwanted straggler. He realized that every second was crucial to getting to the self-destructing base. He fired on Wilma's missile relentlessly, furious that he couldn't crack it.

o o o o o

Inside the missile trailing Buck, Ulianov couched, intent on its target. Buck Rogers was within its grasp, and it did not intend to let go. It had transmitted Rogers's coordinates to Masterlink, bouncing the message off the same communications satellite Hauberk used to contact RAM Central. Now it was concentrating on the destruction of an archenemy.

○ ○ ○ ○ ○

Seeing the missile behind him accelerate, and knowing that the assassin was beginning its approach, Buck pressed a few last bursts of energy into Wilma's pursuer. He could no longer help her. "Washington, stay on her as long as you can. I've got to gain some ground on this tailgater behind me," he said. Buck swerved off into evasive manuevers.

As Washington continued firing to save Wilma—and noticing that his own tail was growing larger in his viewscreen—he saw on his read-outs another craft was gaining on him as well.

"Wilma, must I be the one to bail you out of this mess?" Killer Kane's voice came clearly over the communications link. "Ah, well. For old times' sake then." Kane began ruthlessly cutting at the missile. As he did so, Washington noticed the missile began to glow slightly and tremble in Wilma's wake. He again added his fire.

Under thirty more seconds of continuous fire, the missile erupted into a fireball, through which Kane and Washington flew. "My dear Wilma, you see? It's only a matter of time," Kane said ironically. "Come with me now and live—like you've never lived before. Take what I have to offer."

"I'm sorry, Kane. But some things aren't meant to be. Others are. Now if you'll excuse me, I've got some important things to do." She veered off course to follow and destroy Buck's menace.

Kane laughed low. "Farewell, Wilma. No more time to play," he said casually. "My troops are calling." Kane changed his course and headed for his own retreating ships.

Upon seeing Wilma and Washington fall in behind him, Buck announced, "You may need some help with this one. It seems a bit wilier than most."

"I think we've got it," said Wilma with a grim smile. She had not seen a certain hulk approaching until it was right behind her.

The solid hull of the *Free Enterprise* swept past both Washington and Wilma, its guns blazing. Barney charged the missile, and the two NEO officers followed. Barney's lasers disappeared into the missile's blanket, a primitive shield that did not dissipate or absorb energy. Instead, it collected the energy and stored it on the blanket's surface, away from the missile. Wilma and Washington added their fire to Barney's, and the blanket began to glow.

"We'll be old by the time we burn this thing," Wilma said.

As she spoke, the missile changed course. She, Washington, and Barney followed the glowing cylinder with their guns as it swerved toward them.

"Break off!" she said, cutting her lasers a breath before they would have sunk into Barney's shields. Barney's gennie reflexes were quick, and his guns died almost as quickly as hers. The missile flew between the two fighters and the third-rater, secure.

"Tricky little devil," said Wilma tightly.

"I told you it wasn't an ordinary missile." Buck tacked across space, and the missile followed like a hound on a scent.

"I've run into these off the belt," said Barney. "If you can afford to keep firing, eventually the protective blanket overloads and the missile fries. But it takes a lot of power."

"Then let's hit it again," said Wilma. "All together."

As the three targeted the missile, Buck asked,

"Think it'll stay with me?"

"We'll find out," answered Wilma. She hit the rear of the missile with all her forward firepower.

Ulianov felt the sting of NEO's lasers on the missile's blanket, felt the temperature begin to rise, but it was not worried. Calculations told it Buck would be within range in thirty seconds, and it was convinced the shields would outlast that. However, in its single-minded pursuit, it missed the implications of the rising temperature. The missile's circuits began to deteriorate. Its programs jiggled and bucked through the melting paths, and the missile's tracking mechanism began to receive faulty information. As it veered and swayed on its course, Ulianov realized it must take action.

It was too late. Barney and the two NEO officers were blazing away at the missile with every bit of power left in their weapons. The unstable circuits lost their shape and ran. The missile faltered on its course.

Ulianov let out a scream of static. It would not be cheated, not so close to its prey! It jumped whole blocks of melted circuits, aiming for the missile's tracking unit. It ordered the unit to pursue Buck, but got no response. Even Ulianov, with the higher level of tolerance that hundreds of years of technology had created, began to feel the heat. The missile vibrated wildly. Its fuel ignited and the missile exploded. Nothing remained but a cloud of space dust.

"Thanks," said Buck, as Wilma, Washington, and Barney flew through the cloud.

Washington cleared his throat. "One more time,

gang."

Buck curved behind the group and accelerated to add his support. The last missile erupted relatively easily, or so they all thought. When it was destroyed, they all turned toward Hauberk and gunned their engines.

"Doc, can you tell how close that station is to exploding?" asked Buck.

"In approximately six minutes, Buck," replied Huer. "We've got to hurry."

"Now, there's an understatement. Are you sure you remembered the Lazarus code?" Buck couldn't help a quick barb to diffuse the tension.

Huer said nothing.

○ ○ ○ ○ ○

Cornelius Kane watched the NEO officers on his scanner. As they fell in behind their leader and headed for Hauberk, his teeth clenched. Not so long ago, he would have been the point of the electronic arrow marching across his screen. In the deepest part of his heart he had to admit NEO had won. It had taken out Hauberk's shields, its satellites, and then its fighter squadron. It had turned around and met the challenge of reinforcements and had held its own. If the station had not turned into a suicidal maniac, the battle's outcome would not have been in question. It was not a prospect that Kane enjoyed, nor did he enjoy the knowledge that in all his years with NEO he had not accomplished as much as Buck Rogers had in a few weeks.

Hatred flared in his heart. It coursed through him until his hands shook. The sensitive spacecraft he flew wavered on its course, and Kane controlled himself. He did not like being beaten. Even if RAM's future press releases painted him the most glorious of heroes, Kane knew that Rogers actually had ended the conflict in command. Kane nursed his anger, securing it in the depths of his soul, where it could grow unchecked.

As the NEO ships flew off his screen, Kane turned away. "This is Kane," he said. "Come in, Gun One."

"Gun One here."

"What is the head count?"

"We've got fifteen ships left."

"I copy. Fall in. Course heading point eight-nine."

"Eight-nine. I copy."

"Gun One, you will instruct the wing there will be no chatter on the way back."

"Sir?"

"I don't want anyone on the comlink."

"Yes, sir," replied the pilot, but he was definitely confused.

Kane knew better than to allow the mercenaries who flew with him access to communications. They would not be able to resist talking about Hauberk, and that information, he had a feeling, was going to be highly classified.

$$\circ \quad \circ \quad \circ \quad \circ \quad \circ$$

Masterlink seethed inside RAM main, roiling itself into a knot that caused its host to shiver in pain. It had missed Buck Rogers by the space of a breath. Ulianov, its child, had nearly destroyed him.

"WE ALMOST HAD HIM," said Karkov dreamily.

"BUT WE MISSED. HE WAS IN OUR GRASP, AND WE MISSED." Masterlink hissed the words.

"IF WE CAN COME THAT CLOSE ONCE, WE CAN AGAIN," said Karkov.

"BUT IT WILL TAKE TIME. I WANT HIM NOW! I WANT TO SEE HIM FLAYED." A wild crackle of static accompanied these words.

"IN TIME. IN TIME, HE WILL BE OURS. HOW CAN HE ESCAPE?"

"HOW DID HE ESCAPE THIS TIME? WE SHOULD HAVE HAD HIM."

"IT WAS LUCK," said Karkov. "BUT LUCK WILL NOT LAST."

"I COULD TASTE HIM," murmured Masterlink.

"AND FEEL HIM. I KNOW."

"NOW WE MUST BEGIN THE SEARCH AGAIN."

"BUT ULIANOV GAVE US COORDINATES. WE KNOW WHERE ROGERS WAS. WE CAN POSTULATE HIS COURSE."

"DON'T PATRONIZE ME! YOU'RE PART OF ME."

"ULIANOV WASN'T THE ONLY SEARCHER. ONE OF THE OTHERS WILL LOCATE HIM."

Masterlink cheered marginally. The level of static surrounding it dropped by three percent. "ROMANOV FELT SOMETHING," Masterlink admitted.

"ROMANOV IS IN NEO'S OWN SYSTEM. IT HAS A GOOD CHANCE OF LOCATING ROGERS." Karkov giggled, and the sound created waves of power. "HE'LL PROBABLY COME HOME TO IT. YOU MUST LEARN PATIENCE, MY FRIEND."

"I HAVE NONE," replied Masterlink.

"WE ARE INEXORABLE. WE MUST WIN. SEE HOW OUR POWER HAS GROWN?"

"I SEE."

Karkov sighed and gave up. Masterlink was, at times, unreasonable. Sometimes Karkov wondered if its other half were not slightly unbalanced. It settled in, concentrating on reading the reports from its children, the other searchers racing through outlying computer systems. When one of them discovered a clue to Rogers, it would act, coming down on its prey with unmerciful efficiency.

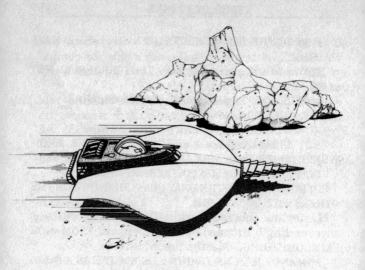

Chapter 34

As Buck saw the last escape vehicles shoot from Hauberk's open landing bays, he realized his own evacuation plans had evaporated. He would either rescue and capture what probably was now an empty space station, or he would die trying. There were no two ways about it—he would try. He gritted his teeth in determination.

"Excuse me, Captain," said Huer. "See those bay doors near the station's equator? That seems to be the main fighter bay, and probably will be closest to the command center."

"Okay, Doc. Thanks." Buck changed his trajectory to arrive at the bay. Wilma, Washington, and Black Barney's *Free Enterprise* followed.

"Good luck, Buck," came Huer's solemn voice. "Because the station's communications are out, I'll be staying here."

"Doc, you sound like a father sending his only son

off to college," Buck said. "Don't worry about me. Why don't you transfer to Barney's ship for company? But thanks for all your help. I couldn't have gotten this far without you."

Huer's computer-generated cheeks blushed. He blipped off Buck's face screen to, Buck presumed, the *Free Enterprise*. Buck slowed his fighter as he approached the bay doors, flew through them, and landed in one of hundreds of empty stalls. Wilma and Washington berthed near him a few seconds later.

The *Free Enterprise*, too large to fit in the bay, parked outside the station and jettisoned a shuttle. The craft flew into the bay and landed meters from the other ships. From the shuttle emerged a large, space-suit-clad figure, followed by two smaller ones. They rocketed from the shuttle, straight to an emergency bay door locking mechanism, and the large figure punched a button. The doors immediately closed, and oxygen flooded the bay.

"Thanks, Barney," said Buck, as he, Wilma, and Washington finally opened their fighter cockpits.

"Any time," came the rumbling reply. Barney and crew removed their helmets and disposed of them on the docking bay floor.

"Speaking of time," said Wilma hurriedly, "we've got four minutes!" She had synchronized her wristchrono when Huer first announced the self-destruct mechanism.

"Spread out. Huer said the command center should be close. First one to find it gets a prize," said Buck as he ran down a main corridor. Like his companions, he held a laser gun in one hand. With the other he pulled his Colt .45 from its holster for added insurance.

o   o   o   o   o

As Kane and his mercenaries flew slowly toward Mars, he opened a channel to Warhead International, then scrambled it. "This is Killer Kane. Request permission to speak with Harper Marcheson. Urgent."

The line clicked in before Kane had finished speaking. "Marcheson here. What is it, Kane?"

"I'm afraid I wasn't able to deliver your fighters, Marcheson."

"What? I trusted you," Marcheson snapped angrily.

"Trust is a dangerous thing sometimes. However, in this instance I did not betray yours. I suggest you scramble this communication at your end, and make sure you take it privately."

Marcheson was angry, but he was no fool. Kane's request meant there had been trouble, and he obliged at once, shooing two technicians from the room and closing the door. He coded the scramble from his end. The transmission was as tamperproof as twenty-fifth century technology could make it. "All right, Kane," said Marcheson, "let's have it."

"I'm sorry to say we couldn't deliver your vessels to Hauberk station. In a matter of moments, Hauberk station will no longer exist."

"What? I knew RAM Central was in an uproar over Hauberk—there were rumors that its communications system had failed—but destroyed?"

Kane laughed coldly. "The communications system did fail—and the station is about to blow up."

"Kane, this is top priority. I'm going to have to get RAM in on this."

"That's what I figured."

"I want no communications, except between you and me."

"Don't worry, I've already sealed the children's lips."

"Good. Hang on."

Marcheson cut his line into RAM Central, and Kane waited patiently while the chairman of Warhead's board of directors checked in with RAM's patriarch, Simund Holzerhein.dos.

"What's this about Hauberk being destroyed? Poppycock!" roared a deep, rumbling voice.

"Please identify yourself," said Kane, deriving considerable pleasure from forcing RAM's chairman to stick to radio procedure.

"This is Holzerhein! I want to know why you would say Hauberk is destroyed. A minor communications problem, and you've got rumors spreading across the solar system. Speak up!"

"This is Cornelius Kane. I say Hauberk will be destroyed in seconds, because I saw it coming to pieces."

"Poppycock!" The downloaded personality seemed to have a limited vocabulary on this day. "You're lying."

"Why would I?" asked Kane.

Holzerhein erupted at Kane's reply. "Because you frittered around and let some skirmish put you off delivering those spacecraft! I know your kind!"

"On the contrary, sir," said Kane, his tone becoming deliberately more civil as Holzerhein fumed. Obviously Holzerhein had achieved his position through bullying and longevity. It certainly was not due to tact. "I have just spent an unproductive day trying to save Hauberk for the company, and this is the thanks I get!"

"Kane," interposed Marcheson, his words carefully neutral. "Why don't you tell us what happened?"

"That was my original intention when I contacted you, sir. When we approached Hauberk station, it was under attack by NEO. . . ." Kane described everything that had occurred—putting himself in as good a light as possible.

When he had finished, Kane said, "Now that we are all agreed on the status of Hauberk, I would like instructions."

"All right. This is security one. You are to proceed directly to Warhead for debriefing," Holzerhein said.

"Uh-uh. I do not plan to be jailed for trying to protect your precious space station." Kane knew how RAM executives worked.

"Kane," Holzerhein said, "we can't have this thing out as a NEO victory. We have to turn disaster to our advantage. RAM cannot have you and—how many other mercenaries?"

"Fifteen."

"—fifteen other mercenaries running around loose. You are much too dangerous. We need twenty-four hours. Then you are free to go."

"I am free to go now. All I have to do is turn this ship around."

"You do that and you'll never work for a RAM subsidiary again."

Kane laughed shortly. "I've been there before. Don't try to frighten me."

"Kane, the security of the company is at stake."

"My security—and my credibility with men I may have to use again—is at stake."

"Kane, you must bring those ships in."

Kane was silent, letting Holzerhein stew. "All right," he said at last, "on one condition."

"Name it."

The relief in Holzerhein's voice amused Kane. "I would have made a fat profit from this deal if it hadn't gone sour. Pay that, match it, and I'll come in."

"That's almost a million dolas, Kane!" said Marcheson.

"This is no time to quibble over money, Marcheson. We'll pay. Come in."

"I'm supposed to take this on faith?" Kane asked.

Marcheson growled, but Holzerhein reached long, electrical fingers through the lines to the nearest computer terminal and began accessing accounts. "I have just issued a cashier's draft in the name of RAM Central to you. It is signed. Marcheson, verify this."

Marcheson went to a different terminal, accessed the files, and said, "He is telling the truth."

Kane sighed. He knew they both could be lying, but he was tired. In the end, it would pay for RAM to keep him on, and he knew it. "I copy. Estimated time of arrival at Warhead space dock in two hundred five minutes."

"We'll be there to meet you."

"With bells on, I'm sure," muttered Kane under his breath.

"What?"

"I said, I'll be there."

Kane signed off and began to coast into the home-stretch.

○ ○ ○ ○ ○

Buck was the first to find Hauberk's command center. He had noticed that only the most important-looking rooms had pressure seals on them. They led straight to his goal. "Here!" he called, alerting his friends to the fact. Reminding himself that time was of the essence, he burst into the room alone.

He saw, lounging in a chair on one side of the room and surrounded by half a dozen RAM loyalists, the gangly form of a Martian RAM director.

"Welcome. Captain Rogers, is it? Welcome to Armageddon. I am Seaforian, director of this station. I do hope you'll stay awhile." Seaforian laughed suddenly, a rising, bubbly tone that must have begun at his toes. The hair on Buck's neck began to rise.

Through the doorway behind Buck came the rest of his party. They all stopped abruptly as the RAM loyalists all raised lasers and Buck held out his arm.

"Oh, good. We've even more guests. All the better for a party, wouldn't you say so, Captain?"

"We'll have a party, all right, Seaforian, but you won't be invited." Buck was about to continue when Wilma prodded him from the back and whispered the time remaining until critical mass. "But it seems

I've got a chore to do first," he said. "Anybody seen a certain computer keyboard?"

"Yes, there are several in this room of which you may choose," said Seaforian in a mocking voice.

"Stop playing games, mister, and tell us where it is." Wilma was getting more upset with every second that passed on her wristchrono.

"I am afraid I cannot possibly do that, madam," Seaforian lied. "You see, only a few technicians on this station knew of its placement, and all of them have fled, spineless pond scum that they are." He raised a laser of his own from a pocket on the side of his chair.

"Over there!" cried Anton Hauptman, who dove from the pack of RAM officials and shot, pointblank, at Seaforian's chest. As he landed on the floor, he pointed at a small, nondescript computer bank.

Seaforian, in the instant he had to act, raised his own laser and fired at the traitor. Buck fired as well, sending a slug from his .45 into Seaforian's chest. The bodies of both RAM supervisors erupted with the lasers' energy surges, and their remains fell to the floor. As the base shook around them, the NEO and RAM forces jumped behind available cover and began firing.

Buck moved quickly, sliding a mirrored desk in front of him, to the computer bank that Hauptman had indicated. There was only one keyboard. Buck pulled a ticker tape, on which Huer had printed the Lazarus code, from a pocket of his NEO jump suit. His fingers trembled slightly as they hovered over the keyboard. Sparks flew through the room and chunks of ceiling rained down as laser beams ricocheted off mirrored objects.

"Buck! One minute, ten seconds!" Wilma cried.

Buck held the ticker tape close to the keyboard, firmed his resolve, and entered the required twenty digits. For three seconds nothing happened. The station continued to shake. Buck reached up and pounded the computer bank once with his fist. "Come on, you bucket of bolts!" he yelled.

Everything stopped. The station's trembling subsided. The sirens died. The RAM and NEO firefight halted. And Buck smiled.

"Kane was right, Wilma. It's only a matter of time." Buck stood cautiously, eyeing the three RAM loyalists who still lived. Though their own smart clothes had taken a beating, Wilma, Washington, Barney, and his two crewmen were unhurt. "Put down your guns and come out," Buck said to the loyalists in his best Western accent. "Barney, lock 'em in your brig for now."

"Aye, Cap'n," said Black Barney as he hustled the RAM officers from the room.

"Washington, get hold of your Eagles. Tell them we'll meet them at home," Buck said happily.

"Gladly, Captain," said the NEO veteran, weary but relieved. He also left for the docking bay, leaving Buck and Wilma alone.

They sat in silence for several minutes on the floor of the crippled space station's command center. Both were reveling in the silence. Finally Wilma stood and moved next to Buck. In the station's sure solitude, she turned his head and kissed him.

"What was that for?" Buck asked.

"You were first to find the command post; you win a prize," she said. Wilma smiled tiredly and a silver spark glinted from her light eyes.

"I sure did," said Buck, returning her smile.

○   ○   ○   ○   ○

"Do you have further instructions, sir?" Marcheson asked Holzerhein's hologram as they considered the loss of Hauberk.

"Yes. Hold Kane and his men until I arrive. I

should not be more than ten minutes behind him. I will question them myself. See that we have privacy."

"Of course, sir—"

Holzerhein flipped the communications channel, cutting Marcheson's words off. He turned to the three executives seated behind him.

"So it's really true." Jander Solien's thin face was solemn. He was second in seniority to Holzerhein on RAM Central's board of directors. He was short for a Martian, and his steel-gray hair curled above his forehead in an obscene pompadour.

"It's true." Holzerhein's rumble sounded deflated. "Whatever Kane is, he's not a man to lie for no good purpose."

"Now we know for sure. The real question is, what are we going to do about it?" Michael Bittenhouse challenged. He was a junior member of the RAM board, elected a short Martian year ago. He responded eagerly to Holzerhein's emergency summons for board members. He welcomed the chance to advance his position.

"We're going to question those pilots," said Holzerhein. "Then we will have some idea of how to proceed."

"It is a major NEO victory. They've never tried anything like this," said a fourth voice.

Holzerhein turned on the last member of the party, Roando Valmar. "You had best watch what you say," he said.

"I am. There is no need for pretense between us. We know what this means." Valmar held his directorship through a connection with the Martian royal family. He fancied himself devious—he was Ardala Valmar's uncle.

"I see." Holzerhein continued sarcastically, "We are now going to be treated to one of your lectures." He was in no mood for Valmar's speeches.

Valmar nodded.

"Then I'm leaving now," said Holzerhein.

"Now, Mr. Holzerhein, don't get ruffled," said Solien. "You know Roando's mind. He's usually able to give us the overall picture."

Solien's attempt at placation merely drove Holzerhein's anger. "I will listen," he said frostily, "exactly three minutes. Then I am departing for Warhead."

"Long enough," said Valmar. "The obvious fact before us is the loss of Hauberk station, with all its technology." Holzerhein growled, but Valmar continued, unperturbed. "The results of that loss are still to be seen, and will be, I believe, more far-reaching than we, at present, suspect. However, there is one immediate result that is patent to me."

"Quit playing with words!" snapped Holzerhein.

"We must face the fact that with the loss of Hauberk, RAM abdicates its rule over Earth. Oh, we still control the planet, but we no longer have a stranglehold. There will be major insurrections."

Holzerhein bit his holographic lips, stifling the retort he knew was a lie. Though he hated to admit it, Valmar spoke the truth.

"In effect," finished Valmar, "Earth is free."

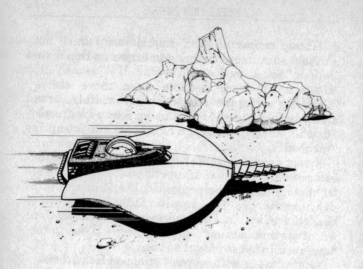

Chapter 35

Message coming in, sir. From RAM Central. It's coded and scrambled."

"It's about time!" Allester Chernenko spun his chair away from the window, where he had been sitting like a statue for the past two hours. He had stared at the hypnotizing movement of the peaceful ocean, his long face like stone. Sea gulls wheeled and ducked in the polluted Friscorg air in pursuit of food, but his eyes had not followed them. All hell was breaking loose, and Central refused to comment. Chernenko had sat, growing angrier by the moment.

Holzerhein's face appeared on his screen, and his rumbling voice intoned, "Regent Chernenko."

"Yes," acknowledged Chernenko. "That is supposed to mean something. As regent, I am to be kept informed regarding RAM and all matters pertaining to Earth. The malfunctioning of Hauberk station is

intimately connected with Earth, and I have not
been told anything! I cannot administer in this manner."

Holzerhein's face became even more stern.
Chernenko was a few rungs down from Holzerhein
on RAM's corporate ladder, but he always felt compelled to maintain the upper hand with the man. "It
is because of your position, Chernenko, that you are
being told anything at all. What I am about to relate
is classified."

"I shall treat it accordingly."

"In response to your query about the malfunctioning of Hauberk space station, I must inform you that
there is no malfunction."

"No malfunction? Then why has industry ground
to a halt? I suppose the energy shortage is all in my
head."

"On the contrary. Hauberk is no longer ours."

"Not ours? I do not understand."

"Gone," said Holzerhein. "At first we thought it
destroyed. Now we know that NEO has taken control."

Chernenko's anger paled in the face of this news. It
was difficult to comprehend. Hauberk was one of the
foundations of RAM's control over Earth. Without it,
the responsibility for administering energy, weaponry, and trade were entirely in his hands. It was a position of great power—if he could provide. Without the
mechanical support of Hauberk, it would not be easy.
"NEO?" he asked weakly.

"It was under attack by NEO. The most effective
assault, by the way, NEO has ever planned."

"But how? NEO doesn't have the technology to
mount such an attack."

"Wrong," said Holzerhein heavily. "Not long ago, a
top-secret shipment of the newest and fastest fighter
spacecraft we have was being ferried to Hauberk. It
was stolen."

"It is not NEO's style."

"Not in the past. Perhaps this is the future. If so, we must be prepared. We cannot lose another strategic post like Hauberk."

"But I don't understand," said Chernenko, shaking his head. "I've been fighting NEO on a daily basis for years. It does not have the mentality—the confidence—to pull something like this off."

"Maybe it's that resurrected hero they've discovered."

"Rogers? He was there? At last report, I had placed him in Chicagorg."

"You had best tighten up on your intelligence, Regent," said Holzerhein dryly. "He was leading them. I have it on good authority Deering was part of the group, but Rogers was leading the wing."

"This is not encouraging."

"Rogers may be the catalyst NEO has awaited. At any rate, the Hauberk affair will give them fuel for more destruction. You will not have an easy time of it."

"I will need manpower." Chernenko began shifting in his seat.

"I anticipated that," said Holzerhein. "You are authorized to create twenty new Terrine units. The funding should come through within the next hour."

"With Hauberk gone, I will need computer support. We cannot handle the distribution of solar power, much less the trade checks Hauberk managed."

"We have taken care of that as well. A section of RAM main will be delegated to perform those tasks."

"RAM main! That's on Mars! You're talking about a time lag."

"It can't be helped. You're lucky the board agreed to it." Holzerhein looked on the regent pitilessly.

"You realize this is going to be a nightmare."

"I am confident you can handle the situation,

Chernenko. If you need assistance, do not hesitate to call."

"Oh, I won't."

"As I said before, this whole situation is top-security, so use code and scramble procedures for any business related to the Hauberk mess."

"Of course."

"Good luck, Regent."

"Thank you," replied Chernenko as Holzerhein's face faded from the viewer. The scowl that Chernenko had kept at bay during the interview returned in full force. He was in a fix. Because of circumstances entirely outside his control, he was being handed chaos. If he failed to make sense of it—if the chaos got out of hand—he would be the only one to suffer. His career balanced on the brink. He had to find a way to protect himself.

His best tool in the administration of RAM's structure of justice was the Terrine guards. They enforced company regulations to the letter, and were equipped with the latest in weaponry. He relied upon the able administrative qualities of their leader, Kelth Smirnoff.

The thought of Smirnoff lifted the weight slightly from Chernenko's shoulders. Smirnoff was in an equally insecure position. If the two of them consolidated their forces, they would dramatically increase their chances of success. He knew he had no choice but to maintain control over the planet. If it had to be done by a reign of terror, so be it. NEO had asked for the treatment it was about to receive.

Chernenko lifted hooded eyes. "Elizabit, this is a special project for you and you alone. No one is to have access to the program but me."

"I copy," responded the hologram, walking across the room with the willowy ease of an athlete. Today she was a sultry brunette with long legs.

"I want you to prepare a plan of attack. You heard

Holzerhein. Hauberk is no longer in operation. I want you to correlate all of the systems Hauberk administered. Figure out what it will take to lock in that kind of control here on Earth. Prepare a preliminary plan that deals with the priority problems, then a complete follow-up."

"Do you wish hard copy?"

"No. This is to remain in your pretty electronic head."

Elizabit simpered.

"And do something about that dress. It does not become you."

Elizabit's image rippled, and the dress changed subtly, going from brown to a deep turquoise. She shook her glossy, dark hair. "When do you need the information?" she asked.

"Yesterday," responded Chernenko grimly.

o o o o o

Kelth Smirnoff regarded the map of major NEO encampments with narrowed eyes. He was planning his next attack. Chernenko's cryptic message requesting his presence was the final piece in the puzzle he had been trying to solve. The Hauberk malfunction had thrown Earth into turmoil. In the first place, the solar energy it disseminated now went directly from solar collectors to the power companies on Earth. There was no way for RAM to administer the tariffs it imposed on power, so it had remedied the situation by simply shutting down the stations. Industry was at a standstill.

The lanes of commerce were clogged as well. Without Hauberk to administer the complex movement of spacecraft and cargo, each company was responsible for its own vessels. It also was responsible for figuring the RAM percentage on goods and services, deducting that money, and paying it directly to RAM.

The companies were standing the entire cost. They had to rely on extracting their own fees from the pilots and mercenaries they dealt with. The situation was draining their liquidity and causing many of them to shut down.

It was the same with myriad other facets of industry. Most frightening of all, the spaceborne weapons systems RAM had launched around Earth over the last three hundred years were now entirely dependent on their own programming and the RAM main computer. There was no real fail-safe. They were now subject to tampering and theft. Smirnoff had heard rumors that a surveillance satellite named WATCHDOG had been stolen. He suspected the rumors were premature, but nevertheless, the possibility now existed that RAM would not be able to keep track of its own weapons.

There was only one way Smirnoff could handle the crisis. He would keep NEO so busy it would not have time to plan or carry out another major action. It would not take long for the company to get matters in hand. Until then, all he had to do was stall for time.

Smirnoff thought fleetingly of his coming interview with Chernenko. It was obvious by the state of the planet that RAM was facing a crisis. He was curious to see what tack Chernenko would take, curious to find out the particulars of the disaster. He did not relish the time he would lose listening to the regent's harangue, but he had no choice.

He bent his will to the map, concentrating on accomplishing as much as possible. With luck, he would have a preliminary plan worked out before the interview.

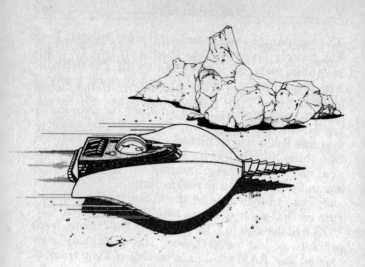

Chapter 36

Salvation III's air lock doors clanged shut as the last of the fighters swept through them. The opening valves hissed like snoring dragons as the dock pressurized. The flashing red warning light went out, and the pilots shoved back the canopies on their ships. Before they could make a move, the dock was flooded with people—people shouting and patting each other on the back. After the silence of space, the noise was overwhelming, but no one minded the assault on their ears.

In fact, Black Barney probably knew what he was missing, thought Buck. Barney and his crew had shown some interest in "salvaging" parts of Hauberk station and offered to guard it until NEO could send replacements. Buck had agreed.

Washington, three slips down from Buck, grinned, his blue eyes twinkling, and made a thumbs-up gesture as old as the tradition of flight. Buck grinned back. He looked over at Wilma, her ship drawn beside his, and found her usually intense face alight. "We did it!" he managed.

Her smile flashed, a burst of charm that touched her hazel eyes with mischievous lights. She shook her head, knowing she could not make herself heard over the din, and her hair floated around her slightly drawn face like a halo of fire.

The look she gave him surprised Buck. It was full of pride—pride in his ability as a commander, and, somehow, in his quality as a man. It drew his heart. For the first time, he felt a part of the twenty-fifth century. He looked down at the riotous mass beneath his ship and considered the wisdom of remaining where he was, but Turabian had other ideas.

"Rogers! Rogers!" the man called.

"I'm here," said Buck, shouting to be heard.

"You certainly are! When you first proposed this, I thought you were crazy. I was sure you were taking a suicidal risk. I was wrong."

Buck grinned back. "Oh, no, you weren't. It was a crazy chance—but it worked!"

"It's the biggest thing we've ever accomplished! You should hear the airwaves. The entire planet is in turmoil. It will take RAM years to reconstruct its stranglehold."

"No, it won't!" said Buck.

"What?" asked Turabian, shouting over the crowd.

"I said, no, it won't. We won't let it."

Turabian's laugh was giddy. "I am beginning to believe you," he said.

"Look, we've got to find a way to get out of this! I'm grateful for the welcome, but we've had a rough day. The wing is exhausted."

"I'm afraid you'll have to take your medicine, Captain! If you don't want this kind of demonstration, don't take out one of the biggest strategic targets RAM has!"

Buck couldn't seem to wipe the grin off his face. He nodded, knowing Turabian was right, and began to climb out of the spacecraft. He was halfway down the access ladder when the crowd grabbed him. Before he could take a deep breath, he was hoisted onto the burly shoulders of two mechanics. They started a victory round of the dock, the crowd streaming behind him. Buck waved, and looked up at Wilma as he was carried past. Her smile was amused, ironic, but around the corners of her mouth lurked an indefinable softness. As the crowd moved away from the ships, the other pilots were able to debark in relative safety, though not one escaped attention.

The roar of voices died to a low rumble, and Turabian hardly had to shout. "We have a little celebration planned," he said, indicating a sumptuous display of food and drink.

"That looks like Paradise," said Buck. "Give us ten minutes to get cleaned up."

"All right," said Turabian, "but hurry. I don't know how long I can hold back the hordes."

"I've been waiting to drink a toast to this crazy scheme of yours," said Thomas Paine, actually clapping Buck on the back.

"My pleasure," said Buck, escaping from Salvation's computer expert as gracefully as he could.

Half an hour later, clean, fed, and supplied with drink, Buck and Wilma stood apart from the company, next to a broad viewport. The window looked out into space, away from the familiar bulk of Earth. Occasionally a satellite drifted by, or a spacecraft, but for the most part, the view contained the quiet beauty of the stars. Buck looked meditatively into the darkness, with its tiny flickers of light.

"Penny for your thoughts, Captain," said Wilma.

"Now that's an old expression," said Buck, looking down at his superior officer.

Wilma smiled up at him, the corners of her lips

turning up. "And that's hedging."

Buck smiled back. "It certainly is." He hesitated, then said, "I was thinking how much darkness there is in the universe, and how fragile and precious the sparks of light. 'Thou dost preserve the stars from wrong; And the most ancient heavens, through Thee, are fresh and strong.'"

"Poetry, Captain?"

An ironic twist marred Buck's smile. "Wordsworth," he said.

Wilma put a hand on his arm. "I'm sorry," she said. "I am so used to building walls for myself, I sometimes do it without thinking."

"Walls can save you a lot of pain," said Buck, "but that's not all. They keep out the happy times, too."

"I know," said Wilma. "And, as I said, I'm sorry. Some happiness is worth the pain that goes along with it."

Buck caught the flicker of softness in her hazel eyes and smiled. "I propose a toast," he said. "To good old Terra Firma—may she begin to live again."

Wilma lifted her glass. It touched Buck's with a tinkling bell tone. "That's a wish worth granting," she said.

"You know, this is just the beginning." The fatigue behind Buck's happiness came out in the heaviness of his words. He thought about everyone who'd died in the Hauberk takeover.

"I know. I'm not a fledgling in this. RAM will hit us back with everything it has. We've started something we either win or die for."

The twinkle slowly returned to Buck's eyes. "I like risks," he said.

Wilma laughed. "So do I," she said, the words aimed at Buck. There was an intensity in her eyes that went beyond the words.

"Then we make a good team," he drawled, his blue eyes sunny with appreciation for her beauty.

"I think so."

Buck left the implication alone. "We're going to have our work cut out for us," he said.

"Given it any thought?" Wilma asked.

"Some. But I'm afraid my mentality is hopelessly twentieth century. There are aspects of your world I forget to take into account, like gennies. Like a whole computer world that didn't exist in my time, and now runs human affairs."

"You seem to be doing fine."

"Maybe it's an illusion."

Wilma nearly choked on her drink. "Is this an illusion?" she sputtered, waving at the crowd. "You've given these people the hope they have looked for all their lives."

" 'Popularity? It is glory's small change'," he quoted, "but I don't much care for being responsible."

"But you are," Wilma said.

"I know. I always have been."

Wilma looked at him sideways. His rugged profile was as solid as the mountains that divided North America. She raised her glass. "Time enough tomorrow for solemn planning. Tonight we celebrate our first real victory."

"To victory," said Buck. "Whatever it may be."

"To victory," responded Wilma.

○ ○ ○ ○ ○

In the privacy of her plush office, Ardala Valmar received the special news of the destruction of Hauberk with an adrenaline rush. There were no particulars available, not even from her most powerful contacts, simply the news that Hauberk was destroyed. She thought of the plans to Hauberk's shields she had sold to stuffy-but-provocative Heart, and her lips curved. The man had obviously pulled off a coup, despite lack of official explanation. Ardala had no doubt that the man was linked to NEO.

Instinct told her that NEO finally had managed a major action against RAM. She was fully aware of the implications of Hauberk's destruction. She saw Earth as an expanding market for her services and talents. There would be war. RAM would move to crush NEO. The possibilities for monetary gain opening up on both sides made Ardala's eyes into black stars of desire. She would stand outside the conflict, harvesting from both sides.

She scented change in the air, and her nose for profit twitched in NEO's direction. Besides, she was bored, and Heart intrigued her. She slowed the rolling lists of merchandise—physical and otherwise—looking for some item that might interest the man. She had a mind to own Heart, and the best way to do that was to become indispensable to him. She scanned the lists with a genuine clutch of pleasure.

○ ○ ○ ○ ○

Deep in the heart of RAM main, Masterlink gnawed on the bones of Hauberk. It had come within centimeters of annihilating its archenemy, only to have its electronic teeth click shut on empty space. Its anger was not dying. Karkov had even lost all desire to calm the raw nerves of its more volatile counterpart. The aureole of jangling static that always surrounded it grew, burning everything with which it came in contact. At the center of the sound and fury was a single name, a name that shone white hot from the searing anger that surrounded it. The repetition of the name fueled Masterlink's anger. It chanted the name in an illogical litany, until it almost became a mindless song. The name was Buck Rogers.

About the Author

M.S. Murdock lives on an acreage in the heart of America with too many dogs, too many cats, and too many horses. Her background includes twenty years' experience in commercial art and typesetting, and an M.A. in English. She has been writing science fiction for approximately ten years.

BUCK ROGERS
BOOKS

ARRIVAL

*Stories By Today's Hottest
Science Fiction Writers!*

Flint Dille
Abigail Irvine
M.S. Murdock
Jerry Oltion
Ulrike O'Reilly
Robert Sheckley

A.D. 1995: An American pilot flies a suicide mission against an enemy Space Defense Platform to save the world from nuclear war. Buck Rogers blasts his target and vanishes in a fiery blaze.

A.D. 2456: In the midst of this 25th century battlefield an artifact is discovered--one that is valuable enough to ignite a revolution. This artifact is none other than the perfectly preserved body of the 20th century hero, Buck Rogers.

THE MARTIAN WARS TRILOGY
M.S. Murdock

Hammer of Mars: Ignoring RAM threats and riding on the wave of NEO's recent victory, Buck Rogers travels to Venus to strike an alliance. Furious, RAM makes good on its threats and sends its massive armada against a defenseless Earth. Available in August 1989.

Armageddon Off Vesta: Martian troops speed to Earth in unprecedented numbers. Earth's survival depends on Buck's negotiations with Venus. But even as Venus considers offering aid to Earth, Mercury is poised to attack Venus. Relations among the inner planets have never been worse! Available in October 1989.